LABYRINTH

LABYRINTH

World of the Stone Maze
Book One

by Shane Lee

Shane Lee
www.ShaneLeeBooks.com

—

There is no light at the end of the tunnel when you are in the labyrinth.

Part One: The Monsters of the Maze

Chapter One

The Walls are filled with darkness.

It is not a complete darkness. The Walls rise high, but not to the clouds. The space between them is often filled with a thin mist, and wide. Five young men like me could stand shoulder-to-shoulder within, and the ones on each end could brush the cold stone with their fingertips.

Light comes in from the sky, but it is bare, diffused, and must travel a long way to reach the ground. Little of it does. The spaces within the Walls are dim and cold, like they are a different part of the world.

It's been like that for over two hundred years. No one I know has been outside the Walls, not even me, Jost, the lone soul from Cartha who wanders the labyrinth. Who goes out into the dark passages to hunt, and who returns alive.

People think that I'm a fool, or that I'm crazy. I like to think of myself as brave and reckless, but the truth is, I'm not scared of the Walls. I'm not scared of the monsters that people say are out here, or the poison that is supposed to fill the air. I've been brushing my hands along the gray stone here since I was eight years old, and in almost twelve years, I had never run across anything to be afraid of.

The people in the city are scared of what is supposed to be out here. The beasts or creatures or malign entities that thrust humanity into small hidden pockets among the Walls. The labyrinth was built around all the cities to keep them safe. The legends are old and confusing, and they name a dozen enemies of man.

I have never seen these things. Perhaps there was once evil that forced this maze to be built, but it's gone now. The Walls are darkness and mystery; mist and silence. I was not afraid of them. I feared nothing in the walls.

Until I found the light.

Chapter Two

It was a day like any other spent in the Walls. Dim and cold. I flexed my fingers and rubbed my hands together, the rasping sound of my skin loud in the calm. I was the only man who roamed the labyrinth, but that didn't mean I enjoyed the weather. I dressed for it. I'd spent a lot on my clothes, and little on anything else. A man who spends his days going miles in the Walls needs warm, strong clothing.

My boots were heavy and worn. I wore long, dark pants of thick fabric sewn to tough leather strips that ran down the legs, some of the best leather in Cartha. My shirt was two layers of linen and wool, dyed a deep black with sleeves that went up to my wrists. It was my hunting shirt. Dark clothing made it much harder to be seen in the Walls, and when I crept upon the ratmoles and burrow pigs that I sold for meat, they would not notice me.

That was today's task—and tomorrow's, if today went poorly. Secure twenty pounds of meat or more.

"More," I said, scratching at my forehead beneath my short brown hair, which was dirty but neat. "You can do more than twenty, Jost."

Talking to myself was common in the Walls. There was no one else. Aside from the unending chill, it might have been nice. No one in the city really talked to me, anyway.

The wooden stringing pole I used to carry carcasses hung over my shoulders, and I shrugged it higher. I was far from Cartha now, almost far enough to need to pull out my map. I knew the labyrinth for a good span of miles around the city, but eventually I always reached a new part.

That would never stop happening, of course. The labyrinth was thousands of miles long, if you believed the stories. And I did.

Not fearing the legends did not mean I wasn't a believer. I was the only one who ventured into the Walls because I was the only one who made it back alive. Ever. Not even one other person had left the city of Cartha and come back to tell the tale.

People stopped trying. They had their own lives to live in Cartha, where the sun did shine and one could grow crops and livestock and pretend the world was like it used to be before the labyrinth, as long as they ignored the hundred-foot-high stone wall that curved around the farmlands and city.

I blinked, casting the sunlight from my mind's eye and returning to the dark mist of the Walls. My boots stepped softly into the wet dirt. I had two small but very sharp daggers strapped on the outside of each thigh, secured tightly to prevent any noise. I smelled the damp soil and the lingering rot of plants that had tried to grow and died, over and over.

I was searching for the burrow this time. Rather than spend days picking up one pig or ratmole at a time, I could find the nest.

"Thirty pounds," I whispered, running my fingers absently along a dagger's sheath. "Forty. Fifty, if I'm quick."

The burrow pigs weren't big, but six or seven would add up fast.

I made a final left turn before pulling my lifelong project from its special pocket inside my shirt. I unfolded it, barely able to read it in the narrow light. The sun had passed its highest point in the sky an hour ago, and this was as bright as the Walls would be for the rest of the day.

My map. As usual, my eyes crawled over it with wonder and familiarity, my fingers holding it like it was a baby bird. Paper was expensive, and treating it to make it durable cost even more, but I paid it for the map.

"Sixty pounds," I muttered to myself, knowing that carrying all that meat back would cripple me. "I could trade for a stack of treated sheets if Gwin is fair to purchase..."

I would have to eat, too, but that could be treated sparingly. My frame was narrow and strong. Walking and hunting in the labyrinth was not a leisurely stroll—stones had to be moved; earth had to be dug up; walls had to be climbed where handholds could be found. The Walls were crumbling in spots, but there was a lot of wall. They would probably crumble for another thousand years.

I looked ahead, holding the map in one hand. I stood where the markings ended, some fifteen miles southeast of Cartha. Between the city and where I stood were three-dozen-and-four turns I'd taken along the way. I knew them by heart.

I had gotten lost only one time, when I was very young. Nine years old, and little Jost felt brave enough to wander farther than he had before. There's no sound of the city once you enter the labyrinth—the stone blocks it all.

I was lost for four days. It was the most panicked and scared I'd ever been in my life. But it was also how I learned that ratmoles could be caught with my hands, and I could eat them alive and not feel bad about it. It was for survival. I learned to map and hunt and where to dig a hole deep enough with your hands to pull water from the ground, if you were lucky. I swore that brush with death would never happen to me again.

And I was right, all the way up until now.

Charcoal in hand, I marked what I saw on a raw, folded sheet that I would later copy in ink to the map. This path stretched ahead farther than I could see, than even the light could show me.

"Haven't seen a straight this long aside from Riverway." I glanced at the long, straight path drawn north of Cartha, which I had named Riverway because I had read about big rivers in books. "I'll need a name for you."

The tantalizing excitement of exploring pulled at me, but there were more pressing matters. I was here to track and hunt, and if the pig burrow was anywhere, it was near here. The pigs wouldn't go too far, and certainly not all the way down this path.

"Longsteel?" I offered, scratching the name down and picturing it looking like a sword from a bird's eye. "No, I can do better. Arrow's Way. No..."

I continued muttering to myself, hardly listening, as I stepped forward in the wet dirt and drew the paths I saw, adding as much detail as I could. I looked atop the sharp corner of a branch path and thought I saw green creeping over the top edge.

Ivy? I marked, and then I saw the small footprints on the ground. Pigs. Easy to track, as long as I was careful not to step on the prints.

"You're lucky there's no other predators here for you, little meat loaves," I said, following the prints down a right turn while marking down the path. "You're far too easy to find."

I wished there were deer here. They were something I'd only ever seen drawings of. Huge, glorious beasts that weighed as much as me. Something you'd need a bow and arrow and true shot to take down. The only reason I carried these daggers was to skin the carcasses. The pigs were easy to catch, and their necks were easy to break.

Down the path, drawing rough lines with my charcoal pencil, it was only when I looked up from my map that I saw, for the first time in my life, light inside of the Walls.

Chapter Three

W hat in fiery hell?"

I stopped dead, my hands frozen on the map. A yellow glow spread a faint but wide circle across the left side of a labyrinth wall. Something was planted in the stone and emitting a light. It was soft, but in here it might as well have been the sun.

I flicked my eyes away from it for just a moment to mark it on the map—*light???*—then got back to my senses and put my things away. I kept my eyes on the light and noticed it pulsed ever so slightly, like it was breathing.

Fear prickled at me, and I hated it. The labyrinth didn't scare me, and nothing inside it should. But this was something I had never seen before; so different from the vast unknown that I'd been chipping away at with my map. The longer I looked at it, the more angry I felt. After twelve years of exploration, I knew more about the Walls than anyone alive. I practically lived here. And what was this newcomer, this intruder?

You're the intruder, Jost. You're in its territory.

"Territory?" I scoffed, but quietly. "It's just a light. It's a little lamp."

But I wasn't staring at firelight; I could tell that from where I stood, some hundred feet away. This was something else. And I was going to find out what it was, and I might smash it for good measure. I didn't need light scaring the pigs away.

I started walking. At least, I thought I did. But my feet wouldn't move. I felt pressure in the back of my throat, and my blood pumped through my neck in heavy pulses.

"By all the denizens," I growled through gritted teeth, "I am not scared of some stupid little lamp."

My paralysis broke, and I moved forward stiffly. I could see now that the mist was gone here, and by the sounds of my boots on the ground, the soil was drying up. Every step I took, things got stranger.

Just leave, Jost. You know the pigs aren't here.

Pigs? Who cared about some pigs? There was a lamp.

The ground was firm beneath my feet; so odd within the Walls. I wanted to look down to see it, but my eyes were locked on the light. The weak thoughts of pigs and meat were driven from my mind, and I found myself reaching one hand forward as I walked, grasping at the yellow glow.

Something was wrong with me. Something was wrong with all of this.

A sickening combination of fear and awe pulled and pushed me, but whatever drew me towards the light was winning. Dry dirt crunched under my boots. I was close now, close enough to see the source, something that was half-buried inside of the wall.

I drank the light in hungrily and reached out for the lamp—while inside I recoiled. I had no idea what this was. It could burn me, or poison me. What the hell was I doing?

I laid my hand on the light and gasped.

A shock coursed through my body, stretching me backward. There was no pain. Energy surged through my fingertips and my body, like I was being filled with rushing water. My mouth hung agape, and my short brown hair stirred like it was alive, making my skull tingle. Lights flashed in my eyes.

I stayed connected to the light for an eternity, though only moments passed. When it released me, I fell to the ground. My elbows dug into the dirt and my hip hit the ground hard, making my teeth knock together. I felt weak, like I'd just run five miles through the Walls and bumped into a few of them on the way.

I went flat on my back and lied there for a moment, finding my breath. The sky above me was narrow and blue, framed by the skyreaching stone, which grew darker with shadow the further down the wall you looked.

I could move, at least. I dug my fingers into the earth and felt it crumble into my palm.

Dry, indeed, I thought. *Like the light took all the water from it.*

Breathing deeply, I sat up, idly running my hands over my arms and shoulders to check if I'd been hurt and finding nothing. I felt battered, but I didn't appear to be broken. I got to my feet, glancing back up at the light.

It was dimmer now. Still bright for the darkness of the labyrinth, but giving off less energy than before, surely.

I had to touch it again.

"What is wrong with you?" I asked, staring at my hand as it reached again for the light, and now I could see it was a round, yellow gem, just barely too big to close my hand around. It was clear and pure. The gray stone and the small pocket within it appeared golden behind the gem.

As far as gems went, even one this big wouldn't get me much in the way of trade, unless I found someone who was an odd and wealthy collector, and there weren't enough of those types in Cartha to keep me fed.

So why was I touching it again?

I braced myself for the shock, but it didn't come. The surface of the gem was perfectly, incredibly smooth. A sphere so unflawed that even the most talented glass-worker in the city couldn't hope to replicate its featureless curve. It was half-stuck in the wall, and at this point I was past wondering why I wanted the damned thing. I was now surmising how I would be able to take it out of the wall without a chisel or a pickaxe.

But when I rested ten fingers on the gem's surface and pulled, it slid free. Shocked, I let it drop to the dirt. It hit the ground with a whisper, like it weighed hardly an ounce.

Jost, what the hell have you found?

<u>Chapter Four</u>

I turned back towards Cartha with no meat and a strangely weightless yellow sphere in my hand. I couldn't stop turning the thing around, looking for any indication of what it was or where it had come from. It didn't have scratches from the stone, nor any imperfections, even deep into its core. I got the feeling that I could smash it against a labyrinth wall and all I would hurt was my wrist.

I wanted to know what this thing was. I *needed* to. I kept thinking of it as a gem, but was it really? Not like any gem I'd ever seen, and there were plenty floating around Cartha. Apparently they used to be valuable, and people hoarded them before the Walls were built.

Hard to believe that something people let their kids lose in the street could be worth anything.

Gwin might know something. He was old, even if he didn't like to be reminded of it, and he'd read a lot of books. I'd go to him first.

Clutching the gem in one hand and following my well-worn path back through the labyrinth, I felt a tingle in my palm. I stopped, pulling it up to my face and looking at it. Deep inside, light was starting to form.

I was so distracted by the lamp that I didn't notice the burrow pig until it ran past my feet, spraying dirt across the front of my boots.

"Hey!" I whipped around, suddenly furious. I never missed a pig.

I tucked the gem awkwardly into my pocket and ran after the burrow pig. The little brown animal was fast, but not faster than me. I caught it as it was frantically trying to burrow into the ground, its only real way to escape. The lamp tingled against my leg, even through my pants, like it was getting ready to shock me once more.

I pulled the beast from the dirt and broke its neck quickly, a practiced motion I'd done hundreds of times. It weighed about eight pounds by feel. A good haul for dumb luck.

While I drew a dagger and began to skin the animal, its coarse brown bristles pricking at my ungloved hands, I realized the gem had ceased its tingling. I wiped the blood on a rag that hung from my pack, strung the animal up, and pulled the gem free again. Its inner glow was gone.

I stared into its depths, seeing my dirty hand clearly through the other side.

I have to talk to Gwin.

Four hours later, I was rounding the last few turns that led me back home, the start of many paths I practically had etched into the backs of my eyelids. As much time as I spent in the labyrinth, the city was something to behold.

Cartha was a grand city. It seemed that way to me ever since I was a child, and it still holds true. I'm tall now, but the buildings around the center farmlands are much, much taller.

It lies within a massive circle of stone in the labyrinth, much the same as any other city. At least, that's what I've heard. There is no trade or visits between cities, not in the last two hundred years. I don't even know if they're still there. Or if they ever really were.

The city is circular, and spans about twelve miles end to end whichever way you look at it. A narrow river sweeps from west to east and cuts almost directly through the center of Cartha. The Walls have a gap just big enough for the water, and steel bars stretching down to the riverbed. They're thicker than I am and have as much space between them as my legs. Between the ends of the city and the circling labyrinth wall is about a mile of grass, though it grows browner and weaker the closer it gets to the stone, before simply becoming the wet, bare dirt that fills the rest of the labyrinth.

There are four entrances into the labyrinth that surround the city—north, west, south and east. They are wide and gated with vast wooden doors sporting iron bands that weigh enough to crush stone to powder. I can't go through them, so I go around them. Or in the case of the eastern gate, up and over them.

It's easy enough. The gates were not built to keep us in.

In the center of the city are the farmlands, the most cared-for area. They are a vast expanse of fertile land where all the crops and animals that feed the city are raised. Cartha's farms are almost forty percent of its land, and the wealthy-by-trade farmers live in the huge homes surrounding them. Before the Walls were built, that land was filled with mansions of the old wealth. Most of them have been cleared for farmland, but there are still some left to house the farming families, and many other homes built for the thousands of people that live here.

From the farmlands, the homes and buildings spread out to become gradually smaller the closer you get to the encircling wall. A network of streets runs outward from the sprawling farmland center, narrow in the northern government district and wide where carts run and people mill about. The roofs are tiled and usually dark in color, but many are patchy with random colors from repairs reusing other materials or discarded pieces from different buildings. Thick, dark wood braces the stone frames of the older, larger structures; newer and less-impressive buildings are mostly gray stone, often salvaged from the Walls. There's plenty to go around.

My house is one of the latter, and it lies on the south side of Cartha, fairly close to the edge. The poorer people of the city live around the outer edge, nearest the labyrinth. Most people hate to be near the wall, but it's all the better for me. The southern part of the labyrinth is the most-marked on my map simply because I have to catch a ride on horse or cart if I want to get to the other entrances in any decent amount of time.

But whenever I do go through those gates, it's a thrill. There's so much uncharted there.

Now, leaving the labyrinth and stepping onto warmer dirt, Cartha looked beautiful. The late afternoon sun was at the point where it peers over the top of the encasing wall, and the city is cast in golden light. The grass stretched before me, a grand, sweeping expanse that appeared to grow into taller and taller buildings until it reached its highest peak in the roofs of the farmers. Between these rows of homes I glimpsed the farms, unobstructed, the streets empty now. Most people were sitting down for dinner in their walls within the Walls.

I had no family to eat with. I had a bloody pig on my back. I had an odd yellow gem that was glowing in my hand. And I had to learn what it was without drawing the wrong sort of attention.

I live in Cartha, and I love the labyrinth. I live two lives, one of which no one truly understands, and most fear. Gwin comes the closest to knowing me. If there is a river between the two of us, then there is an ocean between me and everyone else.

Chapter Five

As I crossed the grassy field, I tucked the gem into my pocket. It would be better for people not to see it. They'd only begun eating the meat I brought back after years of me doing it. Plenty of people still didn't.

Closer to the outer ring of Cartha, the grass was littered with a sprinkling of rock dust and smaller chunks of broken stone, some big and sharp enough to punch a hole through your boot. The houses here stood up mostly straight, and that was all that could be said for them. The stone was old and crumbling, and the roofs often had one corner askew. They stood about eight feet tall until you got a half-mile deeper into Cartha, into the next ring.

My house was on this outer ring, a pile of gray stones that kept most of the drafts out. No wood, not even in the roof, which was made of my haphazard tiling and notched into old iron supports that were comprised more of rust than anything else. I made sure not to sleep under them. The two rooms were about big enough for me to lie down in, and one had a thin, narrow bed that I constantly re-stuffed with straw.

My house was one of the first I walked past as I entered Cartha. I didn't spare it a glance. Gwin was deeper inside the city.

The old man was a trader, the most versed in Cartha because he would trade anything for anything, as long as he deemed it fair.

What went on inside Gwin's head to make these calculations was a mystery, but give him time and he always came back with a price. Sometimes it was enough to make you want to hit him in the face. But he controlled the inventory, so he had the power. He was the only man in the city who could get the paper that I wanted.

He was also the only man I knew that might be able to tell me something about this lamp, and the only one I trusted enough to mention it to.

I only missed seeing Franz because the gem started vibrating so wildly against me that I thought it might explode. I had to stop walking and clutch at it in my pocket in the middle of the street, looking like the crazy person everyone thought I was.

"*What is wrong with you?*" I hissed at the gem, ducking away into a short alley between two outer-ring houses. I leaned back against the stone and stuck my hand in my pocket, trying to still the buzzing thing.

"What you doing there, Jost?"

The jeering call floated in from the street, tickling at my ears while all my attention was focused elsewhere. Still, I recognized Franz's voice. It was high and grating, an irritating combination of pitched and guttural because of stonesmoke roughening his throat. A lot of the builders suffered that. But none of them talked as much as Franz.

"Running scared soon as ya see me, huh?"

Annoying. Even more than this gem. I should have just left in the labyrinth. I'd be telling myself that over and over again before long.

I ignored the gem and stepped out into the street, spotting Franz across from me, an iron pick in his hand. He was working on some project or other. A good builder was always busy, and he knew his way around stone. Franz had a lot of friends in this ring.

He also hated and feared me. It was not a secret.

"Franz," I said, blinking. He was my age, roughly—I never asked him. He had black hair, but it was almost always dusted with gray from working stone. His eyes were dark, and his nose was big and often flecked with tiny red welts from flying chips of slate, though he'd somehow yet to be blinded by them. A shame. He stood a few inches shorter than me and was muscled enough to look stocky.

"What's that on your back, Jost? Huh?" Franz smirked. The expression didn't fool me for a second. I could see the fear in his eyes every time he laid them on me. It was impressive that he managed to bluster past it.

I smiled, shifting my string rack to dangle the skinned burrow pig before him. "Hungry?"

Franz wrinkled his nose. "Keep that labyrinth swill away from me, huh? I told you to stop bringing that stuff into Cartha."

As the gem rumbled against my leg, I felt my composure begin to slip. Usually with Franz, I'd snap back at him a bit, get him flustered, and have him on his way. It was rare we fought. But with growing urgency, I felt the need to shove this bloody animal carcass down his throat. To tackle him to the ground and smash the blade of his pick through his ugly red nose.

I took a step forward, still holding out the pig. I felt my lips stretch into a malicious grin.

"Hey, hey, you keep back, huh?" Franz glared, but to his credit, he held his ground.

Let him. We were going to have this out here, once and for all.

"You won't be so scared if you have a taste," I said, and it came out as a growl. The gem throbbed against me, pressing a circle of heat into the flesh of my thigh and pulsing it through the rest of my body. The setting sun made everything glow in a fiery orange haze. I wondered how soft Franz's eyes were, and how easy it would be for my thumbs to go through them.

Another step. Franz's hands went tight around the wooden handle of the pick. I dropped my string rack off my shoulders, and the bloody pig hit the dirt with a wet thud.

"You wanna do this, huh?" Franz shouted, and now people were looking, people I hadn't noticed in my singular rage, and the gem was trying to burrow into my leg and I ran at Franz and got my hands on him. No, it was the pick, which he had raised to defend himself. I ripped it from his hands and threw it to the ground, where it skittered across dirt and stone, drawing sparks.

Franz got a shot in at me then, and it was a good one, right on my jaw. Bright yellow stars burst in my eyes, but I stayed up and I clutched at him again.

I would deal with him the way I dealt with the rats and the pigs in the labyrinth: with my bare hands, up close. His scabby nose filled my vision, and I smashed my forehead into it. In the back of my mind, order and reason cried out for me to stop. I tasted blood in my mouth where my teeth cut into my tongue.

The builder cried out in pain and tried to pull back, but I had my strong fingers digging into his shoulders so hard I could practically wrap my fists around his slim collarbones. So he thrust forward at me. I lost my balance and fell back into the dirt, biting my tongue again, the pain bursting with the flavor of metal.

You're going crazy. The words crossed my mind. *You're attacking Franz in the street for hardly any reason, Jost, what are you doing?*

I had hissed those words at the gem, just moments ago. Picturing that, it was like it had been done by someone else.

Franz's fist connected solidly with the side of my head, and I didn't think anymore.

Chapter Six

I awoke with blurred vision and a vicious ache in my head. I think I groaned, but I felt the noise gurgle in my neck more than I heard it. I blinked a few times, clearing my eyes, while nausea pushed at the back of my throat.

A face filled my sight. "Jost, you fucked moron."

Cheers, Gwin, I tried to say, but even thinking about speaking made my head throb. I closed my eyes again.

"If I step on you, don't go an complain to me," Gwin said, his voice muffled in my ears as I slowly came back to the world. "Some of us still have to work, can't be wandrin all day and gettin into fights. Dumbest thing I ever saw you do Jost, I swear..."

I let him babble on, half-hearing what he was saying, which was mostly insults to my intelligence with a few knocks to my fighting ability. Whatever. I wasn't even sure I was all the way alive yet.

I opened my eyes again, trying to figure out where I was. It didn't take long to recognize the burgundy cover of Gwin's third-ring market stall. The deep red was the color of the merchant's band here. I hadn't come very far from the first ring, where I had fought Franz. And it was still daylight.

My eyes traveled to Gwin, who was tinkering with something or other on his wide display. The wispy white hair atop his head was completely in contrast to the full, dark beard that sprouted wildly from his face and went down to his chest. The man could have passed for thirty-five years old or seventy, depending on which half of his head you were looking at.

There were wrinkles around his eyes, but they were sharp and blue and often narrowed as he dickered with friend and stranger alike. His cheeks were usually rosy, half-hidden by the beard, and the same color bloomed in his nose. The man could drink five other men under the table—I'd seen it done and had it done to me. Truth be told, I feared what would happen to him if he ever ran out of drink. Based on how often he nipped from his tin, he needed it like air.

Gwin usually wore the sort of leather gloves reserved for smiths, though he didn't work with metal. He said he'd been poked by enough of his collection over the years. The same gloves were stretched up past his wrists now as he sorted through items and dropped more choice words on me. His small belly bumped against the display while he worked.

I took a deep breath and managed to struggle to an upright position, scooting gently backward so that I could lean against the back of the stall. I was inside his setup, hidden from the street.

I slipped one hand down to my pocket and felt the gem. Immediate relief soothed my hot veins; I hadn't even realized I was worrying it was gone. Then I checked my map pocket and found it was still there, too. I saw my pack lying against the back of the stacked-stone wall behind Gwin's stall.

Well, I hadn't been robbed. That was something.

My hand still in my pocket and my fingers around the gem, I looked back to Gwin and opened my mouth to speak. My thoughts died before my tongue could move.

He was sitting on the ground, slumped back against his stall. His face was so covered in blood that he would be hardly recognizable without his beard, which was singed around the edges. Great chunks were missing from his face, and as I looked down his body, horrified, I saw that more were taken from his arms; his torso; his legs. It was like something had taken bites out of him, something with a maw big enough to rip a hole straight through the man.

"Gwin!" I screamed, finally finding my breath as it tore up and out of my throat. I pulled my hand from my pocket, reaching toward him and struggling to my feet. The pain in my head lanced, making me wince and squeeze my eyes shut. *"Gwin!"*

"What in the hell are you screamin about?"

I stumbled upward, standing, and I saw that Gwin wasn't sitting dead on the ground. He stood, half-turned towards me, one hand resting on the apron over his belly. There was no blood. He looked fine, like he had just a minute ago.

"I..." I sat back on the ground. Everything happening today made me feel like I was crazy. "I don't know. Don't worry about it."

"I ain't worried about you, Jost," Gwin said with a little chuckle. "If Franz knocked somethin loose up there, all the better. Prolly would stop ya from gettin killed in the maze."

"I don't want to hear it, old man," I groaned, and I brought a hand to my head to try to ease the pain. Dried blood flaked onto my fingertips where Franz's knuckles had cut open the skin of my temple. Had Franz hit me so hard that I was hallucinating? It had looked very real; horrifyingly real. Real enough to make me scream, and I didn't make a habit of doing that.

"Got a trade for ya anyway," Gwin said, finished up with whatever two pieces of twisted metal he had been forcing together and setting them down on the front shelf. It looked like a child's puzzle. "For your dirty pig that I took up."

Right, the pig. So he had rescued that as well. Gwin would either eat the pig himself or dry it and sell it as jerky, since the market was slim for maze meat. I didn't really have the headspace to argue with him about snatching up the pig, so I just said, "What's the trade?"

"Somethin you need bad right about now, boy," Gwin responded, reaching into one of his apron pockets. "You're damned lucky I was there, you don't need me tellin you that. I was goin to hire a builder to fix up my sixth-ring stall roof, damn thing's crumbling and I need stone. Shame Franz wouldn't take a job from me on account of knowin you, he's the best around—"

"I'm still waiting for the trade."

"—but there's other builders acourse. And I see you lungin at him like you ain't eaten in days and he's a big hock o beef!" Gwin cackled to himself, shaking his head. His beard scratched against the leather straps of his apron. "You sure you didn get your head knocked earlier? I seen you fight Franz before. You wasn't so stupid those other times."

"Damn it, Gwin—"

"Here." He stepped over to me and handed me a small metal flask, which felt full by the weight. "For the pig. An overpayment. I must feel sorry for ya, seein ya get your ass kicked in the middle of the street."

I twisted the flask in my hand, letting the liquid inside swish around before twisting open the cap and breathing it in. The smell immediately made my eyes water.

"I'm surprised whatever is in here isn't burning through the tin," I said.

"That's not tin, ya nin," Gwin quipped. "It's pewter, and prolly worth three of your nasty pigs. Drink up, it'll fix your head."

"If you say so," I said, and added, "Thanks, by the way."

"I wondered when you were gonna get around to being grateful."

"Mm." I tipped the flask to my lips and let a mouthful of the contents spill into me, swallowing. It burned on the way down and kept burning inside for a moment longer. I closed my eyes and leaned back, resting my head against splintery wood. Warmth filled my stomach, leaching the pain down from my skull.

Eyes still closed, I said, "I have to talk to you, Gwin."

"Do ya? Hey—what you got?"

I rested, waiting as Gwin dealt with someone who had come by the stand for a trade. He usually greeted his customers with such warm welcomes as *what you got* and *whaddaya want*. Thing was, he usually had the answer to both already.

"I got plenty of silk," Gwin said.

"I didn't see any silk on six ring," came the voice from the street.

"Well that's six ring, and this is three ring," Gwin retorted. "You wanna argue with me or you want me to point you to someone who wants your silk?"

I smirked, taking another sip from the flask. It was whisky, and good stuff, probably barreled in north Cartha or one of the inner rings. Definitely too much for my pig, but it wasn't like Gwin was going to be able to pull it back out of my stomach.

Whoever he was talking to eventually got on their way. I opened my eyes, wary of what they would show me, but all was normal. Inside, relief cast cool fingers across the warmth in my belly.

"Get speakin Jost, I got trades to manifest." Gwin cracked his knuckles, a loud sound from old hands. "Ya able to stand?"

"I'm fine down here," I said, the whisky making my limbs and mouth pleasantly loose. "I found something, Gwin. In the labyrinth."

"That *is* what ya do for a livin," Gwin said, eyeing me close.

"No, it's different. I need you to tell me what it is. It's..." Unable to find the right words, I reached into my pocket and pulled out the gem.

"What, an emerald? Give it here, I'll tell ya if it's any good."

I shook my head. "It's not—you have to give it back."

Gwin harrumphed. "You think I'm some thief now?"

"No," I responded, not sure why I had said that in the first place. Of course Gwin wouldn't steal it. I held out the gem on my fingertips, and Gwin took it in his own.

"It's—hey." Gwin frowned, his great, bushy beard moving with the gesture. "Thing's glowin."

"Yeah, it does that."

Gwin slid off one big leather glove, setting it on the stall, where it managed to avoid knocking into the many small things placed there. He touched the gem with bare fingers, and I almost shouted to warn him, just now remembering what had happened to me when I first touched it, but nothing did happen.

Except Gwin's hard face was drawing into an expression I had never seen there before.

Fear.

"Where'd ya find this, Jost?" he said, quiet. Gwin was never quiet.

"The labyrinth, I told you." The man was making me feel very uneasy. "It was just stuck into the wall, like someone had forgotten it there."

Gwin's eyes pulled up from the gem to me, the yellow light reflecting in the whites of his eyes and giving him a sickly pallor. "You need to get this gone, Jost. Something like this shouldn be here, not with all these people around. You'll kill us all."

Chapter Seven

"What?"

I was scoffing, but Gwin's grim expression did not lighten. Deciding I'd had enough, I pocketed the flask and stood, giving my head a little shake to clear it.

"I said get it out of here!"

"Tell me what it is," I demanded.

"Gods and denizens, Jost, I barely know anythin bout this kind of stuff!" Gwin cried, thrusting the gem back towards me. I stared. "Take it!"

I did, plucking it from his fingers and putting it back into my pocket. Losing sight of the little lamp seemed to calm Gwin a bit.

"I'm closin up for the night," Gwin said, a narrow beam of setting sun making him squint. "Help me pack."

"Are you really—"

"*Help me pack,*" he repeated, stern and measured. "Then we're gonna take your pig back to my house, you're gonna cook it up, and we can talk. Make it fast, now."

I knew it was too early for Gwin to close, but I shut up and helped him along anyway. It felt like I was living in a dream, and I'd soon wake up and laugh at how surreal everything was. The gem; the fight; Gwin's odd behavior. If my brain was trying to trick me, then it was doing a poor job. Perhaps the strangest thing was Gwin giving me a generous trade.

But even in the fading light of evening, the world was clear. I smelled dirt and blood. The pain in my head had receded, but it was still there like a lingering odor. I felt the lamp against my leg and the whisky swimming through my body. I was awake.

The two of us cleaned up fast, Gwin waving away any peeking Carthans looking for a trade. Some things were packed into the many pockets sewn behind Gwin's apron; most were locked in the three-foot-square iron strongbox braced to the wall. Gwin claimed that the massive thing weighed over a thousand pounds, and even if thieves were able to pry it free of the bracers, they'd never carry it away. The door was thick as my waist. One had to heave with both hands just to ease it open when it was unlocked.

After we finished clearing the displays and locking up, I looked around. "Where's the pig?"

"In the bag," Gwin said, shrugging. "Your rack broke when you fell down."

"You stuffed a bloody pig carcass inside of my pack?"

"I wasn bout to have the damned thing smelling up my stall, now was I? Scare away all the decent people?"

Like you deal with decent people in third ring, I wanted to say, but I held it back. He'd done me a favor, after all, even if he'd ruined the shirt I had stowed in the bag. If I got to thinking about it, the truth was that Gwin had done me plenty of favors since I'd known him. I'd be more grateful if he hadn't screwed me out of just as many good trades. Business was business, but it was better than nothing. I had plenty of nothing in my life.

"Pick it up and let's go." Gwin's eyes drifted down to my pocket, where the gem bulged. "I'm gonna need a drink."

I swung the bag onto my back and heard the insides squelch.

Gwin's home was in the third ring as well, and I was grateful for the fact. For a man who had no qualms smacking people in the head if they got too handsy with his merchandise, he was awfully jittery. I wondered if he might abandon the idea of talking to me, and I couldn't have that. Better to start him talking now.

"So this thing—" I began, before he cut me off.

"Drink first," he said, not even turning his head to look at me.

We walked through the streets quickly, kicking up dust that had already been kicked up thousands of times today. The buildings around us were shorter than the fourth ring and inward, but some boasted second stories and wood braces. Gray stone dominated the sights around, but there were building painters who went to the third ring to work at times. Their coats didn't last long, but some homes were a sheer white or almost-black, or had single strips of color running horizontally around their length.

The people that did come near us steered mostly clear, heading to wherever they were going. I'm sure some didn't notice us and some didn't want to cross paths with Gwin, but I was equally sure that even more were staying wide of me. Even without the string rack of labyrinth meat behind my shoulders, everyone south of six ring knew Jost.

When a woman with her child in her arms did catch my eye with alarm, I peeled my lips back into a grotesque smile and opened my eyes wide. She pulled her gaze away quickly and hustled past us with a berth.

"Hah," I muttered, letting my hand run over the gem outside my pocket. "You'd better run, lady, I'll eat your kid."

Gwin's house was unpainted, a testament to his plain tastes. Certainly he could afford to hire a painter, with the trades he pulled off every day. The man could move into tenth ring, probably, just one off from the farmers, but preferred to live here because this was where business was apparently best.

The stone house made up for its lack of height with width, spanning five rooms across, though the ceilings were low. It was in good shape, with a wood-frame ceiling and thick tiling that would last for years. Gwin cared for his merchandise, his drink, and his house. I'd known him for most of my life, and those facts had rung true through all those years. If he had other friends besides me, I had never met them.

For all his flaws—and they worsened with drink—I liked the man. Even if right now he was pissing me off.

Once we were inside, I went over to his kitchen and set my bag on the cutting table, untying the top and pulling out the pig carcass. I gritted my teeth, looking at the blood and gristle mingled with my possessions, and slapped the dead animal on the table.

"Clean it, light the fire," Gwin said, caring not a bit about the anger on my face. "I'll be back."

"Oh sure, I'll take care of it," I growled, knowing full well he wasn't listening. "Can I season it for you? Do you want it rare or blackened? Shall I run out and pick some sage from the center field and see if they cut my hands off for it? Or will this be plenty for you, master?"

My grumblings carried me through the cleaning and butchering, and I was just laying the cut meat in the skillet when Gwin returned. He sat down heavy in a chair by a wooden table he had hewn and put together himself. It was hideous. I usually would let him know whenever I was here, which was often enough.

On the table he rested two things: a tankard big enough to quench the thirst of four people, and a very thick, leather-bound book. An old one, by the pallor of the severely-yellowed pages, which looked ready to crumble.

If only I could reuse all the paper from all the books in Cartha. Even just one or two of them. My map could cover a thousand miles each way.

Huh. It was the first I'd thought about my map in hours.

"What's that?" I asked him, nodding at the book.

Gwin didn't answer; instead, he drew the dull iron tankard up to his mouth and drank, long and deep. I prayed it wasn't whisky inside. With him slugging away like that, he'd be under that shoddy table before long, and I'd learn nothing. Behind me, the burrow pig sizzled in the pan as the fat melted.

Gwin slammed the tankard down, and nothing sloshed out. He'd drained the whole thing. I rolled my eyes and turned back to the skillet. I wasn't going to be getting anything out of him tonight. My own whisky haze was just about fully faded by now.

"Set it down," he said to me, and his voice was steadier now that he had practically half a barrel of strong ale inside him.

"Huh?" I half-turned from the food. "Pig's not ready yet."

"I ain't hungry. Douse it and set the fuckin rock on the table."

"Are you serious?"

"Now!" He raised the tankard again, finding some dregs in the bottom and swallowing them. His beard shone wet with what he missed.

"You'd better not be playing with me," I said, knowing that he wasn't. I drew from his water hold and doused the fire, letting the pig cook in the still-hot pan. Gwin watched me as I sat at the table, pulling the gem from my pocket and setting it down. The yellow sphere jostled on the uneven surface, turning a few times before settling in an even space.

Gwin made no move to touch it. Instead, he laid a hand on the cover of the book, which was titled in a language I could not read. Interesting. Not that I was well-versed in any language besides native, but interesting that a book in another tongue would be around. I'd only seen two others in my life.

Gwin was the only person I'd ever talked to who spoke better when he was good and drunk. He pointed an accusing finger at me, and then at the gem on the table.

"Jost, you've found yourself an accumulation of raw magic. Probably the most dangerous thing you can hold in your hands. You idiot."

Chapter Eight

I smiled. Gwin didn't take kindly to it.

"Don't mistake me for bein in a joking mood, boy," Gwin said, his voice edging on dangerous.

"If you're not messing with me, then maybe you're just being stupid," I countered, leaning forward and resting my fists on the table. He glared at me, and I glared back. "You think you just get to rattle me around because you pulled me out of a scrap?"

"Ya might need a drink yourself," Gwin said. "Slow that mouth down. Ya can shut up and listen, or ya can leave. Either's fine with me so long as ya don't bring that little ball here ever again."

I wanted to curse him out, but I bit my tongue and felt the wounds there. Then I pulled out the little flask he had given me and I took another swallow, closing my eyes and letting the good whisky burn its way down to my stomach.

"Good. Ya won't have to listen to me long, on account of I don't have much to say. I know how to read, that's about as far's it goes, ya understand?"

I sat back in the chair and opened my palms, waiting for him to go on.

"Now it's...hold on." Gwin shoved his tankard aside and pulled the book in front of him, table splinters scratching at the leather. He flipped open the heavy cover, rustling through the pages roughly. "It's in here somewhere."

It wouldn't have surprised me if he tore the book to bits with the way he was handling it, but somehow it didn't rip. I looked on as he scanned the pages, my own eyes crawling over text that meant nothing to me.

"You can really read this?"

Gwin didn't look up. "Most of it, if I'm feelin sharp that day. Not all of it. S'why I ain't got too much to tell ya."

You feel sharp today, Gwin? Maybe I can get you the rest of that barrel you started? Truth told, I wasn't feeling so sharp myself.

"All right." He settled on a page, his expression grim. "Jost, you found raw magic in the labyrinth."

I grinned, the corner of my mouth creeping up under its own power. "Should I cook it before we eat it?"

"I ain't seen magic in my life, and I'm sure you haven't either, till right now," Gwin continued, ignoring me. "I only know what I read. And magic isn't some plaything. It's not a tool you can just stick in your belt and use at your leisure. It's a hungry, wild animal. It's alive. And it feeds on you and everyone around you. Are ya followin me, or should I slow down?" He furrowed his brow, looking up to me from the page.

I hung in the chair, my head swimming in tiny circles. I definitely took in a little too much drink. "Okay, yeah. It's magic. It's what, it's gonna eat me? And you? I don't think you'd fit."

In one smooth motion, Gwin picked up his tankard and hurled it at me. It smashed into my shoulder and bounced to the floor with a thud. The whisky dulled the pain, but I could practically feel the big, purple bruise forming on my skin already.

"What the hell!"

Gwin just continued as though nothing had happened. "Magic ain't reared its head in hundreds of years. This book ain't that old, but the words inside are. Last we know of its use was around when the Walls were put up. Even that's not much."

I rubbed at my shoulder. "Fine. I'll bite. Let's say it's magic. Let's say these kids' stories about sorcerers and witches aren't a bunch of bullshit. Where'd it all go? How does *magic* just disappear and decide to come back?"

"Yer askin real big questions," Gwin said. "I don't know. No one does. No book does, and I've seen a few different thousand of em. You know who understands magic?"

I shrugged. "Who?"

"The people who use it. You know where they are?"

"...where?"

"Dead!" Now Gwin laughed, a big hearty laugh that rattled the air. "Dead since before your great-great-grandpa was born and found whatever evening-lady started your family line!"

I rolled my eyes, though I couldn't help but crack a grin. That was a pretty good one. And hell, for all I knew, he was right. I never knew my mother or father, let alone my great-great-grandfather.

"So. Everybody's dead," I said.

"You're damn right. The ones who know about magic, and the ones who don't, they've all got the same thing in common, and it's that they're dead. Because magic don't care if you're new or if you're there by accident. It don't care if you've been toying around with it forever. It's there to get what it wants, and that's your life. It's like a great big well that never fills up, but it has arms that reach out and look for more water."

"A well with arms," I said, intending for it to sound nonchalant, but I thought back to when I found the gem, and how all the dirt was dry and there were no plants near the lamp.

"Somethin like that," Gwin agreed. "I'm no poet. But from what I know, this gem here is a pretty big collection. And when I say raw, Jost, I don't mean like that half-cooked pig in the pan back there. I mean that if magic manages to collect itself in one place, this is what it looks like. A little, unnatural collection of color in some shape or other."

I stared at the sphere, wondering what *little* meant in the scheme of magic. It fit in my hand, but Gwin said it was big. Were there tiny magic marbles rolling around outside, or buried in the ground?

"I found it in a wall," I told him. "It was embedded there, like someone had just stuck it in. But I've been in that maze all my life, Gwin. I never, ever saw anything like this before. Not till now."

"Ya never shoulda," Gwin remarked. "Especially in the Walls. From what I know, magic gathers where there's life, if it's gonna gather at all."

"There's a lot of life here," I pointed out. "I've never seen any...*magic*."

Gwin shrugged. "I look like a wizard? I'm just tellin ya straight off the page, and you're lucky to get that."

I reached forward and picked up the gem, rolling it in my hand. Gwin didn't flinch, but his eyes darted to it.

"I'll tell ya once, Jost. This ain't a joke. Don't treat it like it is, and put that thing back right where ya found it. Only bad will come from magic."

"But say I learned how to use it," I grinned, still rolling the ball in my palm. "Say you taught me a few of those runes in that big old book, and I read my way to some kind of journeyman sorcery. I'd be able to...to...climb on top of the Walls!"

"It's not a training manual ya heathen." Gwin slammed the book shut. "It's a few legends about people who didn't know any better than you do now, and now they're all—"

"Dead."

"—dead."

We said it at the same time.

"I have to go," I said, standing from my chair and finding myself a bit unsteady on my feet. "I had a hunt cut short today, and now I'll need to go twice as long to make up for it. Hope you're ready to buy some pig in a few days."

Gwin was silent for a few moments, and I was sure he was going to continue with his speechifying, but he slid the book aside and leaned back. "Depends how this one tastes, eh? You've been bringin back some ratty meat, let me tell ya."

I raised an eyebrow. "You're thinking of the rats."

I left Gwin to finish cooking the pig, clutching the gem in my hand as I left. It was dark now, and the streets were mostly empty. People didn't like to wander around at night beyond the fifth ring.

The thing wasn't glowing anymore, which made it easy to hide. Even if no one would know what it was, I still didn't want to have to try to explain why my hand was lighting up if someone happened to see.

Franz wasn't much the nocturnal sort, either. I was glad not to see him again. I wasn't afraid of him, but I was afraid of what I might do. And the reason I had bolted from Gwin's place so quickly was because I was starting to link things together.

I glanced down at the gem, where it sat dull against my palm, almost invisible in the darkness. Had it stirred up my brain when it shocked me at the first touch? And why hadn't the same thing happened to Gwin? I had so many questions and nowhere to get the answers.

The only thing I knew for sure was that I had no intention of putting the gem back.

Chapter Nine

It didn't take long to gear up for my hunt again, considering that work had been mostly done when I had left earlier yesterday. I had tucked the gem away in my bag, slept like a rock, and woken up with only a mild whisky headache, so the morning met me well. I was able to whip together a new string rack in ten minutes using some mostly-rotted wood I kept behind my house.

I did have to sort out and clean most of my gear and clothing, however, thanks to Gwin's decision to let my worldly possessions bathe in pig blood. When the smell was washed away and the pinkish water was dumped in the alley, I was about ready to go. The last thing I did was pull the gem from my bag and put it in my pocket again. I wasn't sure why, but I wanted it close. I just felt better that way.

It was early, because I wanted to enter the Walls early. I had a natural gift of waking up whenever I wanted to, regardless if I was dog-tired or liquored up. Some kind of internal timetell ticked within me, and it served me well. So I rose with the birds, grabbed my bag, and ate jerky for breakfast on the way out of town.

Leaving Cartha to go into the labyrinth always filled me with a sparkling of wonder and excitement, even though I could plot my path out for the next two hours of walking. The labyrinth had its twists and its turns, and even if I could find my way back from five miles out, there was no telling what I might find along the way. Especially on the hunt. The hunt could lead me anywhere, and I'd follow the meat for miles.

Unless I came across another magic gem, I supposed. Though perhaps one was enough.

The thought made Gwin's face loom large in my mind, and I pushed it away as I stepped from dirt and stone onto bright green grass coated with the morning's dew. Over me, the southern labyrinth wall rose high, plain gray stone squared off at the top. A semicircle of shadow stretched over most of Cartha's circle from the east, where the top of the sun sliced over the wall, a narrow sliver of yellow in the sky. The air was warmer each hour, but the chill of the maze awaited.

The southern gate didn't used to be the easiest one to get through, but over the years I'd been able to shift the stones to suit my needs. I learned early on that if I left a very obvious path to come and go, people got nervous, and I'd often come back to find the hole sealed up with fresh stone, which is a lot harder to work with. So I had to be a little smarter about it.

The iron-banded doors to the south stood about twelve feet tall. From far away, the wall surrounding them looked like it was one massive block of stone, but up close you could see the huge blocks that constructed it, sharp-cornered rectangles two feet high and four feet across. Impossible for me to move by myself, even if they were just sitting in the grass. But closer to the door, where the stone rounded to fit the arched point at the top, the blocks grew smaller and smaller to accommodate. That was where I could work. Specifically, the left side of the door, close to the ground, where there was a small gap between the stone and the thick wood.

With familiar motions, I widened the gap, pulling free bricks as big as my thigh and as small as my palm, and tucking them into the small divot I'd dug into the ground below the door. I got the hole wide enough to slide my pack and rack through, then it was easy enough for me to slip through to follow, tucking the front of my shirt into my pants so I wouldn't scrape myself bloody on the stone.

And then I was back in another world, one that wasn't truly mine, but I thought of it like that nonetheless. Even if I didn't love the cold and the dark, there was no mistaking the fact that this place was for me alone, and no one in all of Cartha could change that.

In the early morning, the Walls were particularly dark. My feet dug into the same soft spot in the dirt I landed in every time I left southerly, and I didn't need light to show me the way. But the darkness made it easy to see the gem glowing in my pocket, bright enough to shine through the thick fabric.

"You're going to be useful, I think," I told the gem as I took it in my hand and held it up. Out here, whatever ill will Gwin had cast toward the little lamp seemed far away and absurd. Standing here in the dark walls, holding it up in my hand like it was a lantern, the orb seemed to be truly in its element. Like it was meant to guide me through these turns and dark corners.

"Where should we go?" I asked of the gem. The burrow that I was chasing before had surely moved on after being so disturbed. I would have to track from scratch. I'd brought enough food to last in here about three days, and that was assuming I couldn't catch a ratmole or something else to feed me on the way. I couldn't cook a grown pig out here, but I had the materials to make a small fire.

I tossed the gem up and caught it again, and it didn't explode or glare its light angrily at me.

"You're not so dangerous, huh?" I said, chiding myself for lending even a bit of weight to Gwin's words. The man knew a lot about many different things, but I wasn't ready to count magic among them. "I wonder if…"

At that moment, the radial glow of the gem shifted and sharpened, pointing forward like it was being focused. My eyebrows raised in surprise, and I stopped talking to the thing. I had been about to say, *I wonder if you can help me hunt.*

If this thing responded to life, and for some reason I wasn't a good source of it, then perhaps it might be able to point me in the direction of other life. Like plump, skittish burrow pigs. Was it doing that now?

I shifted, turning in place and rotating the gem with me. The light stayed pointed the way it was, turning within the gem to remain stationary where it was cast onto the dirt.

"Well, well," I said, "perhaps there's a bit of sorcerer's blood in me, rather than evening-lady."

Sure of myself, I followed the light as best I could. It painted a weak circle on the ground just a few feet in front of me, so it wasn't quite a guide through the labyrinth. It often pointed me right through walls, and I had to make guesses as to where it wanted me to go, taking turns left and right and making the familiar mental notes I always did. It would be many miles before I would need to reference the map.

My heart thrummed a little when the yellow glow fell upon pig tracks in the dirt, and my lips stretched in a smile. I'd only been in the Walls less than an hour, and I was already on a trail! Without this light, I certainly wouldn't have seen these faint tracks. Danger? This gem was nothing but a blessing.

My mind focused singularly on the hunt now, leaving thoughts of Gwin and Cartha and trades for treated paper—the kind that absorbed my ink and didn't smudge—somewhere in the black recesses of my skull. I let the light take me deeper and deeper. I didn't feel the cold air anymore, or the scratch of the stone as I rounded corners tightly to stay on track. I just saw the glow.

When it snuffed out, suddenly and without warning, I stopped dead in my tracks.

My shoulder, I realized, was aching; I'd been holding the gem in the air for...hours? One glance at the sky told me that. As incredible as it was, the sun was high and past its zenith; over my head, I spotted the fading blaze of it as it crossed over the narrow gap above me. Early morning had given way to early afternoon.

Panic scrabbled at me as I became aware that I didn't know where I was. I let my arm fall to my side and looked around, trying to get my bearings. But I didn't recognize anything here. I scoured for the chips I left in the walls as place markers, but there weren't any. Had I wandered so far off my path? It had only been a few hours.

So it's not possible, I told myself, and I tried to calm down. I hadn't felt this panicked in the Walls since the first and last time that I had gotten lost.

I breathed and closed my eyes. When I opened them, I felt a little better.

"Just follow your footsteps back a little bit until you see something you know." The soft dirt made it easy for me to track myself. Unconsciously, I kept the gem out of my sight.

It was only a few minutes of walking before I found a spot I knew, and I pulled out my map just to be sure. I traced the corners with my fingers until the curve of my nail was resting on the spot where I stood.

"Okay," I said, folding the map. My heart was slowed and my energy was right. I was in control again. "Now I hunt."

It would be the last day I ever felt safe in the Walls.

Chapter Ten

The hunt went better than I could have hoped. For some reason, the burrow pigs weren't burrowed—many were running free, which made them easy pickings. Even though the light of the lamp had led me into a brief state of confusion, it had also led me to a golden trough of meat.

By the next morning, I was carrying half my weight in pigs on my back, and there weren't even that many hanging. They were big ones, the kind that normally just stay in the burrow. The den mothers.

"You'll be heading back early, Jost," I said to myself, gleefully hefting the full rack. "There's a lot of skinning to do, but you'll have enough hides to make a blanket."

I was two miles south of Cartha when I heard the sound.

I whipped my head toward it. Sound was a strange thing in the labyrinth; it was hard to tell where it was coming from, and to be truthful, you heard almost nothing when inside the Walls, unless it was right next to you. The dirt and thick stone blocked everything.

So for something to echo so loudly from the direction of Cartha, it would have to be tremendous. It was a crash so loud that it sounded like the wall around the city had tumbled over and crushed everything flat. I stood there for a moment in shock, my mouth hanging open, the sound rolling over me.

And then I ran.

I didn't know what to think. My feet churned the dirt as I followed the map in my head to take the shortest path back to Cartha. The strings holding the pigs' feet snapped as I ran, and one by one my prizes fell off my back and flopped boneless in the dirt. They were driven from my mind as soon as they hit the ground.

It's not good, I told myself as I ran. *Whatever a sound like that is, it's a bad sound. Did the wall really collapse?* I couldn't imagine what else could have caused it. Inanely, I wondered if my constant shifting of the gate stone had weakened the base and led to a fall.

It's your fault, something told me, and I tried not to listen.

As I neared Cartha, the gem began to tremble against my leg. It must have been going for a while without my notice, because by the time I pulled it out of my pocket, the muscle in my thigh felt numb.

"I don't have time to deal with you," I panted. I'd run over a mile by now, and I hadn't heard another sound after that massive crash. But was that good or bad?

My neck being bent down to look at the gem is what saved my life.

Something hit me—*slashed* me—across my face. I pulled cold air into my lungs and fell forward, not even feeling the pain yet; just the shock. I clutched the gem to my chest and tumbled into the dirt, rolling over on my shoulder and landing on my back. Blood swelled from the cut, which ran at an angle from the center of my forehead and down to the corner of my left eye, a hair's width from blinding me.

As the pain found me and I looked forward, I found myself oddly unafraid. My eyes lit upon this new enemy, and it was clear that it was a true denizen of the Walls. I could tell just by looking at it, while I sat up and put my hand on my dagger.

"So the monsters are real after all."

The words came from my mouth, but I didn't hear them. I was transfixed.

The creature was black as night; black as the dirt beneath the dirt. It was like a big dog, if a dog was made of sharp edges and its front legs were long and spindly and twice the length of its back legs. It was so deeply black that it looked flat, like it was a shadow. I couldn't even see its eyes, if it had any. I could just barely see the narrow gleam of light off of the long, black claws on its front legs.

It was, without doubt, a monster. And it wanted me dead.

It leapt at me again, and I rolled. Blood dripped into my left eye, stinging and forcing it shut. I got to my feet, finding purchase in the dirt, but barely. I lost my balance and slammed into the wall. Blood flew from my forehead and splattered against the stone.

The monster reached out one of those freakishly long front legs and swiped at me. It was even longer than it looked, and I wasn't able to evade it. It caught me deeply on the front of my calf, slicing through my pants like they were made of paper.

Fiery pain lanced up my leg, but I gritted my teeth and moved, pushing off the wall. It clawed at me again, snagging at my backpack and pulling me to the ground.

It was unreal. It was fast, it was deadly, and it could reach me wherever I went.

There's only one way to fight it, then.

When it swung at me next, I jumped toward it, getting inside of its legs. I thought it might lunge its oddly-pointed head towards my throat and bite me, but it didn't. And just as fast as this all started, I was able to drive my dagger into its chest, right below its neck. The blade sunk in easily, up to the hilt in no time at all. A savage grin crossed my face as I twisted the blade and dropped the creature to the ground.

When it kept moving, I stabbed it again, and again. Pulling the dagger back and out; plunging it into the darkness that attacked me. The limbs curled, but they couldn't wrap far enough to slice at me anymore. I had an arm around the thing's short neck, holding it steady as I killed it.

It didn't struggle or panic. It just kept trying to tear off more of me, until its blood soaked my hands and my chest and it stopped moving and died in the dirt.

It never made a sound.

When I pulled myself up from the ground, I realized that I had been groaning, lost in the feverish haze of fighting for my life. I sunk my teeth into my lip to make myself stop, and I wiped the blood off my knife before sticking it back into its sheath. My arms hung loose as I stared down at the beast.

I knelt and grabbed it by its flopping, lifeless neck, hefting up the head to get a closer look. The first thing I noticed was that it wasn't as heavy as I thought it should be. The second thing I noticed was that the creature wasn't furred; its skin felt like hardened leather. I was surprised that my dagger had been able to punch through it.

The third thing was that it didn't have a mouth. It had black eyes that were practically invisible and deep-set into its skull, but there were no teeth to be seen. I felt around its short muzzle to be sure, and I found nothing; just a leathery swell of flesh.

It wasn't trying to eat me. The thing looked like it existed just to kill.

I let it fall to the ground and stood up. A shiver wound its way down my shoulders and back, and I leaned against the wall, not feeling the cold at all. This entire encounter had lasted all of two minutes, and even with the evidence in front of me in a pool of its own blood, I was having a hard time believing it happened. The stinging pain in my face and leg helped to ground me, and remind me that there was a reason I was in a rush.

"Cartha," I muttered. I brought the back of my sleeve to my head and wiped the blood away. The smell of it was thick in the air, or maybe that was just because it was coming from right above my eye.

I used the tattered rags of my pant leg to tie up my wounds, just to stop the bleeding. I'd stitch them up once I got back home and found some clean gut, either in my house or from Gwin.

With the bleeding stymied, I cast one glance back at the lifeless corpse of the monster before resuming towards Cartha. I was only a few minutes away now, and my short prayer that I not be visited by another of those creatures in the meantime was, thankfully, answered.

I arrived at the southern gate to find it...gone.

I blinked, my mouth agape. Where there had been an intimidating tower of wood and iron stood nothing. The gate was not *gone,* of course—it had been smashed to pieces. Dust and crumbles and splinters and twists of metal lay scattered across the grass for a hundred yards, like a grand explosion had blown out from the labyrinth and into Cartha.

That explains the noise, I thought, and I looked further still, where at first it seemed that nothing was awry save for the stone carnage before me. But I saw gouges in the grass and dirt, like great shovels had sloppily torn them up. And in the distance I saw...

I saw no one. In the afternoon, even late like it was now, I should see someone. Several hundred someones, even from this far away.

"Everyone must have run inside from the explosion," I said, already climbing over the rubble and out of the labyrinth, automatically casting my eyes toward the groove where I kept my bricks, even though it was buried under the shredded stone and wood. I moved the bigger pieces out of my way and watched the ground carefully so that I didn't end up impaling myself on jagged shrapnel. "I have to find out what happened."

In my pocket, the gem fell silent and still.

Chapter Eleven

I made it past the destroyed gate and its refuse without further injuring myself, though the slice through my calf and my watering, bloodied eye made it difficult. I couldn't quite run the distance of the field without making myself bleed, so I settled on a fast walk. My eyes were cast ahead and my mind was cast back to the thing I'd buried my dagger in several dozen times. Were there more? What if—

What if they had come into the city? As quick as it had all happened, I was quite aware that I had survived my encounter with the black claw—as I'd started to think of it—by the barest of instinct and a thick cushion of luck, and even that cushion hadn't managed to keep all my blood inside me.

Painful as it was, I moved faster. I could see the east and west gates from where I stood, far, far in the distance, and they seemed to be intact. That was good. Nothing else looked off, save the wreckage behind me.

But everything felt wrong, and the gouges in the earth didn't cease beyond the destroyed gate. They kept going, right into the city. And somehow, I knew what I was going to find before I found it.

The grass became dirt, the smooth-packed roads of the outer rings. There were marks here, too, but shallower where the ground was harder to cut into.

"Hello?" I yelled, the word tearing from my lips as my muffled panic burst out into the air. "Hello!? Hello!? *Hello!?*"

Silence greeted me, whole and unbroken. Oppressive. I felt the weight of it suffocating me.

"HELLO!?"

I panted, catching my breath. My throat burned from my screams and my ears burned from the nothing that came back to me. Everything was fine. Everything was here. There was no blood in the streets, nor fires casting streams of black smoke into the sky. It was a beautiful, sunny afternoon, with fat white clouds in the sky and one bloodied citizen of Cartha standing alone in the street.

I went to Gwin's first. My boots scraped along the ground, the sound loud and empty. The buildings on either side of me felt further and further away even as they grew taller, going from ring to ring, as I looked around frantically for something, anything. I didn't know if I was trying to find other people or if I was on the lookout for another surprise attack from a black claw or some other strange being that had emerged from the labyrinth.

Where did they come from? Never—I've never seen anything like that.

The marks in the grass had been far bigger than what the black claw had left on me.

"Gwin! Gwin?" I started talking as soon as I entered, barging into his house and letting the door slam into the stone wall, hitting it so hard that the wood cracked. The snapping sound cut through the air.

"Come on," I said, storming forward, vaguely aware that my leg was bleeding again. Where I walked, I left one bloody bootprint behind me, a narrow outline of my existence. "Come on, Gwin. Where are you, you ugly drunk?"

Panic and fear turned to anger. I grabbed the chair I had been sitting in yesterday and slammed it to the ground. It fell to pieces. I kicked them out of my way as I prowled through the house.

"Gwin! Get your sorry ass out here!"

I stormed through the five rooms of the house twice each before I stopped myself in the kitchen, where I stared at the dirty pan that held the leftovers of the burrow pig. Gwin had eaten most of it, and left the rest out overnight. Maybe he'd had some this morning, and was planning on finishing it for dinner.

"Where the hell are you?" I said, and instead of sounding angry and guttural as I intended, it came out weak and afraid. Gwin's house was just as empty as the rest of the city.

"Fine." I turned, leaving the house and the broken door behind me. I stepped out of the darkness of Gwin's empty house and into the sun of the empty street. I screamed again into the air, loud enough for it to carry through three rings and leave my throat feeling like I'd choked down a bowl of rock dust.

When I was left without a response once more, I snapped. Abandoning Gwin's house, I began to force my way into other people's homes, at first apologizing to nothing and no one, and then simply flinging open doors and yelling with what little voice I had left.

I found nothing but empty house after empty house. And confusing me even further was the fact that there were no signs of struggle. No blood or torn curtains. No broken furniture, aside from the pieces I took out my rage on, which were plenty. All the doors were unlocked, and most of them were ajar. It was as though everyone had simply disappeared.

We're encased in stone, I told myself as I tore through several dozen houses, some belonging to people I knew, most belonging to strangers. *We're surrounded by walls. There's nowhere for people to go. There's nowhere for people to hide. So where is everyone? Where is everyone? Where is everyone?*

And then I thought, *All this time, everyone said the Walls were for protection. Now they trapped everyone in here so there was no escape.*

No escape from what?

Eventually, I collapsed in the street after I stumbled out of yet another house. I was dazed, thirsty, bleeding, and I could taste street dirt in my mouth. I peeled my face up off the ground and rolled onto my back. My leg was terrible; the stinging had progressed to throbbing, and that had advanced into the fiery, painful sensation of my vigor tearing open my wound even further. I had to do something about it. In some small stroke of good fortune, my blind and furious path through people's private property had led me mostly in a circle, and Gwin's house wasn't far. I propped myself up, using the buildings beside me to keep me upright while I dragged my hurt leg behind me.

I fell in through Gwin's open door and pulled myself to his storage room. Thank above and below that I'd worked with the man for so long, because his way of storing and stacking things would have been indecipherable to anyone else but him and me. I knew he kept gut and needle with his leatherworking stores, which were held bundled in his hides, which were inexplicably in a chest with his dried fruit.

"Crazy old man," I gasped, dragging the hides out of the chest and spilling shriveled apricots and raisins to the floor. I fumbled with the twine bindings until I was able to rip them free and toss them aside, then unrolled the hides to find what I was looking for: a curved silver needle and a bundle of animal gut. All I needed to stitch up my wound. Well, all except for one thing.

I pulled Gwin's flask from my inside shirt pocket. The remaining whisky swished inside, and I brought it to my lips and took a small swig. Enough to steady my nerves; not enough to worry my hands.

Gwin had a corked ceramic bottle of cleansing alcohol, the kind he warned me not to drink, not that I had any intention to. The man got himself hurt fairly often, and he was practiced with tidying himself up. Me, not so much, but I could manage.

I wished he was here. I poured the burning cleanser across my leg, groaned, and got to work.

Chapter Twelve

Stitching myself up took the better part of an hour. I cursed my way through most of it, but I took the time to get it done right because I didn't want all the skin to peel off my bones. When I finished and tossed the bloody needle onto the floor, I noticed that odd book he had dragged out yesterday was here, leaning against a dusty crate.

I didn't know why, but I wanted it, even if I couldn't read the words. It was the only thing besides Gwin that knew anything about the little yellow ball in my pocket. I snatched it and I put it in my pack. Maybe Gwin could have it back when he showed his face.

I limped out of Gwin's house for the second time. The sun was going down, and the empty city around me was slipping into reddish darkness.

Something had occurred to me while I was plunging that sharpened loop of silver into my flesh over and over. If the people had fled, then the people would have fled inward. It was entirely possible that everyone was holed up in the manses that encircled the fields, hiding from...something.

Then why aren't there any signs of fleeing? No turned-over chairs or flurry of footprints in the dirt?

I shook off that doubt. Those were questions I couldn't answer. I had to look. So I turned left from Gwin's door and I made my way deeper into Cartha, into the inner rings I almost never entered. Not that I wasn't welcome—although that was at least a little true, depending on who I ran into—but my business kept me in the outer circles.

I moved deeper into Cartha, the city growing taller around me. Wealthier. Wood braced the homes; glass sat clean in the windows. Polished signs hung to denote drinking holes and shops and eateries. The streets began to be paved with stone, tighter and tighter until you couldn't see the dirt. My boots were loud on them, with my awkward shuffle slapping into the stone.

And still, I saw no one. I peeked into the stores and called, but it was half-hearted. I looked through the windows. I let the vice in my chest grow tighter and tighter as I stared up at the mansions rising over everything else and hoped against hope that I would find something there; anything. Even if it was just one person.

But when I made my way to that innermost ring of Cartha, finding the doors there miraculously unlocked, there was no one for me. I walked the entire ring, though there weren't enough hours in the day for me to explore every nook and cranny of the houses there. If the whole city was crammed into them, I would know.

I left the last house and stood in the wide main road of Cartha's eleventh ring, staring down the long path to the houses it met, and the vast beast of the Walls, miles away. Behind me was a house that could fit about twenty of my own, and behind that were farmlands rife with crop. The wind swept over stalks of corn and wheat and barley and dozens of others, bowing them towards the river that cut north and south in two.

I sat down in the road, my legs laid out long in front of me, my freshly-stitched gash reminding me that it was still there. My pack hung heavy on my back, supporting an empty string rack, three days' of hunting gear, and a book that wasn't mine. My little discovery, my yellow trinket that had enamored me up until I came back to the city, was unlit and unmoving like the rock that it was.

I leaned back on my palms and stared blankly ahead.

Strangely enough, my mind felt clear. I had worn myself to the bone, bled and sweated out most of what was inside of me, and the emptiness made it easy to think. But I didn't know what to think. There were no clues, and there were no answers.

The gem was in my hand. I looked at it.

"What are you?" I asked it, not for the first time, but now I wondered what that question really was, and how many more were to follow. Like why it wasn't lighting up now; why it felt dead and lifeless in my hand.

I stared into it and tried to regain my strength. I had never been less hungry, but I knew that I should eat, so I pulled some dried meat from my pack and forced it down, chewing it fast. It hurt to swallow.

If there was nothing else for me here, if the questions weren't going to answer themselves, then I had to go. But was half a day too soon to write off what might still lie in the city?

"No," I said after swallowing a rough bite of meat. "No one's here."

Which meant there was only one place they could be. How could I not see it before? The gaping hole in the labyrinth wall didn't only mean that something came in. It could be that the people fled through it, too.

"The Walls," I muttered, staring at the faraway behemoth. "They're in the Walls. Have to be."

My body was a mess and on the brink of collapsing, but I forced myself to my feet, dropping the half-fist of dried meat I couldn't finish into the dirt. I set my sights directly ahead and I walked, ignoring the pain, ignoring how my legs cried at me to sit down for just a minute longer. I squeezed the gem in my palm and I plunged back through the rings of Cartha.

I didn't stop until I was staring up at the massive hole in the wall that used to be the southern gate.

"Are you in there?" I said, but it was quiet, and not meant to be heard by anyone. Was I talking about my people, the city that had stood in the Walls for over two centuries and had now lost all its inhabitants except for one? Or was I talking about the black claw, the monsters that may lurk yet in the labyrinth, and the ones I hadn't seen? Either I was perfectly alone in the labyrinth, or I was not. Each possibility brought its own horrors.

I entered again. How odd, to walk unimpeded into this vast, intimidating expanse that so scared all of humanity that after it was built, we never went in again. How odd, to stroll past rubble instead of carefully moving blocks of stone and hiding my egress so that the neighbors around me could sleep through the night. I never sought normalcy before. I craved it now.

Onto the black dirt, the chilled air of the labyrinth enveloping me. I couldn't stop myself from noticing the lack of footprints on the ground; the dirt was wet and loose as it always was. Surely no city full of people had trampled through here.

But...perhaps one?

Hm.

I was looking down at a single set of footprints that certainly weren't mine. For one, they were a few inches too big. They were also going off to the right, and into the labyrinth. My journeys almost always started with a left turn, including my most recent hunt.

My heart lifted a little, thoughts connecting to one another in my mind like stacking stones. *One made it out. If one did, more did. Just because the other gates aren't broken, that doesn't mean people couldn't have used them. Were they open, even just a crack? You couldn't be sure from so far away. Someone could slip past them the same way you do. A lot of someones could.*

I was already following the tracks, though I could barely see them and it was slow work. The daylight was all but gone, and the gem was blank in my hand. I shoved it back into my pocket after muttering a curse. It helped me hunt pigs; why wouldn't it help me track something more important?

The footprints went on for a while, and I imagined that was a good thing. This person made it far into the labyrinth, in one piece. But once I saw the blood, the hopeful feeling was gone. There was a lot of it; enough to see in the dim light; enough to be able to smell it. And when I rounded the blood-smeared corner, I knew what I would find.

I just didn't know who.

Chapter Thirteen

The bloodied, slumped-over form of Gwin was such a shock to me that I practically tripped over the dead black claw, skirting around it at the last second where it lied in the dirt. I kicked it, once, just to make sure it was dead. It didn't move; its long, spindly arm twisted slightly with the kick, stirring the dirt, and it was still again.

I drew my attention back to the body, biting the inside of my lower lip. There was no mistaking Gwin, even in darkness like this. He was sat up against the wall, but his torso leaned to the left. There was blood in his hair, his beard, soaking into his clothes, and surely sunken deep into the dirt below him. I saw slashes in his apron—*Even that worked leather couldn't stand up to those claws?*—and in his boots and on the flesh of his brawny forearms.

Seen this before, I thought, and my mouth went dry. I swallowed.

"Hell," I said to Gwin, dropping down next to him. Blood squished in the dirt beneath me, and I felt a little sick. "You killed it with your bare hands, looks like. That's something. A way to go out."

I wanted to reach out and touch him, but I couldn't bring myself to. He stank of blood. So much blood.

When he did move, I almost screamed, shoving back and kicking up clods of dirt.

Gwin grunted. He straightened up slowly, stiff. His eyes were closed; he opened them with what seemed like great effort, staring at me through the haze of blood on his face.

"That...Jost?"

"Gwin, oh god," I choked out, immediately scrambling back to him. "You're alive."

"Not for long," Gwin said, but not before spitting out a wet smack of blood. "Lucky you."

Even in what must have been tremendous pain, minutes from death, I saw that sarcastic gleam in his eyes. Like he was enjoying the look of horror on my face. The stalwartness of his often-infuriating attitude was like a dash of cold water, snapping me back to normal for just a moment.

I knew he was going to die. I didn't bother trying to think of how to save his life, how to stop the bleeding from the many deep wounds that ravaged his body. I spoke quickly, because time was bleeding away the same as he was.

"What happened, Gwin?" I said. I was on one knee, and I leaned in close so that I could hear him better. "What the hell happened to Cartha?"

Gwin shook his head, a slight motion I barely saw. "Dunno," he croaked out. "Wall exploded. Heard it from all the way in. Saw some...things."

"What things?" I said. When he said nothing, I asked him again. *"What things, Gwin?* Monsters like this behind me? Something else? *What happened to everyone?"*

Gwin breathed, shallow. "Fuck, Jost. Dunno. Everyone...started runnin away. Black things in the streets. Like that. Not like that. Smaller...and bigger."

I thought of the claw marks in the ground, deep gouges I could sink my foot into.

"Gwin, there's no one left in Cartha. It's empty. Where'd they all go?"

The old man's eyebrows twitched in surprise. "I got out. Things musta...killed them. Crowd thinned...the further I got."

It wasn't worth it to explain how the city wasn't slaughtered, but instead vacant. "How'd you get out? How'd you get by all the monsters?"

He laughed then, or at least it sounded like he was trying to, as a wet bubble of blood burst in his lips and he groaned in pain from the attempt. "Was like they...didn' even see me. Ran here. Then that thing got at me. S'fine...was never gonna live long...in the Walls. Not like..."

"Not like me, yeah, I get it."

"Jost," he said, and he clutched at me, only he didn't have the strength. His fingers just brushed against my shoulder, then fell back to his lap. His voice found the weight his grasp didn't have. "Ya can't go back. To Cartha. It's found. It ain't safe. You...you understand?"

Gwin's eyes were tired, but they were clear. He raised his hand again and didn't make it as far as my elbow.

It's found.

I tried as hard as I could to make sense out of what he was telling me, and failed. Cartha was no longer safe. Gwin had slipped into the labyrinth in the chaos, inexplicably survived, and knew nothing of anything else that happened.

And now he was going to die.

I reached inside my shirt and found the flask. The gem was awake, it seemed, and thrumming lightly against my leg, but I hardly noticed.

"Here," I said, holding out the polished metal. "Can you drink?"

One of Gwin's eyes had closed. The open one looked at the flask, then at me, and then Gwin said the last thing he'd ever say to me or to anyone.

"Aye."

I spun the top off the flask and swung it to the side; Gwin reached up one shaky, bloody arm and took it. He brought it to his mouth without dropping it, and he tilted it up. There was enough whisky left in it to almost kill me. Maybe it would bring him some peace.

His head slumped to his chest, and I took the flask from him before it could drop. He didn't clutch at it. It was empty.

I screwed the cap back on and waited for Gwin to stop breathing. It didn't take long.

Chapter Fourteen

I sat down next to Gwin after he was gone and I thought awhile. I was so used to the smell of blood that it was like it wasn't even here anymore. I leaned against the wall, where the wet redness smeared against my clothes, and closed my eyes, breathing slowly. If a black claw would come, or some other beast, let them.

People told me that I was strange, when I asked about it, for not remembering my childhood. The farthest I could go back was when I was eight years old. I don't know how I knew I was eight, and not seven or nine, but I did. And I could recall eating a hot bowl of something-or-other and thinking that it was the best thing I'd ever had. Someone was sitting there with me, an older man. My father? Perhaps, though I'd never met the man, nor my mother. I just remember eating from a bowl and someone watching over me, for that brief moment in time.

I tell myself it was Gwin, but I don't really remember, and it probably wasn't, because I didn't really meet Gwin until I was eleven.

Those first few years, I survived in Cartha as a lifter. Another word for that would be 'thief.' Gwin thought the first time he caught me stealing from him was the first time I had ever tried, and I never told him any different.

But instead of beating me to death, he put me to work for him. He knew I went into the Walls—most people did by then. Gwin was a drunk with a hard tongue, but he was just as focused on his business, and he knew an opportunity when he saw it. I'm sure he took far more money from my findings than I did, but it never bothered me.

The dead man next to me was not my father. He was not my mentor nor my savior. He cut me some trade for my work, but I still slept alone in the streets until I could build myself a shack. We didn't share a meal until I was seventeen and he was too drunk to cook without setting his wares on fire. Kind kid that I was, I stepped in to horribly burn some chicken and eggs that his sloshed self wolfed down despite their char.

"If you burned to death in here, where would I get my trades?"

I smiled. I remembered asking him that. I was angry, but the anger had felt different. Like I cared a little bit what happened to the old man.

"You touch my stuff even after I'm dead," Gwin had said, *"And I'll kill ya all the way from the after, ya rat."*

"I stole your book, Gwin," I said aloud to his unhearing ears. "And your gut. I spilled your fruit and I left your needle bloody on the floor. So if you're gonna kill me now, I wouldn't blame you."

I opened my eyes, letting out my breath. "I broke your chair, too."

I turned my head to Gwin. Despite his decade-old promise of posthumous wrath, his body did not stir. My eyes drifted toward the black claw, its shadowy form invisible against the dirt. I was alone here. More than alone; I was surrounded by death.

I felt weak and lost at that moment, a despair that stretched time out long and thin, forming a tunnel with a far, far away end. I stared into nothing and it stared back at me, inviting me forward. I didn't have the strength to get up. I hardly had the strength to think. My hand slipped down to touch the gem, and I felt warmth there, so different from the icy stone behind me and the cold dirt beneath me.

"Magic," I murmured, letting my fingers wrap around the smooth surface. I stared straight ahead into the darkness, feeling the gem and the tingles of warmth it passed into my fingers. I pulled it out and saw that it was glowing so brightly that it practically blinded me to stare at. How had I not noticed before? It was warm to the touch, too; almost hot.

"Lot of good you've done me," I said to the thing, and I briefly wanted to throw it into the depths of the Walls, to lose it forever. Upon that desire, I was swept over by horror at the thought of doing such a thing. Immediately, I pulled the gem to my chest, its weightless heat burrowing into me.

I wouldn't. Never.

The gem thrummed like it was listening to my thoughts. And suddenly, the weight of everything crashed into me—my exhaustion, my injuries. The death of my only friend. The vanishing of my people, and my small, fragile existence beneath the height of these massive labyrinth walls.

I let it crush me and I blinked into sleep, hugging the warm gem close.

Chapter Fifteen

It was still dark when I woke up. At first I thought I had only slept for a few hours, but the raging hunger in my stomach told a different story, and so did the smell of death and decay that greeted me before I even opened my eyes.

My hunger twisted into nausea. I leaned away from Gwin's corpse and vomited, splashing what little contents my stomach had into the dirt. I managed to crawl around my mess to get away from the scene, my ears ringing and my head pounding with each pulse of my heart.

I got to my feet and my sliced leg brimmed with pain; ignoring it, I stumbled around the corner and fell again. It smelled like wet dirt and rotted roots here, the normal scent of the labyrinth. I breathed easier, but my stomach still turned.

I must have been asleep for the whole day and into the next night. For Gwin to have smelled like that...

I managed to hold back my gorge and take a deep breath, pushing myself up on shaky arms and standing again. I pressed my shoulder against the cold stone of the wall and tried to think. I should be grateful a monster didn't find me. Perhaps they hated the smell of corpses, too.

There were two choices casting their long shadows over me. The first was to go back to Cartha, a thought that should have brought some modicum of comfort but instead chilled my bones.

Ya can't go back.

It's found.

If he and I escaped through some small timing of fortune, returning might be the thing to bury me.

The second choice was to flee into the labyrinth, and go deeper than I ever had before. The flickering of excitement that would usually accompany an idea like that was heavily muted, knowing that I had no home to return to. It would be all or nothing.

"Cartha can't be the only city still around," I whispered, grinding my shoulder against the stone while I stared down at the dirt. "I could...I can find something else. Someone else."

Part of me believed that and part of me didn't. I knew that whatever small area of the Walls I had explored represented very little of what was still out there, but I also knew that in my hundreds of square miles of charting, I had never, ever seen a sign of human life. Maybe it was just that whoever else was locked away in the labyrinth chose not to venture—like everyone else in Cartha.

Or maybe they weren't there at all.

The fact was, I couldn't sit in the city. Everyone wasn't just going to suddenly return if I waited long enough. So I decided on both choices—I would return to the city to grab whatever I could carry for my journey, and then I would leave Cartha, probably never to return.

Gwin told me not to go back. He wanted me to survive; to live through this hell. I already stole plenty from the man. I owed him that much.

"Just one more time, Gwin," I said. I straightened up from the wall, facing towards the path that led to Cartha. "Then I'm gone."

I trudged through the black dirt, my body waking itself up one step at a time. I was rested, at the very least. And now that the nauseating stench of Gwin's corpse was far enough behind me, hunger made its straining appearance once more. I pulled some meat and wet root onion from my bag and ate them with big bites, barely avoiding choking. My mind was either blank or my thoughts were running through my head so fast that I couldn't make sense of them.

What do I need? I finally landed on that thought, seizing it like a rope. I should have some idea of what I would grab from Cartha. I'd taken a thousand trips into the labyrinth, some hunts lasting several days. But I had no idea what to take with me for a voyage like this. Unknown and permanent.

"Food," I said, though I could hunt in the labyrinth. "Firestarters. Clothes...a new lantern..."

It's not stealing if everyone's dead, I told myself, and I thought that might bring a laugh out of me, but it didn't.

"A weapon," I said, tasting the word. I had my daggers, but with what I knew was out here—and what I didn't know was out here—it might do good to have something else. There were a few swords and bows around Cartha. They were expensive and useless, used for show or competition or decoration. I'd never in my life heard of someone killing someone else with a sword in the city, but I'd read about it and heard plenty of stories. I'd shot a bow once or twice. I had no confidence with either weapon.

I emerged from the labyrinth and back into Cartha. Muted, late evening light made the buildings look black and featureless, and I heard the breeze roll across the grass and slide between the green blades. It was a pleasant evening. I hiked my pack further up on my back and strolled into the silent city.

I went to the second-ring butcher's first. His meat was still out on the wooden display shelf, never pulled in from the day before. I didn't want the fresh cuts, much as I might enjoy them any other day. I pushed in through the ajar front door and around the counter to the dry storeroom, a place I'd slipped into many times as a young lifter. I'd never been as an adult. It brought back strange and sad memories I didn't care to linger on.

I filled three pockets with dried meat and I left, closing the doors behind me. I looked to the left, deeper into Cartha, and realized that anything I would need would be at Gwin's.

"One last bout of thievery, is that okay, Gwin?" I said, setting off toward his home, which was just a few minutes away. A thought struck me, and an excited smile actually settled onto my face. "You have treated paper, don't you? Sure you do. Oh, Gwin, just one more haul, but I am going to clean you out. Sorry, friend."

What better time to expand my map than now? I was surprised the inclination had taken this long to grab hold of me. It put a hustle into my step. I'd make my map ten times as big, if I could. Maybe even more. It would fill a book!

When I neared Gwin's, I didn't see what lurked nearby. But I heard it, and I flattened myself against a wall in shocked silence. Strange claws scraped against the dirt.

It hadn't seen me. I slipped around the wall as quietly as I could and tucked myself between two houses.

What the hell were you thinking, coming back here? I shouted inside my head. *Now you're dead. You're as dead as Gwin, you just don't know it yet.*

I peered around the corner and saw a black claw in the street, incredibly hard to spot were it not for its claws, scraping along the hard ground and catching what little light there was. I watched it, wondering if my heart would start beating loud enough for it to hear.

The monster was walking close to a nearby house, practically touching the stone wall. As I watched, it reached out one of its long arms and scraped gently at the stone. The noise made my ears twitch. Was it searching for survivors?

Another horrid thought: was it waiting for me to come back?

I shook my head. *Don't be stupid. These things aren't smart, and you're gonna make a mistake if you think they are. They're monsters, and they don't care about you except to spill your blood. So get out of here, Jost. Get out.*

It was stupid. It was irrational and reckless, but there was no one around to judge me. I wanted that paper.

I took my pack off and laid it on the ground, letting the strap slip through my fingers slowly. I was only a few houses down from Gwin's, and it would be a lot easier to move in stealth without the bag.

Before I moved toward Gwin's, I dared another glance at the black claw. Something about its behavior bothered me.

The creature was pushing its arms into the wall, its claws sinking through the stone. It rotated them, carving out a chunk of the wall, and let it fall to the ground, where it hit with a dull thud. Then it dug its arms in some more.

I blinked, not sure what I was seeing. Maybe it was trying to burrow its way inside. To think that its claws were strong enough to cleanly cut stone like that...I shouldn't be alive right now, and I was about to risk it all again.

But I was already here.

I pulled back from the street and crept through the alley, very aware that I could stumble across another creature lurking here. Thankfully, the alleys were clear. I laid my hand on the wall of Gwin's home.

In and out, I told myself, taking pains to not speak aloud as I often did. *You know where it is. Storeroom lockbox. Unlocked, because Gwin knew I was the only person in Cartha who cared about buying loose paper, and he trusts me. Trusted me.*

A twinge in my chest. I moved into the street and I didn't see the black claw until it touched me.

Chapter Sixteen

How I didn't scream, I'll never know. The odd, leathery hide of the creature grazed across my hip like a deadly wind.

I froze, wishing I had gone for a weapon first, or that I'd at least had the foresight to walk around with a dagger in my hand. But it was too late for that. I took a step back and waited for the monster to attack.

Waited, reaching slowly for my weapon.

Waited.

The attack didn't come. Somehow, the black claw didn't seem to have noticed me. I took long, slow steps backwards until I reached the alley again and quietly let out my strained breath.

The window, Jost, just go through the window.

The wall on the opposite side of the house had a shuttered window, just a square cut into the stone, which I should have used in the first place.

I hurried back around the house and shoved at the shutters. They didn't move. Locked. So I pushed harder until the narrow hook lock splintered off the wood and the shutters flew inward. I pulled myself through and fell hard onto the floor, not feeling the pain.

Watching the window, I got to my feet, expecting the monster to follow after me. Surely it had seen me. In close quarters, here, I could win. I'd done it before. The thing's clawed legs were too long to be of any use in a tight room like this.

I stepped backward and something squished under my boot. Grimacing, I whipped around, thinking, *How could they be inside here, too!?*

It took me a moment to realize I was stepping on the dried fruit I had spilled on my earlier endeavor. I sighed. The window stayed empty and I closed the shutters, though they hung ajar.

For the time being, I felt safe. And when I realized that I could see in what should be total darkness, I pulled the glowing gem from my pocket and grinned.

"Look at you," I whispered, holding it before my face. "Finally helping out when I need it."

The gem did not reply; it just held its steady yellow glow, bright enough to help me search for what I needed, and hopefully not strong enough to peek through the slat in the shutters.

The strongbox was up high, atop a stack of small crates that almost reached the ceiling. It was funny, because Gwin wasn't that tall. I pictured him climbing on these crates to get the box, or pulling a ladder over from another room just to reach his own wares.

I still had to boost up on one of the shorter crates to reach the small metal box. I opened it to find a thick stack of treated paper. I ran my tongue over my teeth as I touched it, feeling the smooth surface, confirming it was real. My map, as it was now, was composed of eleven paper sheets, attached at the borders and scrawled with tiny, neat lines and writing. This stack here had forty sheets, at first glance.

I closed the box again and put it under my arm, landing back in reality. I had what I came here for, and now I had to get out. The window would be best; back the way I came, grab my pack, and slip through the alleys until I reached the field to the destroyed southern gate.

I opened the shutters and managed to pull myself up along with the box, looking first to the left, figuring the black claw would be in the direction I'd come from. But looking to the right, I saw that it was there, and that it hadn't been a black claw at all.

This monster was black, too, and hard to see. It should have been impossible to make out in the night, but it was surrounded by some narrow glow, like it was outlined in very faint white. The shape it drew against the darkness was wretched and unnatural. Unlike the black claw, which somewhat resembled a four-legged beast, this thing was a mishmash of smooth lines and rigid angles, like an ooze that had clung to and trapped a bunch of planks, and now they stuck out of it at jarring angles.

As I watched, it moved these stiff limbs as though they were spider's legs, pushing its spattered body up from the ground by just a couple inches. Its glowing outline moved fluidly, like it barely contained the seeping liquid that comprised this being. Did it notice me? Was it looking at me, staring me down, deciding how to kill me? Impossible to tell without seeing eyes or a face or a mouth—why didn't these things have mouths, what in the name of the denizens were they?

If it could see the lamp glowing in my clothes, surely I was doomed. I knew it was still lighting itself, and I had no idea how to stop it.

Fast but silent, I let myself slide back down out of the window and into Gwin's home again. I'd have to take my chances out through the front door, which had managed to close itself when I last burst out of the house.

I crept to the door of the storeroom and pushed it open slowly, somehow convinced that one of the black claws had burrowed through the wall and into the house, but all was clear. Unless one of them was tucked into a corner, invisible in the blackness...

Ears alert. I tried to keep my breathing quiet, which wasn't an easy task, and I tried to keep my boots quiet, which was even harder. Stupid, ungainly things. I should have done this barefoot.

I reached the front door and rested my hand on it, looking down slightly and listening for any hint of what awaited me outside.

Listening for the sound of claws on stone, or for more pieces of the building across the street being pulled off and dropped.

Quiet.

Go now or stay here forever.

I pulled open the door, unconsciously thanking it for moving smoothly and without groans or squeaks. The street was empty, but what stopped me in my tracks was the absence of the wall across from me. The house that faced Gwin's was gone. Not like it had never been there, because it had, and I could see small crumbles of stone scattered around the ground. But the walls, the roof, the front door...

Don't go insane, I told myself, blinking and hoping something would change. *Don't go insane, Jost, you can go insane when you get lost in the Walls but don't go insane now, even though it would be really easy to go*

I turned to my right and started walking, my mouth dry and my throat blocked.

Don't go insane.

Right through the alley, two more lefts and I was opening my pack and sliding the box inside before I put it over my shoulders again.

Get out.

It felt safer to move through the alleys than the street, so I did, but I was starting to lose it and my pack was bulkier than normal and I was bumping into barrels and getting caught on the walls, snagging on rough stone or knocking my elbows on the corners.

Everything I laid my eyes on made it harder to grasp what was happening. Did Gwin know? Did he know what I'd be coming back to if I returned?

Black claw. I heard its uneven movements somewhere near me. But was it in the street or in the alleys? I was in a labyrinth of sorts among the houses here, and sound was a tricky ghost. I put my left hand flat against the nearby wall and tried to listen, and that was when it emerged from around the corner in front of me.

I bolted, praying that I could outmaneuver it among these narrow spaces and cursing my bloated pack for slowing me down. My legs didn't get cut out from underneath me, so I must have been faster than I felt.

When I stopped, I was probably a half-mile west of Gwin's, but I couldn't be sure. I'd have to take to the streets to get a sense of direction.

I slipped out of the alleys, my watchful eyes scanning left, right and forward, very aware that I would only be able to see these things if I was lucky. At least I was able to get a better sense of where I was, and I could move south.

But south seemed to be the only way I could not go. I saw a black claw in the street, and then another in the alley, so I had to turn and flee. It happened again and again. It was frustrating and horrifying and I could only imagine that they were pouring through the southern hole, somehow just hours behind my exit into Cartha.

"West, then," I said, falling back into the habit of talking to myself in my fear-driven delirium. "Have to go west, I'm closest, I can get around the gate and be gone."

I don't know how I made it out alive. I saw many black claws and other things, but they didn't seem to be interested in me. They were scraping and cutting. Destroying stone; destroying homes. Bringing down walls. I heard more thuds around me, and louder crashes. I pictured roofs crumbling and shattering the beds and tables underneath. I pictured the butcher shop collapsing, the skinned carcasses squelching under heavy stone. I pictured my house, gone, its shape imprinted in the dirt.

The grass of the western field greeted me at last, the ground soft under my feet. Darkness sat before me like a thick fog, perhaps hiding nothing at all, or hiding my death. It wouldn't matter if my house was gone if my blood was all spilled out in this field. It wouldn't matter if my house was gone if I could never come back to Cartha again. But it still hurt me, and at this moment, staring towards the wall, I knew I was looking at my future. I could never turn back.

My steps were unhindered, and I crossed the field in the absence of starlight or moonlight, my journey covered by some errant cloud.

The sky cleared when I reached the western gate, casting nighttime light onto the wood and iron. It was unbroken, so utterly normal compared to everything behind me. I turned to say goodbye to my city.

The cityscape was familiar. Whatever damage had been done wasn't yet widespread enough to make it unrecognizable. But deeper in the city, within the inner rings, there was something else. It was no black claw; no glowing, viscous shadow. It was a monstrous, massive, malign entity, and it rose above even the farmer's mansions, blocking their roofs and the fields behind it.

I watched this thing rest one gargantuan, misshapen hand on a two-floor building and crumble it down to the ground. I stared as it did it again, and again, in slow but smooth motions, as though it were flattening flowers in a field.

I turned and I left Cartha.

Part Two: Into the Labyrinth

Chapter Seventeen

The labyrinth greeted me with cold silence. I hadn't been to the western gate in some time, but I knew I could make it a few miles without needing to glance at my map. Of course, I now had to go beyond that. There was nowhere else for me to go.

"At least I don't have to see Gwin's body again," I said, casting a glance south toward where his remains laid. "That's something."

And I have all this paper.

A humorless smile crawled across my lips. The weight of my pack pulled on me like it wanted me to stay in Cartha. I drew it up higher on my shoulders and put my footprints in the dirt, one after the other. My ears were strained and alert for a sound, any sound, whether it was the sound of my city collapsing or the scratches of claws on the stone around the corner, but all was still. I could hear my breath, thin and alone.

I outlined my map in my head as I walked, curving widely around corners and staying focused on the path ahead. Surely there had to be some monsters still here; they couldn't all be in the city. I could be inches from death and not know it. It was so damned dark, and the gem was unlit once more.

This was crazy. I'd been to this part of the Walls dozens of times, yet it felt different. So many shadows that could be hiding darker shadows with sharp claws.

With fear gripping me, I reached not for my dagger nor my pack, but for the gem, where it sat mute in my pocket and rested likewise in my palm as I held it out.

"Light up," I said, giving it a little shake. "Come on. Glow. I need the light."

With each second, the darkness pressed in on me heavier. I'd dealt with the dark of the Walls for years just fine, but now it was oppressive and heavy. I squeezed the gem, its unyielding surface hard against my fingers.

I was very scared very suddenly, and I closed my eyes and tried to squash that feeling but couldn't. It was like every hair on my body was standing up, like I was surrounded and I knew it and I was just waiting for the world to collapse in on me.

I need light, I thought. *I need it.*

And when the fear stopped my breath, when I opened my eyes again, I had it. The gem was alight, and it chased away the shadows for ten feet. When I tried to see beyond those shadows, the light crept further.

I breathed again.

With the light around me, my anxiety ebbed away. I was still scared—only, the fear was now resting up for its next visit.

Something's wrong with you, I thought, *and there's not a thing you can do about it except try not to go crazy on your way to dying in here.*

"Easy," I said, and I managed to stop talking to myself for a few miles until I was breaking into new territory. All the while, the gem kept its glow for me and seemed to brighten whenever I looked at it.

When I took my first step past the lines on my map, I was already looking at the paper with a pen clenched in my teeth and the gem awkwardly tucked into my palm while I held the papers. The iron taste of the nib tickled at me, not yet wet with ink. I lowered the map from my eyes and looked ahead.

I tended to halt my explorations at straightaways, and this western line was no exception. Above and beyond the top of my map stretched a length of hall that went on, surely, for at least a mile. I remembered seeing it in the daytime weeks ago, how far it stretched, most of its mysteries now hidden in the dark of the night.

"And there are branches, branches and branches," I said, glancing down at my map and quickly but carefully sketching in the barest length of lines to note where I stood, and indicate the distance which laid before me. I held the gem between my shoulder and neck while I penned with my free hand. Despite its light, it was cold as a buried rock.

I would go forward as far as felt right, I decided, and put the map under my arm. If a path looked clear, I'd take it. But the goal was to cover as much ground as I could. Sleep would come soon, but I still had some energy.

Before moving on, I dug into my pack and found some trap netting, old stuff I hadn't gotten around to using on the hunt. I tied a portion of the net into a small sling and secured it atop the strap of my bag, then put it back on. I was able to set the gem inside of it so it hung from my shoulder and rested against my side.

"Now I don't need to grow a third hand." I smiled, and the smile left me when I began to walk, marking my progress with straight lines as I moved forward and westward.

Like the other parts of the labyrinth that had once been new to me, this farther-west area was just as dark, cold, and full of dirt as the rest. After marking a few branching paths down, I took a right turn. If I started curving back east, then I'd readjust.

The last thing I expected to find as I broke into this wing was a body. I yelped, shocked, as the gem's yellow light crawled over the corpse. My first thought was that maybe the person was alive, but of course no one whose arms and legs were bent like that could live. The body was facedown, like the head was being absorbed into the dirt. Not only was it dead, but violently dead, its legs bent at such sharp angles that I could practically hear the cracking of the bones still bouncing around the walls.

I turned immediately. This was not the way I wanted to proceed. I went back to the main hall at a fast walk, ignoring the other branches I'd marked along the way. The image of the twisted body laid in the back of my eyes, blinking in and out of existence. I felt that nausea come back, and I bit down on the insides of my lips.

Are you from Cartha, or somewhere else? How long ago did you die?

Left. I'd go left this time.

I placed my hand along the wall, dragging it across the stone. I came to the third left-side branch in the hall, having passed over the first two. The light pulsed gently as it bounced off my ribs. It was as unsteady as I felt.

I had never seen a dead body in my life. The last hours had brought me across two, and as my flat gaze fell upon a third, sprawled here in the dirt, one arm reaching forward, my mind reeled away from reality. I spun and I ran, clinging to one thought only.

Don't get lost.

I held my pen and map while my light thrummed like a heartbeat, hurrying back the way I had come. Anywhere that wouldn't take me to a corpse.

But everywhere I went, there was a body waiting for me. Or two. Or several. And soon my mind was empty and I was just running, tired, my body aching, my wounds throbbing, and my hand miraculously working the pen across the paper so that I wouldn't forever   wander   this   labyrinth   as a lost soul, waiting to join the people half-buried in the dirt.

The branches off this main path were infested. Infested with the remains of the dead, people I might have recognized if I were to study their faces long enough, because surely they had to all be from Cartha. Where had my city gone? Well, now I knew, and I should never have asked. They had fled to the labyrinth and been killed off, and I was here to find them and flee. Was I truly the only one left? The only one alive? Why me?

But that was obvious. I was the labyrinth wanderer. The oddball. The one who was feared and hated by more Carthans than I would ever be able to number. And my lust to navigate the walls had saved me from the very things they were always rumored to contain.

Saved me for now, at least.

I was being funneled down the straightaway and I didn't realize it until I slowed down, gasping for breath. I had been running—for how long? Time was a blur and behind me was blackness. Only the map could tell me how far I had come, and the lines I looked at were long. Miles long, in the scheme of the paper. The kind of distance it would take me months, maybe even years to cover if I was thoroughly mapping it, and I'd run it all.

My chest burned like I'd swallowed flaming pepper. I tried to catch my breath and couldn't; I dropped to my knees, cold dirt pressing against my legs. The map fell to the ground next to me, and the gem swung back and forth under my shoulder. I stared straight down at the dark ground.

The light bobbed beneath me, and my eyes latched onto it while I got air into my lungs. It was swinging oddly. It was faint, but something was wrong. Like it was reaching for something.

I rolled onto my side, then onto my back, letting my bag slide off me. A black claw could come for me now while I was prone and helpless; I didn't care. I felt like I was inches from death, like my body would wither away.

Resigned to the earth of the labyrinth, I thought. *Fitting for me.*

I needed sleep. If I didn't find it, it would find me. There was no energy within me to put up a tent or cover; not even to reach into my pack and pull out a blanket. I lied in the dirt and stared up at a sky that I couldn't see until my eyes closed. Faintly, at my shoulder, I felt the gem tugging, straining slightly against its harness. I ignored it; the sensation was far away and unimportant.

When I fell asleep, I don't know how long it lasted, but it had been enough for the sun to barely emerge. It gave the Walls their eerie cast of early-morning light; whatever was left as the rest of the world took its share. I opened my eyes and took it in, then I looked around and I realized a few things.

I was somewhere else. Not where I had fallen asleep. My shoulder felt pinched and raw. And there was a track in the dirt trailing from me, like I'd been dragged to wherever I was.

I took this information in within about one second and I was up on my feet in the next, turning to find whatever or whoever had taken me here.

As I swung around, the gem in its harness smacked me in the chest, and I slowed. My left shoulder stung; I'd fallen asleep with my pack half-off, the left strap still slung around me, where the gem was attached. I remembered feeling that tugging sensation as I'd drifted off.

"You?" I whispered, taking the quiet gem in one hand and rubbing my shoulder with the other. "You pulled me this way?"

I wasn't dead or injured. Nothing and no one was around. It made no sense at all, yet it was the only explanation. I marveled at it for a second, then—

Don't get lost.

Panic swelled up. I checked my map pocket, but I knew it was empty, because I'd dropped the map when I'd collapsed last night. If it was gone, and I didn't know where I was...

"Breathe," I commanded myself, the word weak and choked. "Follow the track. You know...exactly where you came from."

And I did; it was marked in the dirt. I just didn't know how far I had come, and if the track would still be where I hoped it would be. The Walls didn't tell me where I was. It all looked the same, unless you knew what to look for. Here, I didn't.

Both in front of and behind me were sharp right turns; I was standing in a short hall between them with no idea what waited on the other side. If I had been dragged all night, it might be a long journey before I found out.

I could worry about the why later. I had to find my map.

I moved quickly, my feet light with the odd weightlessness that panic brings. I rounded the corner, following the scraped path my body had made through the dirt, praying to anyone that might answer to guide me back to my map.

And then...there it was. Everything. The map. My pen, that I had also dropped. My imprint in the dirt from where I'd slept. I'd barely gone anywhere at all. Just around the corner, a corner I hadn't seen in the craze of the night before.

I let my breath out in a rush and snatched my map up from the ground. The dirt didn't stick to the sealed surface. My pen was dirty, and I shook it off, batting it against my thigh. Immediately, I marked the twin corners on the map as I muttered to myself about how I was going to go crazy. I was surprised I hadn't already. I'd been attacked by monsters, I'd watched my only friend die in front of me, and my city was being pulled apart piece-by-piece as I fled. By now it could already be gone. Maybe I was already crazy, and this was the result.

A comforting thought.

The map now told me that the best path forward was through those corners. Behind me, I knew, laid body after body after body. I could walk over them, past them, but...I didn't want to. Following a trail of corpses couldn't possibly lead to anything good.

Calmer now, but still confused about my short, involuntary trip, I turned around and followed my trail once more, a quick walk to where I had awoken. The moment I stepped beyond that spot, the gem woke up. Still hanging from my shoulder in its snug harness, it glowed bright enough to make me squint. And then it stretched forward like it was being pulled, or trying to get somewhere on its own, tugging at the strap of my pack.

"Unbelievable," I whispered, while at the same time standing my ground, because the force was strong enough to move me if I let it. No wonder my shoulder had hurt.

I could resist it, but should I? What alternative was there besides back through the bodies?

"You've lived here longer than I've been alive, I'm sure," I said to the gem. I was now well past the point where it felt strange to talk to this round yellow rock. "You know better than me about this place. I'm just a map maker. Pig hunter. Bad trader." *Lone survivor.*

I followed the pull, marking my map as I rounded the corner. I stole glances at my paper to make quick lines, keeping my attention focused ahead. The morning light showed me some, but not all. This corner led to another sharp left turn. I marked it and I took it.

And then the gem fell flat against me and I stopped dead in my tracks, because set into the right-side wall some hundred feet ahead of me was something I never really believed I would find—at least not so soon.

After hundreds of miles and a life of wandering, I had found another gate.

Chapter Eighteen

It was just a few miles beyond my map's western border. My jaw hanging, I traced my finger along the path that had brought me here, triple-checking to make sure I hadn't somehow circled back to Cartha. But this was no Carthan gate.

"Just a year...maybe two," I muttered in disbelief. "I spent so much time in the south...but eventually I would have come this far west. Two years and I would have made it here. It was this close, all this time..."

Not that close. You ran a dozen miles last night, Jost, and that's why your legs feel like raw meat.

A gate would mean a city. It would mean there were people besides Carthans—people besides me. I knew there should be other cities, everyone did, but no one had ever seen one. I assumed I'd never get to find one, and certainly no one else was trying. If I had found this earlier...

I shook my map, the sharp sound of the paper bringing me back into focus. That was useless wondering. Anyone who would care was dead now. Probably. That wasn't what this was about; not anymore.

"Hey," I said, realizing something. I pulled the gem out of the harness and held it before my eyes. "You led me right to this town. You...you knew, somehow."

I was smiling, holding the thing and looking at it. It felt warm, and there was a tiny, tiny glow in the center. Just enough to know that it was there.

"Wish I could give you a treat," I told it, and then I tucked it back into the strap and stared at the gate. It was much smaller than Cartha's gates, perhaps twelve feet tall and rectangular, two wooden doors that looked to have not moved in years and years. There was no iron banding around the edges, but they looked well-set into the wall.

I was hesitant, and I didn't know why. This was exactly what I wanted, was it not? Exactly why I came into the Walls and abandoned my city—to find another one. And then I would...

What? I'd live in this city as a stranger? If I could even get inside; if they even accepted me. If they were even alive.

My pack felt heavy. I sat down, sinking into the dirt. The labyrinth slowly grew brighter around me as the minutes passed, and the gate remained unchanging.

Survival had driven me this far, and I'd pulled myself forward on its rope. Now that it was in my grasp, I was looking for something else: what that rope was tied to, and where it would lead me. Where I could go.

I didn't want to die. If I did, the opportunity was generous. Did I want to wander the labyrinth forever with no place to call home? That didn't sit right, either, just the same as living on the other side of this gate chafed at me.

I lowered my head, catching sight of the gem, and understood that there were two things I wanted.

I wanted to learn more about this jewel and the magic it possessed. Gwin might have taught me a thing or two, but he was dead now. There had to be someone else out there who knew something. Every little thing about it surprised me, and I craved that knowledge. Like I held a tiny labyrinth in my hands.

And I wanted—*needed*—to know what happened to my city. Whether it was the age-old monsters from the stories finally come to feast, or...or something else I didn't understand.

"You," I said again to the gem, looking down at it. "You're involved in this. I'm sure of it. I just don't know how. I'm going to figure that out, too."

The magic, the gem, did not seem evil. Nor did it seem good. It was just small and yellow, and it would become more if I learned my way around it. I touched one hand to it and asked it to give me light, and the glow surged out.

There. One thing that I knew. One tool that would help me.

"Enough," I said, and the glow faded to its inner speck. I got up, brushing dirt from myself. I would go into this town, yes, if it was there. I would see what they had to offer; if they knew anything of monsters or magic. And if it wasn't everything I needed, then I would move on. There was a lot of world left to explore.

My mind crystallized behind my eyes, and at last the jumble of horrid images, morbid thoughts, and fear dissipated. At last, I knew what I wanted. It wasn't anything I knew how to get, but it was a place to start. That was all I needed for now.

I took a breath and the air tasted wet and good.

"All right," I said, approaching the gate. "What can I do to get by this thing?"

After waking into confusion, stumbling into panic, and then retreating to my thoughts, I stood before the wooden doors with renewed energy. I scanned the edges of the stone and ran my hands over the wood, feeling for weakness. I also flicked my eyes to the right and left to ensure that I wasn't about to be ambushed.

The door was sturdy, not unlike the gates of Cartha. And like those gates, there was a small area of wear towards the top. Whether it was from improper building, poor weather, or perhaps ancient use of the door itself, I didn't know, but I recognized the damage. It was the

kind of wear that a skinny climber like myself could get through with
the right amount of shifting and sorting.

My pack would have to be left behind, though, for now. I set it
down without much qualm; nobody would be coming to steal it. I did
take the gem and settle it back into my pocket, then flexed my fingers.

The Walls were mostly smooth and not made for climbing, but
there were spots. Chips; flaws; markings. Particularly near the gates.
Insignificant to the grander scale, but plenty big enough for me to
shove the toe of my boot in, or dig in my fingers. The further you got
up, the fewer flaws there were, so a climb could only get you so far.

This climb was easy enough—where the stone was lacking, the
wood offered many holds—but working the gap atop the gate was
much harder.

I approached it with my feet resting easily on a thick cross-
plank adorning the front of the gate, so I had plenty of leverage. The
gap between wood and stone was about a foot wide, top to bottom.
Side to side, the room was plenty; enough for three of me to slide
through. So I just had to work on the vertical space.

Eager, I put my head into the gap, trying to see what awaited
me on the other side. But it was dark there; it was like I was staring into
a black curtain, despite how bright the light was on my side. By
labyrinth standards, it was a sunny day. Not something you could farm
with, but not dark enough to obscure my vision completely.

"Doesn't matter," I told myself, though quietly, like someone
on the other side could hear me. "I'll see it soon enough."

Like the walls around the Carthan gates, the spaces here were
comprised of smaller stone blocks that could be worked free. Not
without effort, and not without time. I expended both of these
liberally.

After the first couple of blocks, sweat was dripping down my
face and wetting my shirt. I had to jostle them free of their crevices,
which took several hundred small wiggles at minimum, and each block
weighed around fifty pounds; enough to crush my hands if I wasn't

careful. I dropped them to the ground one by one, careful to miss my pack. They sunk deep into the dirt.

The parallels, at this moment, between myself and the creatures that disassembled Cartha, were not lost on me. I chose to ignore them.

The sun had crossed overhead by the time I climbed down from the door to rest and eat. I was hot, tired, and grateful that direct light in the Walls was short-lived. I took shade against the opposite wall and sat to eat, staring at the gate the entire time.

It had been a strange couple of days. To my knowledge, I was the last of my city left alive. The last thing I had done was get in a very public fight with Franz, and lose badly. After that, things happened so fast that it felt very normal to accept that I was staring at the gate to another city, despite the fact that Carthans—and all people, as far as anyone knew—had not been in contact with one another in centuries. Compared to what I'd been through, this was low on the list of strange happenings.

"No one goes in the maze, Jost," I managed around my food, blinking slow. "Just you. So who else would find it but you?"

I took the water from the back of my pack and I drank.

What would I have done if I'd found this a week ago? Would I have broken into this city the same way I was trying to now? Would I slam a loose rock on the gate and announce myself, hoping that someone would hear me? There was no one else from Cartha I could ever convince to come into the labyrinth with me. I would have had to deal with this alone no matter what.

I finished eating and rested my hands on my lap. Tickling at the edges of my consciousness was the fact that I was on the brink of breaking into truly new territory—an idea I'd toyed with over time, imagining how I might mark a city on my map—but never one I really believed I'd experience.

I was used to being an explorer. Now I would become an invader.

"If there's anyone there at all," I whispered to myself, reciting the same worry that had been running through my head. "If this isn't just a door to nothing."

I would be faced with a civilization unlike my own, or be driven back into the endless recesses of the Walls. Amazing how the same goal that had inspired me to strike out into the maze and survive another day was so blackly frightening as I stared it in the face.

"You deserve a good dose of fear, you lucky bastard," I said, standing up once more. "You've lived too long without it."

Easy to say now, compared to last night or even this morning. But I could say for certain that that last thing I would do would be to turn away from this gate. If I did that, then I might as well just dig my own grave here and lie down in it.

I stepped past the blocks I had already dropped and climbed the gate again. There wasn't much left to do; looking down at the mess I'd made below, it was clear I'd gotten farther than it seemed. Yet even with all these blocks and chunks of stone pulled, even with the hours I'd spent here, I still heard nothing from the other side.

The gates in Cartha were far from the city, I reminded myself, looking into the blackness of the hole and straining for something I couldn't see. *There's something there.*

I dropped the last block into the dirt and placed my hands on the rough surface of the gap.

It was time to go in.

Chapter Nineteen

I pulled myself up and over the gate, feeling the scrape of the jagged stone around me. Nothing I wasn't used to. The space was big enough to move through, and long enough for me to almost fit in lying down. The gate was as thick as the wall.

I listened for any sign of life or movement on the other side but came up with nothing. Even buried in this wall with my fingers curled around the outside edge, I couldn't see a thing. On the other side, it appeared to be the middle of the night, while muted daylight laid across my boots.

Feels wrong. I stayed there for a moment, shifting slightly as the stone poked into the parts of me it could reach. How could something like this feel right?

I exhaled quietly and pulled myself forward. The scrape of the stone was very loud around me, and I couldn't shake the image of a pack of black claws, invisible in the darkness, turning their mouthless heads toward the sound.

Once I was partially out of the hole, I could turn and get my legs out. Now my waist pressed into the edge and the toes of my boots rested against the inside of the gate. I was still at least ten feet up; not a comfortable height to fall from, especially in the dark. My shoulder twinged as I lowered myself and looked for a foothold, trying to be quiet, which is difficult to do when blindly feeling along with the toe of your boot. But I found some ledge, probably a cross-plank, and it took my weight. From there, I was able to lower myself until my hands were gripping that same spot, and I worked my way down to the ground.

I thought about dropping once I was a few feet down, but I decided I wanted to feel earth under my feet before I let go.

When I planted my feet in the dirt, I turned around fast. How could it be so dark here? I couldn't even see anything above me, despite the fact that a few feet behind me, the dim light of midday filled the Walls.

I closed my eyes and I waited, a habit I'd picked up many years ago when I first started going into the labyrinth. Coming from bright Cartha sunlight into the dim light of the Walls took some adjusting for my eyes, and this sped up the process.

This wasn't quite the same, but it couldn't hurt.

It was a long ten seconds of staring at my eyelids, and when I couldn't take it anymore, I opened them to find that everything was still black.

"What the..."

Hold on. There. I could see something, something pretty far off.

Yes...yes! It was a roof, it had to be. I followed the faint shape, which must have been over a hundred yards away, and saw that it led to others.

"There's really a city," I breathed, my mouth open as my eyes confirmed what my mind struggled to believe. "There's something here."

Something, yes, though I could barely see it. I had to get closer. I couldn't quite see the ground, but it felt the same as the labyrinth; soft, wet dirt, whereas Cartha's land was much drier because of the sun. Where was the sun now?

I walked slowly, hoping I could see well enough to not stumble over something. The buildings in the distance looked quite small. The outer rings of this city? Was the darkness hiding the taller structures; the expanse of this place? I'd find out soon enough.

"..."

I froze. I'd heard...what had I heard? It might have been the wind, but I felt no wind. It was like a whisper. And another. Many.

I no longer felt alone in the darkness.

Shuffling steps, too many to belong to just one or two creatures. Or...people? I fell back, knowing the wall was not far behind me. Should I climb back through and wait for daylight?

It's daylight now—there is no daylight here—

And then the shapes emerged from the dark, close enough for me to see. They weren't Carthans and they weren't black claws. I saw pale skin, so pale I wondered how I couldn't have seen it even without light. Upright, standing, humanoid, but with long, thin arms and fingers, most with short hair or no hair, talking to each other or to me but saying nothing that I could understand. There were many of them. Ten? Thirty? More, hidden behind bony shoulders?

I had been wrong. This was a town of monsters. And before I could run, they descended on me, a wave of smoky flesh converging from the edges of my vision.

I cried out as they touched me, a sound of anguish and fear. I lost my footing and fell to the ground. Something climbed on top of me, wrapped fingers around my forearm. I reached with my free hand towards my dagger. The sheath strapped to my leg was impossibly far away. I reached up to push the thing off me and touched bony edges and cold skin.

I pushed hard, panicked, and was surprised when the task was easy; the thing was light, and I heard it fly back and tumble. I drew back and made a fist, swinging mostly blind, and connecting solidly with what felt like a skull. My knuckles flared in pain, and another attacker fell off me.

I shook my gripped arm, pulling hard. The fingers fell away, and I was able to elbow that one off of me, too.

They're not strong, I'm stronger, a lot stronger—

Soundless light erupted, a flare bright enough to make me turn away, and the pulsing in my pocket made it clear it was the gem. I turned back to see the shapes bathed in yellow light, all covering their faces and turning.

Not wasting a moment, I snatched my dagger free and reached my left hand out, grabbing the enemy I had just knocked off my chest. I rolled over and raised the dagger above its prone body.

It screamed. I saw its eyes, wide and black, circled with a narrow band of white. Its hair, short, black, and dirty. It was a girl. It was a person.

"Stop it! Stop it!"

Calls from behind me, no longer senseless whispers, but words, and I stalled. I held the dagger up and I looked back, where the other people were running towards me, and the gem flared again. All of them—twenty or more—fell to their knees and their moans of pain mingled together in the air. The gem was hot in my pocket, buzzing.

The girl below me, quiet now, twisted her face in fear and pain.

I dropped the dagger. It stuck into the dirt beside the girl. I plunged my hand into my pocket and pulled out the gem. It felt hot enough to singe my skin, but I didn't care. Something was wrong.

"No," I said, my voice hoarse. "Whatever you're doing, don't do it. I'm fine. I'm okay."

Was it listening? *Could it listen?* Or was two straight days of talking to it enough to make me think stupid things like that?

It was still hot and yellow. I smelled my own burning skin. The groans of pain around me were growing weaker, and it became very clear that the gem was killing them. All of them.

"*No.*" I gripped the gem tight, not sure if I was talking to it or to myself. "*No. This is over.*"

At last, the heat faded. The light faded. The pain in my hand swelled, and I dropped the gem into the dirt. I moved to the side, off of the girl, and looked down at her.

"Hey. Hey. Are you okay?"

Her eyes were closed; they slowly blinked open.

"Are you okay?" I repeated, glancing over my shoulder to see the other ones. With the light gone, they were hard to make out. I plucked the gem from the ground and it lit for me, showing the others rising to their feet.

"You're talking," she said.

"So are you," I said, trying to remain calm despite my pounding heart. "So did it...did I hurt you?"

"I'm okay," she said. "I thought you were a monster. You're not."

"I..." It felt wrong to say that I thought the same of her. "I'm not."

Looking at her now, and even at the others, I was amazed that I hadn't seen that they were just...people. In the midst of fear and darkness, my mind had refused to accept it. They were pale and thin to the point of extremity, but they were people.

To be fair, they were people who had tried to kill me, and likely still wanted to. But between the gem and the fact that they all appeared very physically weak, it seemed like they couldn't. I got up and turned towards the swell, holding up one hand.

"I'm not here to hurt you!" I yelled, a very loud declaration in the black silence.

My words made them all hesitate. I saw them cast glances to one another, then up to the glowing gem in my hand.

I looked to the girl, the only one I'd spoken to. She was still lying on the ground, staring up at me. There was fear in her eyes, but it didn't feel the same as the desperate violence that pulsed in the crowd. So I held my hand out to her and I waited, watching her dark eyes.

She put her hand in mine. It was light and cold and bony. I helped her to her feet; she weighed less than my pack.

"Go on," I told her. While the gesture may have eased them slightly, it would be better for them not to have one of their own so close to this stranger. To me. "Go."

With a small hesitation, the girl slipped away from me to rejoin her fellows. I watched her disappear into the crowd and waited for them to attack once more. But the rage didn't come. They simply looked at me.

"I'm not your enemy," I told them. "I'm sorry that I trespassed here. I'm from another city in the Walls. It's...I'm the only one left. I came looking for other people."

Silence. I was starting to realize why it was so quiet when I came through here. They were just lying in wait, having heard my stonework. When I emerged, they came for me, and now they found themselves overwhelmed. Overpowered. I didn't know how to make it right, but putting the gem away was a start. It dimmed inside my pocket.

At last, someone stepped forward. A man, I believed; he was tall, and that was about all I could tell without more light.

"Say again," he called to me.

"My name is Jost. I'm from another city," I told him, loud enough for them all to hear. "Cartha. It's some miles east of here."

"You came through the labyrinth? From another city?" His disbelief was palpable.

"Yes." I could understand the doubt. I'd lived with such from my own people all my life. But unless he believed I'd sprung up from the ground, it was the only remaining explanation. Monster or not, I had to have come from outside.

"Why have you come here?" he asked, and his people murmured.

I didn't have a good answer for that, so I repeated my words once more. "My city was attacked. I was the only survivor. Monsters came from the Walls and...everyone is gone. I had to run. I hoped to find another town and..."

I trailed off.

"You say you're not here to harm us," the man acknowledged. "You don't look a monster. You're different, but you're no monster."

I stayed silent. What was I supposed to say—thank you?

His words were strange to me. They had an odd affection, almost harsh-sounding. The girl had sounded like that too, but softer. Did they all speak this way?

"And whatever magic you have there..." The man flicked his wrist, extending a finger toward the gem in my pocket. "It's powerful. We want no part in it. We can't fight you. But you should leave."

He knows of magic, was my first thought, and then I heard the rest of his message.

I would be the first to admit that this had gone wrong. But I apologized, and they seemed to understand I didn't want them dead. Now they wanted me to leave?

This man—none of them—none of them had any idea what I had been through. The past days dragged on me like years. I'd seen things I would never forget. But my first glimmer of hope had come. Shrouded in darkness, yes; barricaded by bony bodies, yes; but still hope.

"I have nowhere to go," I said, gritting my teeth. "My city is gone, and the Walls are filled with monsters."

"There is—"

Someone put a hand on the speaker's shoulder, cutting him off. "Lud, think for a second. You brought us here for an enemy. Now you're talking to someone that came from outside Iyes. You'd chase him away?"

The man—Lud, apparently—shrugged off the hand. "He attacked us all."

"He's not now." The one coming to my defense stepped forward, in front of Lud. "Jost, you said?"

"Aye."

"I'm Mort. I have—we've not ever seen someone come from the Dark. You're really from a city? Somewhere else?"

"I am. Cartha."

"That's incredible," Mort said, fascination coloring his voice. I couldn't see him well, but he was a bit shorter than Lud and his head was bald. "Explain the light you carry, and what it did to us."

I grimaced. "I admit that I don't know much about it. I found it in the Walls—outside."

"See?" Mort turned to Lud while pointing a finger at me. "He's a boy who came across magic and doesn't know what to do with it. It's just acting on its own."

They know? My heart skipped a beat. I didn't want to shout my ignorance for the whole crowd to hear, but a million questions bubbled up inside of me.

"That's worse," Lud snapped. "That's more dangerous than the alternative. We'll all be eaten alive."

Mort turned back to me. "This is a strange thing, Jost. You're here, and that's a miracle itself. But you come with danger."

"I can control it," I said immediately. It wasn't entirely a lie. I could make the light work for me, and I had put a stop to whatever it was doing to the people. "I won't let it hurt you."

Mort went back to Lud and the two of them spoke quietly. I waited, somewhat anxious but mostly firm. If they told me to leave, well...maybe I would. But not right away. I was incredibly lucky to find this place. I had to at least see it, and try to talk to someone who wasn't afraid of me. Mort, too, seemed to know about magic—astonishing. Was he the only one, or were there more?

No, I wouldn't be leaving. Whether they liked it or not.

Chapter Twenty

Mort and Lud arrived at their conclusion, and Lud spoke. "Stranger—"

Jost, I thought.

"—we agree that we can't make you leave, if we tried. Not without some of us getting hurt." Lud seemed miffed at this fact. "I got no curiosity about the outside. Some of us do. I'm more concerned with the safety of our people. That as it is...we are—I am—sorry to have attacked you."

"If we hadn't, this whole thing might have been avoided," Mort added.

Probably true, I thought, though I wondered if the gem would have done its thing anyway. Unless it was simply protecting me?

"Maybe," Lud said to Mort. "Maybe not. But we don't want any more fighting."

"I understand," I said, "and I agree. I won't impose on you. I'll sleep on the grass by the wall. I might stay some time, but eventually...I will move on. I'm just looking for answers about what happened to Cartha."

"You're not gonna find them here," Lud said, "but do what you have to do."

As a group, they turned away from me and they went back to their town. Which, if I had heard correctly, was called Iyes. Like the things I could barely see out of right now. How could they live in this kind of darkness?

I stood there and let the adrenaline finish with me. My eyes were getting used to the lack of light, so I was at least fairly certain that none of them had lingered.

I pulled the gem from my pocket, keeping it dark. In that respect, it was like the little thing was listening to my thoughts. But it still was doing plenty outside of my control, and that was something I couldn't admit to these people unless I wanted to scare them off or have them try to kill me in my sleep.

"But would you stop them?" I whispered. This magic jewel had dragged me across the dirt while I was unconscious, but it didn't try to slam me through the gate. It had stymied an entire horde of people on their way to pull me apart, but it didn't kill them, though it might have if I hadn't intervened.

Magic. These people knew it when they saw it, which was more than I could say for myself. Lud was wrong. There were answers here, and I'd find them.

"Stay quiet till I need you," I told the gem, and I put it away, certain that I would never break the habit of talking to myself and to things that couldn't talk back.

Relaxed for the moment, the experience finally washed over me. I was looking at another town, something no one had seen in hundreds of years. Something no one had even been sure was out there! I was always a believer—how could Cartha be the only city to have survived the build?—but there was a difference in seeing and believing. I was warm. I was anxious. I wanted to see more.

I walked toward the town of Iyes. Being cloaked in darkness, even more than the rest of labyrinth, made it difficult to see the scope of the place. Was it as big as Cartha? I couldn't tell for sure, but I had the feeling it was not. The smaller buildings and the size of the group that had come to confront me lent to that. The air here felt slightly damp.

More of the town emerged to me as I pressed forward, peeling back the layers of darkness. For the first time, I cast my glance upward and I saw slits and dots of light high, high above me. It was like a starry sky, but with long streaks of light here and there.

"Is that the sunlight?" I asked myself. A hundred feet above my head, something blocked out the sun, allowing the barest stretches of light to poke through.

Looking back down, I could get a better sense of the town. The buildings were indeed small; I couldn't count a single two-story structure among them, and I could see a few hundred feet with confidence. The line of buildings curved slightly, not indicative of a true circle like Cartha's, but they were surrounding...something. What?

Before I entered, I wanted to get a sense of how big the place was, so I backed up to the wall and followed it. There was no curve, and it wasn't too long before I found a corner.

"Is it a square?" I pondered, running my fingers over the stone. I ran back the other way, crossing past the gate, and running until I found the opposite corner. It took less than ten minutes. But how deep did the town stretch?

I instinctively reached for my map pocket and laid my fingers on the paper, but remembered that my pen was back in my bag. *Damn it.*

I'd save marking for another time and just try to remember as much as I could. The borders established, I finally approached what would be the outskirts of Iyes, just a few hundred feet from the gate.

The grass thinned as I neared, but it still grew sparsely on the dirt roads through the town. I wondered how it grew when it was so dark. It must have been different from the grass in Cartha.

The homes were mostly quite small, made of stone and a surprising amount of wood. I didn't see this much wood in Cartha outside of the wealthy inner rings. Everything smelled of dirt and water, a bit like the Walls but...nicer, somehow.

I wasn't afraid, even walking into a town filled with people who might want to attack me. After Cartha's fall and the horrors that I had come across in the labyrinth, this was nothing.

Besides, a fight seemed to be the last thing on anyone's mind. Word must have spread about me, because the people I did see weren't shocked at my presence. I got stares, but mostly I was ignored and given a wide berth.

Small town, I thought, watching a pair of skinny men cast me a glance and move further away. *Easy enough to hear about the stranger.*

That was fine with me. Would I trust any of them to come into my ring? Or what was left of it, anyway?

I drifted to the left—north. All the buildings looked the same, even the ones over here that didn't seem lived-in. The roads had more grass and there were hardly any people about, but the homes were still mostly wood and a little bit wider. Storage, perhaps?

The smell of water grew stronger as I walked. It wasn't something I was used to. Cartha's river was narrow and shallow, enough to keep our town alive. Here in Iyes, it seemed different. When I reached the edge of the last building to the north, I noted that the wall was visible from where I stood. This place was a little more than a mile wide, at most.

It was when I was about a mile deep into Iyes that I heard the water, though I couldn't see it yet. Gentle splashes; not running water like Cartha's river. The grass grew lusher and thicker, and the homes were further apart, leaving more open area for me to walk through. Residents disappeared outside the reaches of my vision, slipping out of my sight like fading lights.

Something was odd here. I could see slats of light on the ground ahead, despite the fact that nowhere else in Iyes did the sun seem to penetrate all the way to the ground. Here, the dapples of light were frequent, dotting back much farther than I could usually see.

It took me a moment to realize I was about fifteen feet from stepping into a massive lake. I blinked. The water was reflecting the snatches of light from a hundred feet above. It was like a sheet of black glass, undisturbed, stretching farther than I could see.

But no—there were people here, out on the water. Around the vast curve of the waterside were wooden walks built out into the lake, reaching as far as a hundred feet, with thick wooden supports that thrust down into the water. People sat on their edges, holding something in their hands. With some, their feet dipped into the water, moving idly.

It was a sight I'd never seen. I watched the water for a long while, its cool air rolling slowly over me. Everything here was very different from Cartha. It was small and it was dark. It was quiet, almost as quiet as the walls. I could hear people talk, but they were mostly whispers.

I rounded the lake to find that it stretched all the way to the walls on either side, and it might extend a hundred miles forward for all I knew. It was too dark to tell. So the town was half-composed of a lake, or maybe more than half.

It might have been nice, living here. As it was now, I felt trapped, with water on one side and a world of hostile beasts outside the gate. I retreated from the water and back to where the grass thinned and the muted sounds of talking and movement were more familiar to my ear. With the lay of the land painted in my mind, I wanted to try to talk to someone.

A group of three villagers were gathered out front of a small house with a pointed roof that rose two feet above their heads. All of them were sallow with shaven heads, and they all gave me the same look as I approached. Stony.

"Could I ask you some questions?" I said, trying to keep my voice quiet as it seemed the polite thing to do.

They simply turned from me. News of my coming didn't bring fear to Iyes, just guardedness. Like I was a stray animal they were intent not to feed.

I moved on past the group, searching for someone to meet my eye. I followed the sound of voices, but whenever I neared them, they would stop. I became aware of how loud my boots were on the dirt, and noticed that the villagers of Iyes were barefoot. One could barely hear them move. I must have sounded like a thunderstorm.

I wound my way through Iyes until I could have sketched out a street map from memory. It wasn't complicated, and yet everyone I came across found some clever way to disappear from my sight before I could talk to them. Those I did reach were not receptive. They didn't speak a word to me, not even to usher me away.

"Do you know where I can find Mort?" I asked one, a woman I saw crouched in the grass toward the lake, digging at something. She snapped her head at me, which was more acknowledgement than I'd gotten from anyone else. But then she just turned back to the ground and continued to gather whatever she was collecting, throwing small pieces into a wooden bucket one by one.

Clunk.

"If you could just point me in the right direction."

Clunk. Clunk. Clunk.

A minute later, I was pacing around the lake again, and now the sunspots were gone and it was just a black hole that ate the horizon. If there were people on the walkways there, I could try them, but what was the point? If I fell in the water, I could die. I didn't know how deep it was.

I went back to the gate, walking directly through Iyes and listening as sound disappeared around me like I was pushing through a thick fog, the wisps separating across my shoulders. I clenched one fist and tried to slow my breathing, but it was all incredibly frustrating.

Tomorrow would be better. Tomorrow, someone would talk to me.

For now, I would get my pack before it soaked up all the dirt-water in the Walls.

Getting in and out of Iyes was much easier now that the hole was already made. My pack was right where I left it, and there was no greeting party of monsters or fresh corpses. I climbed back up the gate and hated how the labyrinth seemed much more familiar and welcoming than the town full of people I had dropped into.

Back inside Iyes, I settled down somewhere between the gate and the northern corner, resting my head on my pack and staring up at nothing, hearing nothing. Without the ground under my back, I might have been hanging in the night sky. It was too dark to do any map work, and if I lit the gem, they would see it and distance themselves even further.

I lied there deep into the night, thinking, unmoving.

It was some hours into the dark when I heard the footsteps.

Chapter Twenty-One

There was only one, I was sure of it. Quiet as these people were, they couldn't be completely silent. Was it a detractor, coming to break their tacit agreement of safety and plunge a dagger into me while I slept?

Reaching for my own dagger might alert them. Better to let them approach—if they ran off, I'd never know who it was. So I let them come, closer and closer.

I turned my head slowly, looking to the right. The nighttime in Iyes was thick like pitch, so dark that I was sure that even a villager couldn't see me without getting within five feet. Once they did, that's when I'd make my move.

As the steps grew near, the unexpected happened. A voice.

"Is that you? J...Jost?"

I froze at first, unsure how to react. The voice was familiar, which meant it had to be Lud, Mort, or that girl. Or some haunting specter from Cartha, come to take revenge on me for surviving.

"Who's there?" I called out, coming up to a sitting position, ready to spring.

"Of course it's you. Who else'd be out here?"

She came into view then, looking taller than before. It was girl that pounced on me; the one I might have killed if things had gone farther.

I got to my feet, my muscles tense. Ironic that I'd spent all day searching for someone to talk to me, and now that one had come to find *me*, I was on guard.

It must have been obvious, even in the black of night.

"My name is Atell," she told me, her palms upturned in an easing gesture. "I just want to talk."

"That would make you very different from everyone else here," I said.

"I am," she responded.

I wanted to see her. On impulse, I reached for the gem, but it was already lighting in my pocket, growing brighter until it lit us both in the barest of light, shielded by the heavy fabric around it. Could the villagers see it from hundreds of feet away? Maybe. Probably not. I noted, mentally, that this was the first time I was able to control the light without touching the gem directly.

Atell looked much like the other villagers I had seen, at first glance. She wore her black hair shorter than the other women I'd seen in Iyes, very close to her skull. Her skin was pale like her fellows, her nose small and her lips thin. Her shirt clung close to her skin, and her pants weren't pants at all, but cut short above the knees and hemmed.

Her eyes were green and curious.

I found it difficult to tell how old she was, but my first impression of her being a younger girl—when she attacked me—was definitely wrong. She could have been my age, or a little older. Like the others, she was very thin, but she moved with energy and she spoke fast.

Different.

"Magic," she said, nodding at my pocket where the gem glowed. "You don't know much about it."

"How do you know that?" I asked her.

"I've been following you all day," she said with a little shrug. "Half the questions you asked were about your light."

"Okay." Had she really been on my trail the entire day and I didn't notice? "So you came out here to find me at night. You don't want to be seen talking to me. Why risk it?"

She cocked her head. "Please. Why are you trying to talk to everyone else here? You're from the outside. All my people want nothing to do with you. I'm the only one who appreciates this. It's like two different worlds coming together. I didn't even know anyone else was alive from the outside. From the Dark. Now here you are. Why wouldn't I talk to you?"

It sounded like something I would say. Maybe it wasn't only bad things that were allowed to happen to me. A town with probably three hundred people in it, and I find a kindred spirit.

"We call it the Walls in Cartha," I said, as a trickle of exhilaration slipped through my body and out to my fingertips. "Used to, I guess."

"What's your city like?" Atell asked immediately, stepping a little closer.

"Hold on." I lifted my hand. "What do you know about magic?"

Atell shrugged again. "Just what I've read. I'm one of the only people in Iyes who can read some Lillitan."

"Lillitan?"

"The old wielder language. From the north, before they built the maze. You don't know about it? With magic in your pocket?"

"I've never heard of it," I said, shaking my head. "Maybe you could show me some of your books, or..."

I trailed off there, suddenly remembering what I had in my pack. I turned and dropped to my knees, opening my bag and rifling through it until I had the book in my hands. Gwin's book. I turned back to Atell and stood, holding the cover in the light.

"Is this Lillitan?" I asked.

"Wow," she breathed. "Yes. That's really...that's a book! All I have is some pages. Barely any."

"You can read this?"

She nodded. "Some of it, yes. Probably not all. Depends what's in it."

I opened the book, the paper shuffling quietly amid our breathing. "Here."

"Not now." She straightened up, looking away from the pages and to me. "I'll read some of your book. But you have to have something for me. I have questions, too."

I had seen how her eyes had lit up at the book. She wanted to pore over the pages the same as I wished I could. But arguing wasn't the right thing to do. This girl was the only chance that I had to learn something here.

I shut the book. "That's fair. So what do you want to know?"

"A lot," she said, and then she looked over her shoulder. "But—hell. It took too long to find you. They'll notice I'm missing. They'll know what I'm up to. I have to go back."

"Tomorrow, then."

"Tomorrow," she agreed. "Come to the water. No one does any fishing on the deep south end. We can talk there."

I didn't bother to ask what that meant; I just nodded, and she took one last look at my book before she was off, running through the grass with almost silent strides. She disappeared from my light, and I let it go out.

Despite my uneasiness as I drifted off, no one else came, neither to talk to me nor to kill me in my sleep.

Chapter Twenty-Two

Morning came, and the world was brighter—something I wouldn't have noticed if I hadn't spent the last day here. But it seemed there was light in Iyes, after all.

I rose and stretched, more comfortable now that I could see more than five feet around me. It was still dim, of course; dimmer than the Walls. But the smells of grass and water made it feel much different.

Something struck me in the head and fell to the ground.

I turned, somehow expecting to see someone behind me, but of course it was just the wall, blank and tall. The top of my head stung. There was no one around.

"What..."

I saw the thing lying in the dirt. I grabbed it between my finger and thumb and pulled it close to my face. I thought it was a rock at first, but looking closer at it, it looked like some kind of...nut? It had a hard, smooth shell, and there was a crack running along one curved side. Probably from when it had smacked against my skull.

It wasn't like any nut we grew in Cartha. It was huge; I doubted I could fit four of them in my palm. Any bigger and it might have knocked me out. It had fallen straight from the sky.

I dropped it to the ground, put my pack on, and moved away lest I be hit again. It was time to go meet with Atell, as far as I knew.

Was it too early, or even too late? Just being able to see didn't tell me what time of day it was, and without the sun, the best I could do was guess.

"Deep south end," I murmured, swinging to the right around Iyes and taking the long way to what I assumed was our meeting place—the south side of the lake where the water and ground met the wall.

The morning here was as quiet as the previous day, but I could hear the sound of the water when I got close, and I saw people on the wooden walkways like they had been yesterday. I'd have to ask Atell about 'fishing'—was that what they were doing?

I walked through the grassy gap that separated the town proper and the endless lake that stretched east for miles unknown. The sunspots that lit into the water were captivating; bright, and they would sparkle on occasion, usually from the corner of my eye.

The southern side of the lake wasn't far. Maybe it was earlier in the day than I thought, because there was no one here in the field. Just the few people on the walkways over the water.

I crossed to the opposite wall and worked my way down to the lake, close enough to the stone to brush against it. The curve of the lake was gradual at first, and then steepened, so there was actually quite a bit of ground heading along the wall on the south side. I traveled far enough water-side to where I could no longer see the town when I turned.

It was also deserted. The grass was lush and undisturbed, and I had passed the last wooden dock a hundred yards ago. To my left, the water stretched out into the dark, and ahead of me was an ever-narrowing strip of grass. Where was Atell?

Once the land got to the point where I was practically stepping in the water to walk forward, I stopped. I looked around, though I'd been doing that the whole time and I'd seen nothing. Should I call out for her? It seemed...rude, almost, like it would disturb the tranquility of this place. I hadn't heard anyone yell or shout since I'd first come down from the gate. Not even to haggle over a price.

After one more glance around, I sat down on the grass and leaned my back against the cold stone wall. I tapped my foot on the ground, annoyed. Maybe I would shout. Maybe I would light the gem as bright as I could, so I could see everyone and they could see me. What would they do about it? Nothing. They couldn't do a damn thing. And if they—

Movement. In the water, just a few feet out from me. Before I could stand up, the surface broke and out came Atell's head.

"You took long enough," she said, drifting to the shore and walking up in the time that I got to my feet. She ran her hands backward through her short black hair, pressing the water out, where it ran in rivulets across her bare shoulders and neck. It soaked into the thin fabric of her shirt, which was really just a tight-fitting band across her chest with a small overhang that draped over her ribs.

"It's..." I shook my head, still acclimating to the sight of someone emerging from the water. It was not something that happened in Cartha. "It's hard to tell what time of day it is when it's dark all the time."

"You think it's dark here?" Atell said, her eyes lighting up. "Do you see well outside?"

"You mean in the Walls?"

"Why do you call it that?" she asked me.

"We always have. It's a bunch of walls, is there a better name for it?"

"Hm." Atell walked toward the wall and sat down, moving one hand through the grass. "Just different, that's all."

Her hunting hand found what it was looking for—a small, dark object she pulled from the ground. I recognized it as one of the same things that had hit me in the head this morning. As I watched, she felt along its surface, then stuck her fingernail in a crack in the shell.

"What is that?" I asked her.

"This?" She pressed on it and it cracked cleanly in half with barely a sound. "It's a branchnut. See?"

Atell held the shell halves up, and I knelt down to get a better look. I sat back down and said, "You eat them?"

"Of course," she said, and she plunged her fingers into a shell half, pulling out the nut inside and taking a bite of it. "If you're hungry, just look around. You'll find one."

"I'm fine," I said.

Atell shrugged, finished the nut, and ate the other half just as quickly. She scooped some dirt out of the ground and buried the shell in the small hole. "Swimming makes me hungry."

I wasn't sure where to begin. Pulling out the book again probably wouldn't get me anywhere, so I just sat and waited while she finished chewing. Let her get out what she wanted to say.

"All right," she said, leaning back a little and putting her negligible weight on her hands. "You want me to read your Lillitan book. Right?"

"I do."

"I probably can. I already said that." Atell's eyes flicked to my pack where it hung off my shoulders, then back to mine. "And I will. At least so you can learn something. And won't kill us with your magic."

"I'm not trying to hurt anyone," I said, a little indignant.

"You seem fine," she said, "but if you can live on the outside, there's something dangerous about you. I can't read your mind. I'm just—foolhardy, is what others would say. My parents. Really, I'm curious. So tell me what it's like. The Walls."

I let Atell interrogate me for a while. She didn't write anything down, or ask me to repeat things; she just took it all in, watching me strangely the whole time. I felt like an insect trapped in someone's cupped hands. Her questions were short and they came one after the other, as soon as I'd finished an answer.

I told her what the Walls were like, and what Cartha was like, and what happened to me over the last couple days. Some things she wanted more details on—"How many people lived in Cartha?"—and for others, not so much. I was certain she'd ask me more about the monstrosities I saw, but she wasn't interested, moving past them quickly. Most of her questions were about the city and its people and what life was like there. I must have gone on for an hour.

When Atell dug another nut from the ground, ceasing her questions, I pulled some meat from my pack and we ate in silence for a moment. The book was on my mind, but her questions had stirred up some of my own, and I couldn't resist asking.

"Why is it so dark in Iyes?" I cast my gaze upward, where it was too dark to see anything but the lack of light. "Even in the labyrinth it's not this dark."

"It's the branches," Atell said. "You told me Cartha's open on top. It sounds like it was big, and I don't know if branches would get that big. But here, they cover us up. That's where we get the branchnuts from. They fall, and we eat them."

"You can't farm without sunlight," I said, the realization coming to me. "So you eat these nuts, and…"

"And fish. There's a lot in the lake, and everyone here can fish. Not as well as me." Her pride was unabashed. "Besides, some plants grow here. The grass grows. Some other food, but it's small. I can show you."

"I'd like to see that," I said, and I wondered what kind of grass this was that grew without sun, and what a fish would taste like, because we didn't have those in Cartha. The river was shallow and had no denizens. We drank from it and we watered the crops.

But I had to abate my curiosity for now, because there were more important things to attend to. I pulled the book from my pack and set it down on the grass between us.

"That's enough from me." There was plenty I'd like to learn about this town, but none of it was going to help. I needed the information in these pages. "The book, now. Can you teach me the Lillitan?"

"Maybe." She didn't sound very sure, which was the first time I'd heard her tone change. She stood up and came over to me, sitting down next to me so that we could both see the book. "That's a lot. I never tried to teach it to anyone. I could teach you to fish better."

"If you can try," I said. "I'll settle for hearing the pages from you, though."

"Hm." She pulled the book closer to us, sitting on her knees in a posture that I couldn't possibly replicate. "It's called *Breath*. Or it could be *World's Breath*, or *Breath of the World*. Depends how you read it. It looks very old."

She opened the cover, running her fingers along the pages. "I'm surprised it didn't fall apart. It must never have gotten read."

"Could be." Gwin had read it, or at least some of it. How much could he have told me? His dead body floated in front of my eyes.

Atell was silent, looking over the first page. In her intensity, it was like she had forgotten I was there. Then she snapped her head up and looked over at me. "You don't know anything at all about magic, do you?"

Lying wouldn't help me. "I don't."

"Well, this isn't going to help you." She closed the book and slid it away.

"What do you—"

"Your elders didn't talk about magic?" Atell stood up again, stretching her arms and legs. "Someone just gave you this book for no reason?"

"Yes," I said. "Yes to all of it. So are you going to help me?"

"We know magic here, but we don't go after it," Atell said. "I would maybe. But that's—it's not our way. It makes the branches grow and it brings the fish in, but it's dangerous. It's like fire. This book is...a big fire. There's a lot I don't know even just on the first page. You can't use it. Not now."

I gritted my teeth and snatched the book up, standing. "You're saying it's too advanced."

"Too advanced," she said. "And even worse than that if I can only read half of it."

"Well, thanks for nothing, then." I tore open my pack and stuffed the book inside. "You're really the only person here who can read this? Who else can I go to?"

"We just need to start somewhere else," she said, ignoring my question. "Let me—hey. Hey! Your pocket is burning!"

I smelled the smoke as soon as the words left her, and then I felt the searing heat as the gem tried to burn through my leg.

I pulled it out. Expecting it to burn me, I immediately dropped it to the ground and prepared to kick it into the water if the grass started ablaze, but there wasn't even any smoke. The gem wasn't lit, and when I hovered my hand near it, I felt no heat.

"Oh," Atell said. "You're mad at me."

Chapter Twenty-Three

The statement was so out of place that I froze with my hand over the gem. Crouching, I looked up at her. "What?"

"You're mad at me," she repeated, shaking her head. "That affects your bond. So either you wanted to hurt me, or the magic wanted to hurt me."

"That's..." I let out my breath and picked up the gem, keeping it firmly in my hand. "I do *not* want to hurt you. How many times—"

"Then the magic does," Atell said, flicking a finger at my fist. "That's worse."

"Okay. Okay." I tried to get a handle on my frustration. She might as well have been speaking...Lillitan. "I found this gem in the Walls. It was stuck into the stone, and I took it. That's all I know. So tell me something useful!"

"You just...touched it?"

"Yes!" I snapped, and I held it up in the air. "Just like this!"

She was nervous, like it was just occurring to her that this whole time, I'd been telling her the truth. That I knew nothing about what was in my hand, and that part of me was realizing I had stumbled onto something powerful enough to kill a village full of people and I didn't know how to control it.

I lowered my hand. "If you can't help me with this, I have to leave." I reached down and grabbed my pack, tying the top again to seal the book inside along with what little food I had left.

"Don't leave!" Atell said. "I can help you. I think I can. I can at least tell you something."

I left my bag on the ground. "Then do it fast, before this thing acts up again."

"Someone tried to climb the wall here. A long time ago," Atell said. "Before I was born. He made it all the way up the stone somehow. And he grabbed onto one of the branches. And as soon as he touched it, it killed him. He fell from the sky and his body broke into pieces.

"It was the magic in the branches. It just tore through him and left him empty. And you say you just touched this gem and you're okay." Atell shrugged.

"That's what happened. I..." Thinking back; the moment I saw the light. Following it, and reaching out. "When I touched it, something *did* happen. It didn't hurt me. It didn't *tear through me*. But it was like there was lightning in my skin. It knocked me down. And when I got up, I could hold the lamp. The gem."

"That's incredible," Atell said, staring down at the gem. "That story is the story of Thom, who tried to climb the wall and died. Everyone learns about that when they're kids. But my grandpa told me what he was trying to do was *bond* with the magic. And to do that, you have to touch it. And most of the time it kills you. Especially if the magic is too...big."

"Big," I repeated.

"Big like this," she said, pointing upward. "There's a lot of magic up there. And in that gem—you can fit it in your hand. It's powerful. But it's not the same as the branches. Maybe that's why you lived."

"So if I climbed up your wall and touched the branches, I would probably die."

"Yes," she said. "And the magic is...I've never bonded with magic or touched it. Obviously. No one here has. No one I've heard of has, not in a long time. Since before they built up the outside. But it's not like a weapon or a tool. It's alive, and it does what it wants. Bonding with it can help control it, but..."

We were both thinking of the night I came in, I was sure.

"I can control some of it," I told her.

"Like what?"

"The...light." I squeezed the gem. "Just the light."

"That's harder than you think." Atell smiled. "Just touching that thing would probably kill me. And when you're bonded with your magic, your emotions can take it over. You came through the gate and we attacked you. You were scared. You were fighting us. And the gem felt that."

"But I didn't want to kill you," I said. "I mean, I wanted to defend myself, but once I realized you were just people—"

"I believe you," she said simply. "So maybe the gem did. That's what magic does. What it wants. And usually what it wants is more magic. To get bigger. It's not a nice thing."

"It's like a fire," I echoed. "And fires can be...can be built, and be controlled and...used. But they can also go wild."

"Exactly. And good luck putting this fire out if it does."

I pulled in a deep breath of wet air. Tiny little pieces were falling into place in my mind. Some of this was starting to make sense; as much as anything like this could make sense.

"When I first found the gem..." I stopped. I was thinking of when I attacked Franz. I had been so angry. "I wasn't acting like myself. I—I don't know. I got kind of hotheaded. Can it do that to me?"

Atell shrugged, a gesture she seemed to enjoy. "I'm no wielder. It seems like it. Or maybe it just made your feelings stronger. Are you a hotheaded person?"

"Sometimes."

"Sure." That smile again. "But now, you understand what you're holding."

"A little bit."

"That's all I have." *Shrug.*

I wanted to say something about how Gwin touched the gem and nothing happened, but was that even true? He didn't die, but his face had been...as soon as he'd touched it, he knew what it was. There was so much he must have known. Things I never would.

I couldn't talk about him now.

I came out of my reverie to see Atell turned away from me, a little farther down the narrow stretch of land. She picked up something from the ground and came back over.

"I have to fish now," she said, carrying a rod which must have hidden in the grass. "We can't talk. It'll scare the fish."

I had enough to try to wrap my mind around now, anyway. I pulled my pack onto my back. "Thanks for the help. There's still a lot I want to talk about, just later."

Shrug.

"Where could I do some trading?" It would be nice to get some hot food, and there had to be something in my bag of value to the people here.

"We don't have trading streets like in Cartha. So...with anyone, if they'll talk to you." Atell twisted her mouth. "So maybe with no one."

"Right. I was hoping to try a fish."

"You'll have to trade with me, then," she said. "Branchnuts. Bring me twenty for a fish. Twenty-five, I'll show you how to cook it."

It wasn't like I had anything better to do. "Okay. And listen—I don't care if the book is too much for my little brain to handle right now. It's all I've got from Cartha, and I need to know what it says."

Atell just nodded and slung her rod over her shoulder. "Twenty-five. I'll be on the farthest pier this side. Find me soon. I catch a lot of fish fast."

Gathering nuts, I thought, watching Atell as her quick feet carried her around the curve of the lake and away from me. *I took magic, I killed a monster, I found a town in the labyrinth, and now I'm gathering nuts to trade for a fish.*

It better taste good.

Chapter Twenty-Four

How did you find this many?"

The number of branchnuts that would fit into my pack, around my other possessions, was close to two hundred. That was also close to how many pounds my pack weighed when it was stuffed to the top with these things. They were dense.

"The light," I told her. We were crouched on the shore by the easternmost pier, my bag between us. "Do you all usually hunt for these in the dark?"

"Usually." Atell tapped a fingernail on a nutshell. "Even with fire, this is a lot. The magic must have helped you."

"Maybe. It seemed to shine bright off the shells." So maybe I'd been unconsciously controlling it. Not the grandest use of such a thing, but it had worked. "I'm thinking we can strike a deal here."

"I'm not giving you all my fish."

"No. Take all the nuts—I still want one fish—and we're looking at the book together. Whatever you can tell me about it, I want to know. I need to." I stood up, lifting the pack and grunting at the weight. "Are you done fishing?"

"Yes." She had her haul wrapped in wet fabric, sitting on the grass. With how it smelled, I was a little less eager to try it.

"Then let's do this now." I had plans for tonight, and they didn't involve tucking myself into the far corner of Iyes and sleeping on the grass. "Not waste any more time."

She was agreeable, at least. "I have to get the fish back. And I can't carry those."

"Just tell me where they go."

Atell mused on this for a moment, shifting her wrapped fish to the other arm. "Come with me. We'll take it to my house. Don't say anything to anyone."

"Fine." I carried the pack in my arms, worried that the weight would put too much strain on the straps. My back would recover, hopefully.

Atell lead the way from the lake back to town, a five-minute walk that felt much longer with the weight of the pack. By the time we set foot onto the sparsely-grassed streets, I was sweating, despite the cold wet air.

Mercifully, Atell lived close to the water. We passed a few people and I got some looks, but true to my word, I kept my mouth shut. Not that talking would have been easy. And besides, getting looked at was quite the step up from being completely ignored.

"Here."

We stopped before a house that looked like every other one here, seven feet tall with walls of wood and stone. I'd noticed in my jaunts around Iyes that there were fallen branches every so often, some of them wider around than me, which would explain where they got all the wood from. I supposed the magic left them when they broke off the main canopy, but I wondered how many people they had crushed.

"Inside. Stay behind me. Don't say anything." Atell was already opening the door, a thin board that was silent as it swung inward. I followed her inside the small house, which was surprisingly much warmer than the outside. If there was a fire burning somewhere, I had missed the smoke in the general darkness.

"Father," Atell called, though it was quiet. "I have my fish. And more. The stranger brought us branchnuts."

From a side room emerged the man who must have been Atell's father. Like most of the Iyes residents, his gaunt frame made it hard to tell his age, but there were signs. His skin sagged at the elbows where they stuck out of his shirt. His hair was in a graying ring around his head. His eyes were sunken and milky white. Blind.

Atell didn't wait for him to respond, instead pulling a huge woven bowl from the floor and putting it on the small table in the kitchen.

"Ya brought him here?" her father said.

"Listen." Atell turned back to me, beckoning. She pointed at the bag, then at the bowl. As quietly as I could manage, I hefted the bag over the bowl and let the haul pour in, all of it. It took some time.

"That's all. I have to go back." Atell pointed at the door, and I left with her close behind me. Once outside, she didn't slow her pace, and now she went up through the town, toward the gate. Her stride grew quicker with each step.

Still tired from carrying the bag, I managed to keep up with her. "What's going on?"

Atell seemed rattled. She wasn't looking back at me, or around to anyone we passed by. She was just walking fast, light and quiet as a feather.

"He's angry," she said finally, though she still didn't look back and it was hard to hear her. She slipped in a narrow space between two houses and I followed her through, tucking my elbows in till we emerged out the other side.

"He didn't seem that upset," I said, but the words were hollow and I knew it. I couldn't know her father—or anyone here—better than she did.

"He knows how I am. So does mother. They don't like it. People see me with you and they don't like it. I brought you into the house. I thought a gift would help. He didn't care."

We were out of town now, walking in the thicker grass toward the gate wall.

"There's no secrets here," Atell said. "Doesn't matter if I'm at water's edge, or at the gate, or swimming. People see you, they know. I thought I could sneak around and learn from you. But I was just being stupid. I live in a box. So it'll be easier this way."

"I hope you're not going back on our deal," I said.

"No." She stopped once we were near the gate, off to the side towards where I had slept the night before. "Turn your magic light on and let's read."

"The light. Really."

"It's easier," Atell said, "and being sneaky doesn't work. So if they don't like it, too bad."

It was clear that no one else in Iyes would be happy seeing me work any kind of magic, even well off in the distance like we were. Was I willing to damage any hope I had of a future relationship with these people? If I *were* to try to stay here, if they *were* to come around, and I could survive here while exploring the Walls further, finding other towns, learning more, that would—

That would be ideal, I thought, and I understood I was being naive, and possibly even stupid. I was not living in an ideal world, and things were not going to work out the way I wanted them to.

I had one friend here, and even if I was just some little project to her, some diversion from her life that she was latching onto, she was still the sum of everything I'd found in this town. And I'd rather have Atell, here and now, than some vague wish that things would be better if I waited long enough.

"If they don't like it, too bad." I grinned, and so did she, and I lit the lamp with the barest thought, holding it in my hand. I dropped my pack on the ground and fetched the book, which she took into her thin fingers. The warm light made her paleness look healthier; made the green of her eyes stand out.

We sat down in the grass.

"*Breath,*" she read again, opening the cover. She sat close on my left side. "It's a story. I don't know who wrote the stories. But all the magic pages I read are like this. It's a story about a wielder, or wielders. And you learn from it. I think that's the point. Maybe all this stuff really happened."

"So this book is like some kind of children's cautionary tale?"

She shrugged, shifting the book in her lap. "I haven't read it yet. I'm sure there's caution. And adventure, and other things. The wielders don't sit around in their houses."

The wielders. Am I a wielder now? "Who are the wielders?"

"Well..." She looked up from the book. "There've been a few, over time. Not a lot. I could name perhaps a dozen. My grandfather, maybe a dozen more, and he knew a lot. The names wouldn't mean anything to you. They don't to me. But there weren't many, ever. And probably none now."

"Are they just people who..." I searched for the word. "People who bonded with magic?"

"Yes," she said. "But also no. They're the people who bonded with it and used it and grew it. They're the people who learned about it and wrote the stories. Like this one. They're the people who built the outside."

"So you think the Walls are magic."

"Obviously," she said, raising her eyebrows. "Did all of Cartha think the old people built them by hand?"

"It's just a bunch of stone," I said. "Life was different before the labyrinth was built. A lot more could have been possible. Who knows?"

"It's magic," she said with confidence. "And your gem only proves it. You found it in a wall out there, you said. It was part of it."

"I've never seen magic out there except for this," I told her, shaking the gem. "Ever. And I've walked hundreds of miles out there."

"I don't believe you," she said. "The outside is filled with magic. Dangerous magic and monsters. It's why we don't leave."

"Don't try to tell me what's out there," I said. "Look at this."

I dropped the gem into the grass and took my map from my inside pocket, unfolding it and laying it on the grass. I rolled the light closer, illuminating my life's work.

"What..." Atell's mouth was open, her fingers limp on the book. I took some satisfaction in seeing her speechless. "What is this?"

"It's the world that I've seen with my own eyes," I told her. "And in Cartha, we say it's dangerous. That it's filled with monsters. And it's—well, it wasn't true. Until now."

Or was it only a matter of time?

Atell read the map for some time, silently, running her thin fingers over the paper. She hovered over Iyes where I had marked it, then went to Cartha, tracing a larger circle around the shape of the city. She looked to the edges, where my branching sketches ended or faded toward the steps I'd yet to take.

"This is...unbelievable. It really is a labyrinth. You made this, Jost?" She spoke without looking up at me. The gem's light gleamed off her eyes as they moved around the pages.

"I'm making it," I told her. "I'll probably make it for the rest of my life."

Quiet breath as she read the map. Finally, she turned her head. "You're going out there tonight. Right? You were in a hurry to read. Are you leaving?"

"I'm—" I couldn't believe how easily this woman saw through me. "I'm going out, yes. But I'm coming back."

"I'm going with you then." The words were fast and certain, and when she saw the look on my face, her next words came just as quickly. "That hole you came through. It's there because of me. I tried to get out and explore. But I couldn't move all the stones."

"Atell—"

"You're welcome," she said. "If you don't take me with you, I'm just going to follow you. I've been thinking about it ever since you opened it up."

"It's dangerous," I said. "Deadly. I've almost died out there."

"I almost died in here," she said. "I almost drowned when I was small. You almost killed me. If I was scared of dying I wouldn't do these things."

Could I argue that? At best I would be a hypocrite. If I couldn't stop her from going out there, then she should be with me. I could protect her. Maybe.

Or I could just be forced to watch her die.

I liked her. She reminded me of myself. And I needed her alive. So I agreed with her, on the condition that she follow my direction exactly while we were in the Walls.

"You showed me around in here," I said to her. "It's going to be different out there. You don't stray, and you don't choose the path. We're not going far."

"Okay," she said.

"It's serious." Atell wasn't exactly lighthearted, but I was grim. "We are not alone out there. If I have to leave you for dead, I will. And I won't lose any sleep over it."

Chapter Twenty-Five

I t's about a wielder named Fire," Atell said. After our short discussion about our upcoming excursion, we were at last reading the book. Well, she was, and I was taking her at her word, which I mostly trusted.

"His name is Fire?"

"Her name. It's a woman."

"Fire. Do all the wielders have names like that? Because it seems..." I waited for a better word to come to me, and it didn't. "...stupid."

"Wielders earned their names," Atell said, sounding a touch horrified at my response. "And they wore them proudly. She had a different name before. But that was someone else. Before she really became a wielder. And when she did, she got her name from another wielder. Someone strong. Like Brander or Scrit, maybe. It doesn't say."

Brander. Scrit. I didn't bother to inquire.

"The name comes from the talent. Fire. It could be destruction or art. Or something we can't even fathom. The story will tell us."

"Okay. Go on."

"I'm trying. There's a lot here." Atell fell silent, scanning the first couple of pages side-by-side. "It starts like ones I've heard. How she bonded with her magic. But if this whole entire book is about her...her story must be legendary. It would take weeks to tell it full.

"She bonded with fire. With flame."

"No surprise there," I said.

Ignoring me, Atell continued. "A magical fire ate—no, consumed her town. And everyone in it. When she was very young. But she..." Silence while she read on. "I don't know this part. But she lived and took the fire inside of her. Too late to save the town. Maybe she's named for that deed. Something she did as a child. Without even knowing how."

Atell read for me—for us—as time passed into night. As she had warned, not all of the Lillitan was clear to her, but enough came through for both of us to understand. The story started with the short tale of Fire's origins, and then skipped ahead to a ferocious battle between her and something called an ice elk. I commented that I'd never heard of such a beast, and Atell said it wasn't a beast at all, but a northern people who lived in frigid weather and didn't feel the cold like we did.

"Grandfather's stories were all fights and battles," Atell said, excited. "I can read almost all of this part."

Fire won, of course. How could she not have, with so much book still left?

Fire's magic, though bonded, had a *temper*, as Atell described it. It would listen to her, but it would also overreach her command. She would ask it to lift a rock, and it would tear up the earth. These incidents, rather than growing better with time, only grew worse.

"Why?" I asked, trying not to look at the gem that was giving us steady light.

"I don't know," Atell said. "It might not say. There's a lot here I—"

"I know," I said. "Keep going."

We stopped when both our gnawing bellies reminded us we needed to eat. I waited for Atell while she went into town.

She took longer than I expected, but returned with a wrapped board loaded with so much food I was amazed she could even carry it.

She set it down on the ground and pulled off the cloth. The gem was still shining, muted and steady. I could see easily, but I wasn't quite sure what I was looking at.

"That's the fish," Atell said, reading my face and pointing at a pile of three fat, silver-bellied, cooked fish with their heads chopped off.

"I know," I said, and it became clear she was teasing me. "It smells good. How did you catch ones without heads?"

She laughed at that—it was short and quiet, but it was the first time I'd heard laughter in this town. She moved her hand over what appeared to be a mushy mound of green slop. "This is waterweed. It grows in the lake. We pick it from the bottom."

"Ah." It wasn't the most appetizing...pile.

"And these are some branchnuts," she said, hovering over the last edge of the board, which was piled with dark shapes she must have scraped out of the shells. How many, ten? A dozen? I couldn't remember the last time someone had prepared a meal like this for me, including myself. I ate an awful lot of dried meat.

"Thank you, Atell," I said.

"It's nothing. I still owed you a fish. Now you have two."

That fish, it turned out, was delicious. The meat was still plenty warm, and I followed Atell's method of peeling back the scaly skin and eating the meat around the bones. I was ravenous; one taste of the fish awakened that in me, and it wasn't long before I had cleaned their bones. I was less excited about the waterweed, but hungry enough to try it without hesitation. It was very wet, almost slimy, but had a similar taste to the fish and was refreshing.

It was the branchnuts that were the most surprising. I bit into one of the chunks and found it dense and satisfying, almost like a slab of beef. It crunched between my teeth when I bit in, but the inside was tender and the flavor was reminiscent of the nut cakes I used to buy from a bakery in the second ring.

Even between the two of us, we couldn't finish all of them. Still, when the time came, I wouldn't take my final leave from Iyes without loading my pack with branchnuts.

The tale continued, though it frustratingly lacked the kind of information I was craving. It really was just a story, not the grand guide I was hoping it would be. Fire lived, she defeated the ice elk but didn't kill him—instead, she sought their elders to learn to control her magic. But they turned her away because with the temper inside her, she was a danger to them all.

"Maybe that's why she was named Fire," Atell said. "Not because she used fire magic. But because everything she touched got hurt."

"Maybe." I was growing disinterested, and time was sliding by us rather quickly. Night was here in its total darkness, escaping even the light of the moon and the stars underneath the vast canopy. "We should go, Atell. Thanks for reading all of this. But it's time, before we get too tired."

Atell closed the book quickly and looked me in the eyes. They were shiny, the green tinged with yellow from the light.

"I've never been more awake," she said.

Chapter Twenty-Six

I went through the gap first. Most of my time here had been spent by the wall, and I knew there was no chance for the people of Iyes to have resealed the hole, but it was still good to see that it was open.

I understood how Atell could feel trapped here, in a small, dark town that was one-hundredth the size of Cartha. I probably would have gone crazy if I couldn't get out.

All was quiet outside. I scraped across the stone, moving carefully to avoid being snagged on some broken cropping of rock, and awkwardly shoving my pack through to drop down first. I had asked Atell if she needed help getting up, but she assured me that she didn't. And soon after I made my way down to the ground, I looked up to see her head coming through the hole, her face in the shadow of the moonlight that stretched from above.

"It's so bright in here. Is your light on?" Her voice was quiet and quavering, brimming, ready to jump out of her throat and bounce around the walls, yet scared to do just that.

"It's the moon," I said. "The moon and the stars. It's hardly any light."

She shifted; twisted. Her clothes scraped the stone, and she looked upward, facing the sky. I watched as high, high above her head, Atell saw a slice of the moon for the very first time. A white, shining sliver arching softly around the top of the wall, grazing us with pearly fingertips.

"Atell," I said. "Come down."

She descended, slow to move, grabbing each piece of rock and edge of wood carefully until her feet touched the dirt. Normally bare, they were wrapped in the heavy cloth she had used to cover the food. I had recommended it for this little journey.

Atell leaned back against the wall, glancing up once more.

"Are you okay?" I asked her. She was breathing fast, but there was no sweat on her face.

"It's..."

She didn't look good.

"Sit down," I told her, kneeling when she did. "Are you hurt? Did you get cut on the way down? Twist something?"

Atell shook her head.

"Deep breath," I said. She was practically wheezing.

It took a minute or two, but she did get her breathing back to normal. All the while I rested on edge, ears alert for the slightest movement; eyes scanning for lurking shadows.

"Sorry," Atell said. Her eyes were closed, the back of her head pressed against the firm wood of the gate. She opened them slowly. "It's...just a lot bigger than I thought."

"The Walls?"

"The..." She lifted a limp hand, palm up, then let it fall back to the ground. "The sky. The world. The walls too. I didn't realize how far up they went. And this is all...a small part of your map."

"Yeah."

She had been born in darkness, in a box with a closed lid. She'd lived there her entire life. An adventurous spirit wasn't enough to overcome a shock like this. I couldn't imagine seeing the sky for the first time and what I would think, even if I knew it had been there all along. I imagined, for me, that finding Iyes felt like one small piece of what was coursing through Atell's mind and making her weak at the knees.

"If you want to go back in—"

"No. No." Atell straightened up a bit, pushing her palms into the dirt. "Definitely not. This is all I've wanted. I'm a little embarrassed that it all hit me at once. But I'm fine."

I stepped back, eyeing her. "Can you stand up?"

"Yeah." She said it and then she did it, and she didn't look as shaky as I expected. "I'm fine. I can walk. So...what are you coming out here for?"

I watched her for a moment longer, then spoke. "Exploring. Before...all this, I was doing it just to do it. I wanted to make my map, plot out the whole labyrinth. I never thought I'd really find another city or town. But now I'm looking for answers. Someone, or some people, who can tell me what happened to my city. And..." I thought back to the empty streets, the ghost town Cartha had become. Not a soul in sight, with monsters on the prowl. "My people. Some died. But I can hardly account for all of them. They could be alive, and if they are, I want to find them."

"I thought your city was destroyed."

"It was." I was already taking out the map and unfolding it. "And I saw very few dead people, even though the place was overrun. They were just gone. So they're somewhere else."

She didn't say anything; just blinked.

"It starts and ends with the map," I said, pulling it out and giving it a shake. "I need to push out and expand what I know, and I need a record of it. So that's what we're doing. And it's a lot more dangerous now than it ever was before. I don't know what did it, or if the monsters were always here, but something woke them up. And honestly, I hope that if we both survive this little stroll, you never come back into these walls."

"That's nice that you want me to live." Atell's energy seemed to be back, sarcasm hot on its heels.

Slightly annoyed that I couldn't rattle her, I just turned and said, "Let's go," keeping the map out and ready, because even the first step past this gate was a step I'd never taken before.

Quiet, with wet air and almost total darkness when a cloud passed over the moon. I knew we couldn't trust the quiet, that the black claws could move in silence over the soft dirt, so we had to rely on our eyes.

It was nice to have an extra pair, and one that was used to living in even darker walls. It saved my neck the soreness from constantly looking up and down at the map. I told Atell that if we spoke, it had be quick and hushed, as we didn't want to draw anything to us, nor did we want to miss any warning sounds. For being full of questions before, Atell was mostly silent now. Drinking in the outside world, perhaps. Save for the deadly creatures, it was duller out here than it was in Iyes.

Except for that constant, invisible twinkle of the horizon—of knowing that you could keep walking and walking and walking and nothing would stop you from going forward unless it killed you. That feeling of being surrounded by walls yet being more free than you'd ever been back at home. It was an energy that I only ever found out here. Even falling into Iyes for the first time didn't drive me like the Walls did.

Atell watched over my shoulder as I drew out the map, pressing in fresh lines. Beyond the gate, this path stretched beyond sight. The door to Iyes was set into the eastern side of a very long, straight hall. Far down—almost too far to see—was a branch opening to the left.

"Onward or over left," I said, staring down at my map as we pushed on, well past the gate. "Onward or over?"

"Huh?"

"Oh." I glanced back at Atell for a second. "Nothing."

"Okay."

Try not to talk to yourself when other people are around.

We pressed on, leaving our footprints in the dirt and finding no traces of anything else passing through. I had the gem glowing, strapped to my shoulder like it had been before. Would it pull me towards the next town like it had with Iyes? What if the small towns were clustered together, separated by walls rather than by distance? It was possible. Anything could be possible out here. That was the overwhelming beauty of it, covered by an ugly facade.

We stopped before the branch. Incredibly, the northern path stretched on. I didn't have to check the map to know that it was the largest, practically-unbroken straight line that I'd seen in the labyrinth. If I had the time, I would have jotted some notes about that—*Why? Building around something? Common pathway?* But now wasn't the time for that kind of wondering.

"What do you think?" I asked Atell softly, as we were poised at the corner of left and forward. "Onward—" I pointed my pen into the reaching darkness, "—or over?" I flicked it to the left.

"How should...how would I know?"

"You don't, and neither do I," I responded. "What does your instinct say?"

"Left," Atell said immediately, and I nodded.

"I was thinking the same. This northern path could go on for miles without a break. Left it is."

We broke west and moved into new territory that felt more like the labyrinth I knew, with short paths and frequent branches. Rarely did we walk more than one hundred feet without coming to a turn. And as we went further and further with no sign of other life or trouble, ease crept back into our movements.

The map was fleshing out; growing deeper into the western walls. It felt good to be able to do this again.

"What's that?" Atell's voice was a sharp whisper, cutting at me while I hovered my pen over the paper. I had heard the noise too—a soft shuffle that I was familiar with.

"It's just the burrow pigs," I said. "Little animals that live in here. They dig their homes in the dirt and they don't see very well. I would hunt them and sell the meat and hide. Mostly the meat. The hide is bristly and small, not very useful."

"Are they dangerous?"

"Not in the least," I told her. "They don't even have teeth. I'll catch one for you, maybe next time. And you can try the meat. It's very different from fish."

By my markings, Atell and I had covered two miles of branching paths and turns before we found something. We didn't hear it, and it was only by the luckiest trappings of skylight that I was able to spot it, but I did.

"Don't move." The words slipped from my mouth, and I twisted my palm backward toward Atell. I stopped us before a sharp corner to the left. To the right it was clear, and straight ahead was a blank wall. But creeping around the corner to the left, I saw the pitch-colored leg of a black claw, almost invisible in the dirt.

The gem dimmed down to nothing.

Is there time to run, or does it know we're here? Why didn't I have Atell bring a weapon, or give her one of my daggers?

We couldn't creep over two miles back to Iyes with this thing at our backs. It had to be killed.

"Monster?" Atell whispered, barely audible.

"Monster," I said, and I drew my dagger.

Chapter Twenty-Seven

The black claw wasn't moving. It didn't hear us, which was beyond lucky. Had we caught it in its sleep? Did these things sleep?

We'd take it quick; not give it a chance to fight back. I kept my free hand pushed back toward Atell for just a moment, silently urging her to stay put. This wasn't a fight for her, weaponless and new. She almost lost it coming out of the gate.

I went from stock-still to moving in a flash, stepping around the corner with my dagger pointed up. I would leap on the thing before it could react and I would drive my dagger into its throat, ending its life in one quick stroke.

But when I came around the angle of stone, I didn't see an upright black claw like I expected. In disbelief, my foot caught the corner and I fell hard, past the monster and into the dirt, and I rolled to the side. Atell gasped and called my name.

"Stay there," I said, my eyes never leaving the monster. "I think it's dead. I think they're dead."

It wasn't just one black claw here. It looked like two, slumped over each other, unmoving. Getting to my feet and shaking the dirt off myself, I relit the gem and saw that there were actually three of them, still and lifeless, piled over one another.

I walked up to one and kicked it, holding my dagger at the ready, but I knew it was dead. Sleeping things didn't look like this. My boot connected with its oddly-firm flesh and shuffled its corpse a few inches across the others. There was no blood on them, nor was there any in the dirt.

Could have been swallowed up by the earth, I thought, and then, *How long have they been here? What killed them—and how close is it to us?*

Atell came around the corner now, eyeing me briefly before turning to the dead claws. The sight stopped her dead at first, but she quickly overcame that and knelt down. "I've never seen anything like this."

"Neither had I." Enthralled as she was by the dead monsters, I was setting my sights on the open spaces stretching to either side of us. There were no strange tracks in the dirt, no sign of anything having been here recently. Probably, we were safe. As safe as we could be in the Walls.

Atell reached out and touched one, laying a hand on its long front limb, tracing fingers down its hairless, slightly-pebbled skin until she reached the long claws curving into the dirt. "You really killed one of these?"

"Yeah. And I'm worse the wear for it." At least my leg had been healing well. "If these three had been alive, we would be dead. Probably in pieces."

"What killed them?" Atell was still touching the monster, lifting its limb to test the weight.

"I don't know," I said, and before I could speculate further, the sound of a crash rolled over us like thunder. Atell bolted upright, and the hairs on my neck stood straight up.

"What was that?" Atell whispered, panicked and hushed.

"I don't know," I said again, but I did know the sound because I'd heard it before, only a few days ago, when I was hunting burrow pigs to bring back to Cartha.

It was the sound of a labyrinth wall breaking.

"We have to go," I told her, sliding my dagger back into its sheath. "Now. We have to go now! Stay with me!"

I ran, looking back only once to see Atell following me. The gem banged against my chest in its harness. I pulled the map out on the fly and found our course quickly before folding it away again. There was no time to do anything but run as fast as we could. If I was quick this time, if I was fast enough, then maybe...

Atell had more stamina than I expected. She was on my heels every step of the way, and she could have outrun me if she didn't have to follow me through the maze. Our feet churned the dirt and left a messy trail. The silence was thick and unsettling in the wake of the boom that had echoed from the direction of Iyes.

I prayed we wouldn't find what I expected.

The path back was clear, devoid of obstacles or monsters, the same as it had been when I fled back to Cartha that night. We ran, sucking in breath, taking turn after turn and kicking up dirt in our wake until we came to the gate, or what was left of it. The rubble was cast inward, the ragged hole in the wall so big that twenty people could have walked through it at the same time. Any remnants of wood and iron were buried in shattered stone.

"No, no, how could this happen?" Atell cried.

"There's no time," I said, nausea coiling in my stomach. "It's an attack. If we're going to save anyone, we have to hurry."

"No, no," Atell said, and she kept saying it even as she leapt past me to get past the rocks, even as I caught up to her and shoved my second dagger in her hand.

"You stay with me," I said, holding her forearm tight. I could feel her bones with my fingers. "You hear me? *You stay with me.* The magic must be what kept me alive in Cartha. I don't know how, but— you have to stay with it."

Atell's trailing murmurs tapered off. "Okay," she said. The dagger was trembling in her hand, loose and threatening to fall.

"Hold it tight," I said, "and use it if you have to."

We moved over the rocks. The air was filled with stone dust, making us cough as we passed through. I remembered Cartha, and the eerie ghost town that had met me when I emerged from the labyrinth. Iyes was as quiet as the city had been. Quiet and dark but for the spare moonlight that drifted in through the wreckage of the gate.

"Don't call out," I warned Atell. Her footsteps were going quicker, carving ahead of me. I remembered screaming into the silence of my city. "We're going to look around. Carefully."

The sick feeling in my stomach grew stronger as we entered the town, walking through pitch-black streets. Atell's rattled nerves displayed themselves in every motion she made, but her goal was clear. She was heading straight for her house, towards the water.

I stayed alert, but I wouldn't be able to see a white wall in this darkness, let alone a black claw. I hated it. But there was no sound besides the two of us, and I knew we were traveling through an empty town. We made it to the other side and didn't hear or see a thing. Just darkness and the occasional movement of the water as the fish lived their lives, oblivious.

Atell threw open the door to her home and barged inside, any semblance of discretion lost. I waited outside, getting a handle on the surroundings. It was clear that exactly what had happened to Cartha was happening here. The gate smashed; the people just...*gone*. Not a sound around us, or any evidence except the giant hole in the wall. This time, Atell was the townsperson who happened to be outside during the...the what? Attack? Kidnapping? What kind of phenomenon was this?

And why? Why was it happening *again*?

Chapter Twenty-Eight

Gone," she said when she emerged, leaving the door open behind her. "It's empty."

"Yeah," I said.

"I'm checking the other ones," Atell said, immediately going to the next house and throwing open the door.

I let her go through the next seven, eight, ten houses, all the while thinking, *How long until the monsters come? How long until the black claws take this place apart? Till the rest of them move in? Till that huge creature stomps this whole place flat? How long?*

When Atell came out of the next house—was that number twelve?—I grabbed her by the arm. She struggled against me, trying to dig her narrow fingers underneath mine and pry me off.

"Atell," I said. "Atell. Please, stop. There's no one here. We have to get out of here before they come."

"What are you saying? Let me go!"

"It's just like Cartha," I said, my voice dead, the gem silent and dark against my chest. "There's no one left. And soon the monsters are going to come, and if we're here when that happens, we are dead."

"They're here," Atell growled, and she yanked at her arm. "They're here, Jost, there's nowhere else for them to be. Let me go!"

Atell had the dagger in her captured hand. She twisted her wrist, bending it back, and the tip of the blade dug into my arm. I hissed and pulled back and she broke away from me, running. East, toward the water.

I pressed my thumb over the wound and felt the blood trickling out. A small cut. She probably didn't even realize she had done it. But if she would have just listened to me—hell! We were both standing on the brink of death, and I hadn't gone through all this to get killed trying to coax someone else into acting logically.

That's not fair. She's losing everything, just like you did.

"I don't care," I said, dropping my arm and letting the blood drip down to my fingers. "We're out of here. I'll drag her if I have to."

I stomped through Iyes, flattening grass and leaving heavy boot prints in the dirt. Forget being quiet, that bubble was already burst. I pushed through the blackness, onto the grass leading to the water, looking for Atell. The way it was here, I would probably trip over her and stab myself on my own dagger. Or blindly fall into the lake and drown. How the hell could these people live like this?

The small sounds of the water told me when I was close, though I couldn't see Atell anywhere. Even though I was sure the whole town was empty, I couldn't shake the feeling that just out of my line of sight was a creature blending into the darkness, waiting for me to get close enough to grab. I kept my dagger out.

I neared the edge of the water where the ground began to slope in, and I stopped. No Atell. Maybe she was checking the piers, seeing if anyone had withdrawn to safety atop the water. Or maybe I misread her entirely and she had circled back to the town around me and was barging into another few dozen homes.

"No, I'd hear you," I said to myself. Dagger out, I walked, peeling to the right, towards the area where I'd met with her the day before, when she came out of the water. Guesswork, all of this, and I was tired of it. I was wandering in the dark in every kind of way. The closest thing I found to light was a gem I knew nothing about, and someone else to read a book that told me almost nothing.

"She knows, though," I said, skirting around the end of the lake. "She knows, and we're getting out of here and she's gonna tell me everything."

The first pier jammed its upright post against my thigh, and I cursed and grabbed it to catch my balance again. A loud curse pushed at my lips.

My gem flickered then, a dim light that seemed like a massive torch in the darkness. I made it quiet. Now wasn't the time. I walked onto the pier, the sound of wood strange underneath my boots. Tiny noises splashed up at me from the water, the movements of the life within. If I wasn't so hurried and angry, I might be afraid of what was beneath me. If there was a hole in this pier, I would sink like a rock to the bottom of the lake.

But I didn't find my death nor anything else. Just the sudden end of the walkway that would drop me into the water. I retreated to land quickly, my heart dancing a little behind my ribs.

I came to the next pier and decided, the hell with it. I pulled the gem from the harness and held it out, facing down the walkway like I was challenging it. And when I called the light, it came as a beam roughly the size of the pier itself. It cast the wooden boards in yellow light all the way to the end. Nothing. But the light shaped for me, and that was something new. Something Atell would like to see, I was sure.

The next pier on this side of the lake was the last, some hundred feet from the place where the ground narrowed too much to walk without getting your feet wet. I cast my light there just the same, where it fell on nothing and no one.

I rounded back, faintly aware of the gem pulsing in my hand even though I had recalled the light. Time was wasting away, and as much as Atell was to blame for that, I was too. I should get out of here and leave her. There was no benefit to being pinned down to die alongside her just because she couldn't accept the truth.

Like you could live with yourself if you left yet another person to die.

"I didn't leave anyone to die," I spat, stomping past another pier, the first one I had checked. The lush grass made my boots quiet despite how deep my footprints were embedded in the ground.

Left your whole city to die, Jost. Left Gwin to die.

"Gwin died in front of me," I said, and then, "or was I asleep? I don't remember. But I didn't leave his side."

You just told Atell that your people weren't dead. Just gone. Who can't accept the truth now?

When would the sounds come, the horrid etchings of curved claws against stone? The splintering of wood as the homes were crushed and collapsed, flattened like a field for planting. What would I see this time, and would it be enough to crack my mind in two like a—

"Branchnut," I muttered. The stiff curve of a shell pressed into the sole of my boot. I stepped harder on it, pushing it into the ground, looking down at my feet. And when I looked back up, I saw Atell sitting at the edge of the water, her legs bent underneath her, staring out at the black surface.

She heard me coming, surely, as I walked over, but she didn't say or do anything. She just kept looking at the water.

"Atell."

"Jost." Eyes straight ahead.

"What are you doing?"

Shrug. "What is there to do?"

"Leave," I said. "Survive."

Silence. She didn't move a muscle. I wondered how far she could see, having lived here all her life.

"There's no time—"

"I don't belong out there." Now she moved, to turn her head back to me, and the faint light of the gem shone across the wetness of her eyes. "I thought I might. Now I went out and everything is ruined. Like I climbed the wall and touched the sky."

"So what, you want to die here?" I snapped, and the gem flared like a struck flint. "That's your plan, Atell? How about you get the hell out of here with me? There's all kinds of time to die later. It doesn't have to be now. It doesn't have to be like this. And I—"

I stopped, my breath heavy and harsh, my throat suddenly tight, making it hard to speak. But I knew what I wanted to say.

"Don't make me go out there alone again," I said. "Come with me."

The Walls were different now. Still filled with darkness. Misty wetness. And other things. I'd walked them alone my entire life, but even just a few hours of having Atell there with me made it into something else. I wasn't prepared to lose that yet. I'd lost so much already.

"I wish I had taught you to swim," Atell said, and her eyes were back on the water. "There wasn't enough time. The lake leads somewhere, you know. The fish come and go. I hear the water move. There's a big tunnel going under the wall and it leads out. Maybe to another town."

Her voice was wistful, her shoulders slumped. "If I could hold my breath long enough. I could swim to the other side. I never tried. Once you try, there's no going back. You either make it or you drown."

"Atell—"

"I'm sorry, Jost," she said. "I can't go with you. I was wrong about everything. I'm sorry."

"If you think I'm leaving you here to get killed, you're out of your mind." I strung the gem back into its harness. I reached for her.

I almost got her.

Chapter Twenty-Nine

If I had grabbed her first, if I had wrapped my hand around her arm, what would have happened? Would I have held on, or would I have let go? Either could have killed her. Holding on could have killed me.

But that doesn't matter, because I wasn't fast enough.

Something burst from the water and took her. It was almost too fast to see, a crash of sound and blackness in the blackness. It snaked out a fingerless limb that was thin like a flapping, black ribbon, and it snaked up her arm in a spiral. It all happened in an instant. Her eyes went wide, she reached for me as I reached for her, and then it yanked her through the air and down into the water.

"Atell!" I scrambled, pushing into the water and wading in until I was up to my waist. But what could I do? I couldn't swim. I couldn't fight some kind of water beast. I was stuck. I watched the water for something, anything, but it was as quiet as it ever was. One moment, one second, and she was just gone.

"Atell," I said, almost pleaded, holding my hands above the water, very aware that I could be taken just the same at any moment. The gem was lit and it was hot against me; I barely registered it. It would protect me or it wouldn't. Was everything completely out of my control?

A minute passed.

Then two.

Then five.

I left the lake half-soaked and bewildered. I knew time was dragging on, that I could be walking into a field of monsters, and I felt a lot like what I imagined Atell felt like as she sat on the ground and stared at the water.

Hopeless. Alone.

Iyes was empty. Dead. The same as Cartha, just that it hadn't been dismantled yet. And just like in Cartha, I had to watch the only person I cared about die in front of me.

I pulled my boots off, dumped the water out of them, and slung my socks over my shoulder. They would take some time to dry. I marched forward barefoot. The grass felt good on my bare feet, and the sensation practically made me retch. Why did I deserve to have grass between my toes, to be breathing the cool air while Atell's lungs were filled with water?

I bit the inside of my lip.

When the grass thinned and my feet grew dirty, I was grateful. I would walk barefoot in the Walls, too, and let half-buried rocks slice into the bottoms of my feet. I would bleed into the dirt. If the black claws could smell blood, let them come. I had plenty more to give.

I came across my dagger where Atell must have dropped it as she ran. Thin blades of grass sprouted up around it; some were crushed underneath. My blood had dried to gummy stiffness on the tip. I picked it up from the ground and wiped the blade out of habit before re-sheathing it.

I walked past empty houses, some with doors hanging open. Atell's work, or the people of Iyes' final disappearing act? It was so quiet.

Now past the town, I could see that the mist from the broken gate was drifting in from the Walls, slowly creeping across the grass. The damage gaped, a hazy mound of moonlight. Like a ghost, I drifted there.

I looked back at the town, a wave of buildings and wash of water that I knew was there but couldn't see. Boots in hand, I left it behind, stepping over jagged wreckage and embracing the pain it brought to me. The monsters weren't here yet, but they would come. I might as well be gone.

There was something in my mind. A tickle that was growing to an itch. Something I didn't want to investigate while Atell was with me, but now...

The gem. Quiet, resting against me. I hadn't told Atell, but it had been doing *something* while we had been out. Heating up. And as impossible as it seemed, it was growing. The harness twine was tight against it, and some of the narrow strings had snapped. Thin, but noticeable if one looked, and I did.

I immediately turned right when I entered the Walls, map in mind. I had come from the left—south. I knew what was there; what I had seen and what I hadn't seen. What I was looking for had to be elsewhere.

The dirt was cold and wet under my feet, so unlike the comforting grass. I tied my boots to my pack, letting them hang upside-down while I walked so that I could handle my map. I was pushing into uncharted territory once again.

Down the long hall I went, the unbroken straightaway that led north, away from the former gate. I knew when the curve would be coming, now, because I knew the size of Iyes. The sharp right turn marked the edge of town, and I took it without slowing, drawing careful lines on my map and not caring what I might be walking into. My suspicions formed a lump in my throat and a sick weight in my stomach, the same feeling I had when Atell and I first heard the crash.

Because it was—it really had to be—all my fault.

My map bore straight lines and the barest nudges towards other paths. My destination was not further from Iyes, but nearby. I didn't know for sure. Cartha's was farther away from the city, but maybe that was because it was bigger?

Atell might have known something about it, but then wouldn't she have figured it out? Wouldn't she have cast me away the moment it occurred to her?

I would have.

My heartbeat quickened with my steps as I mapped out the wall, heading directly east towards where the lake was pinned inside the walls of Iyes. If it was here, I had to be getting close, unless the lake stretched much, much further than I had imagined. I hated the fact that inside me, there was hope I wouldn't find it. That it—

Splash.

Ice-cold water on my feet made me gasp and step back. I'd been storming onward, not paying any attention, and I'd walked right into...water?

I called the light and it came, soft and yellow, projecting forward. And it showed me that the lake was not at all pinned inside of Iyes, that in fact it went under the wall and out, filling this hall with water. Shallow? Deep? The surface told me nothing.

I rolled my pants up and trudged forward. The ground dipped slightly, but not in the severe way it did within the town. Either this was an outer edge and the lake likely didn't span into the next hall, or this puddle-deep expanse was an overflow that was growing outward, maybe even as I walked through it.

It would be here, then. If the water was this huge, big enough to pass the wall and go farther beyond, then it would have to be here.

"How would you know, Jost? It would have been hundreds of years ago," I said, sloshing through the water and churning up the wet dirt below.

"I know because I felt it," I answered myself, lightly touching a finger to the gem. The broken twine poked at me. "I know because you felt it. And you stole it, didn't you? You stole it all."

I came upon it not long after, the scoop in the wall, the hollow where the gem would be, just like the one outside Cartha. A city like mine might have several, I surmised. Perhaps one for each gate. But

Iyes had only one gate, unless there was some kind of port for a boat that would never come. And it would only take one gate to be broken, would it not? That was all it took for my city.

I sloshed forward through the water, my feet and ankles rolling waves forward, small swells swirling with flecks of dirt. I stood before the socket and ran my fingers over it, feeling the smooth curve, the perfect half-sphere. Empty.

The sickness in my stomach, dragging me down, closing my throat. I crouched, pushing my hand into the water, searching, and I found it. I pulled my hand from the water and opened my palm to see a broken, colorless gem.

If gray stone could be made clear, it would look like this. Lifeless. It lay in two pieces on my palm, sitting in the tiny pool of water collected in my hand.

I let it drop back to the water and I left, staying upright until I reached dry ground, where I fell to my knees and the sickness came out of me and splashed into the dirt. My throat burned with each powerful retch.

It was me. I took the gem from Cartha and disrupted whatever sort of magical protection it had given us. And now I'd come here and done the same—by accident, but it happened. My gem, greedy and strong, must have sucked this other gem dry, pulled its magic out until it cracked and fell from the wall. Just hours ago.

Everything I had learned about magic, I learned too late. There was more blood on my hands than I could possibly imagine.

I retched again and there was nothing left, so I screamed.

Chapter Thirty

I don't know why I took the broken gem, but I did. I turned from where I had splattered my insides across the ground, went back to the water, and fished it out. Even if I could repair it, if I could begin to comprehend what would go into a task like that that, it was already too late. Maybe I'd carry it as penance. A reminder of what I'd done.

My mind was fuzzy, like it was being pulled apart and I was seeing through the webbing of strings that held it together. I left the water again and eventually I found myself at the pile of dead black claws, the three that Atell and I had stumbled across earlier.

I had no memory of the journey here. I stared down at them and wondered again what had killed them. I thought of going to Iyes and climbing through the rubble and sitting in the center of town and waiting. Or maybe I'd sit inside someone's house, someone's empty house with their abandoned furniture and food and clothes and everything else they'd never touch, and I'd wait for it to collapse on top of me.

One blink of my eyes and maybe I'd be there. But they closed and opened and I was still staring at the pile of dead monsters and now I could smell them like I couldn't smell them before. It was like rotting plants, like a harvest that spent too long in storage. When I was younger, in Cartha, I'd broken into a harvest shed to steal some food and come across a messy pile of decayed slop that smelled so bad I couldn't make myself eat the whole next day. This reminded me of that.

"Some way to go, huh?" I told myself. "Take out a city, then a town. Then just lay back and die, nice and easy. Very convenient for you."

I looked at the dead things and breathed in that awful smell and chewed the inside of my lip bloody. Metallic tang flooded my mouth. I gnawed at the wound and drank it and decided that death was too simple. Far beyond what I deserved.

What was to be done? I couldn't go looking for another town and let the same thing happen again. Even if I left the gem behind, what if some monster found it? A dumb one could swallow it and carry it in its belly and steal all the magic in the labyrinth without even knowing it. A smart one...

There had to be intelligent creatures behind what was happening. The black claws, the odd tangled mess I had seen in Cartha—those things felt like lackeys. Maybe the big one was in control. Maybe there were others. But leaving this behind to be found couldn't lead to anything good. Look what happened when I found it.

I took the gem out. At some point I had moved it from my harness to my pocket.

"I can control you," I told it. "I've done it before. I stopped you killing all those people in Iyes. I use your light. And if you start eating other magic, then I stop you. If I can't, then I walk the other way. There's nothing here *but* other ways."

Wanderer, that would be me. I would wander the Walls and safeguard this gem, keep it out of hands that might otherwise use its power. I would dedicate whatever years fate had left for me to clearing these Walls. I'd kill every monster I saw. I'd live on burrow pig and roots and rain. I couldn't take back what happened, but I'd do everything I could to help the people that were still alive, even if I didn't know them or where they were. Even if all it amounted to was a pile of three dead black claws stacked on top of each other in some unknown corner of the Walls.

I heard the noises then, the indication of the horde's final descent onto Iyes. The echoes of crumbling stone and fallen walls. The loud splintering of thick wood that might have been standing in its spot for a hundred years. It wouldn't take long for them to erase Iyes from existence.

"I hate you," I told the gem, "but if I could use you the way Fire could, I'd go back to Iyes and kill every single thing there."

No response from the gem, the little concentrated ball of magic that ruined my life in exchange for being able to see in the dark sometimes. I listened to the not-so-distant sounds of Iyes being torn apart and thought, if this was really the gem's fault, I wouldn't hate myself so much. I got involved with something I had no business in. No knowledge. Would I get mad at a dog for eating my meat if I walked away from my plate? Maybe, but that wouldn't make it the dog's fault.

I couldn't stay here. I needed to leave those noises far behind me.

I harnessed the gem and I walked. Map in hand, pen in the other, I stepped forward once more into new, dark places and marked them down. It was like old times, except not at all.

Wanderer. It didn't matter where I went, but the general direction of north felt right. Cartha, or what was left of it, sat in ruins southeast of where I stood. Iyes, just a couple miles behind me. The northern reaches of my map felt much emptier than the network of passages I'd scrawled to my back. If I was to die out here, be it today or years from now, I'd cover as much ground as I could and mark every single step.

I let the passages take me.

When darkness came, I slept for a few hours. It was all I needed or wanted. I was hungry, so I ate some flavorless dried food and thought about hunting. There were signs of burrow pigs here, many miles from Cartha, so I would find some. Maybe I'd find new meat. Maybe I could even fish somewhere.

The thought wrenched my chest. I stood and I stretched and I walked. Further north, I found another dead black claw. Just one, this time, and its death was apparent and violent—its limbs were broken in many places, mangled and turned back in on themselves like the monster had been twice rolled over by a boulder. It was almost too grotesque to look at, but I did, and I talked to myself.

Like old times.

"Must not have been pleasant," I commented to the dead thing while the gem watched from my shoulder. "Looks like you got in a fight with one of your bigger cousins. It folded you up like a blanket."

I marked it on my map, same as I'd marked the other dead pile.

When I found another dead black claw to the west of this one, something stirred in my mind. I'd come a fair few miles from Iyes now, and I thought—*If these things are working together to dismantle cities, why would they turn on each other in the Walls?*

This black claw smelled burnt, a tinge of acridity that did not cover the awful rotting-plants smell that accompanied its brethren. There was a smudge on the wall near it, which I'd taken for blood at first, but now I saw that it was soot.

"Marked," I murmured. I wasn't quite sure what to think, and none of the possibilities were pleasant. Other monsters, maybe. Things I'd never seen before, *doing* things I'd never seen before—maybe. Other people, strong enough to kill black claws and leave no trace of themselves?

"Maybe," I said, smelling the air. "Wonder if they'd take kindly to me."

Three scenes of death, the only dead ones I'd seen besides the one I'd managed to kill. Spread out, but still near each other...

It meant something. Right now, I didn't know what that was, but I would find out. The only thing to do in the meantime was to keep moving. North.

For being aimless and lost, I covered a lot of ground quickly. I didn't find any other creeping bodies of water in the Walls like where I had found the gem. I looked for signs of burrow pigs, craving hot cooked meat, but there were none.

I'd just seen some with Atell, I thought. Or did I only hear them? *Have I come so far? Are there none in this part of the labyrinth?*

Seeing more dead monsters and marking them on my map stirred that tickling again, that needling sense in the back of my mind. It was the way I felt when I had to decide between a left and a right turn, or when I had to decide how much food I had left during a long journey in the Walls and if I could make it back home without having to hunt again. It tickled, but I didn't know why. I let the itch build.

I was snaking northward as best I could, not wanting to beeline. The map would be hideous, useless, if there were just an inch-wide swath of me walking north and marking all the paths I passed by. If there was one thing I could do right, it was this.

The tickle grew maddening when I literally stumbled across my next corpse, my boot catching the soft, dead limb of the thing and flinging it across the dirt. Calmly, I looked down at the messy pile and wrinkled my nose. This was no black claw and no wild animal, but certainly a monster. It had the pitch-black skin of the rest, like a shadow brought to life and turned ugly. What must have been its skull was cracked open and sprayed across the dirt, blending in but for its jagged edges. Its many legs crossed over each other randomly, tipped with sprigs of bent, pointed claws. It resembled a giant spider with a head sticking out of one side. I felt strongly that if I were to see this thing alive and moving itself along with its flower-burst claws, I would go at least slightly insane.

I marked it on the map and finally scratched at the tickle, unfolding the full width of my papers and staring at what I'd done.

It was the deaths, of course. It had taken only a few more markings to see plainly in front of me that there was a pattern; a distribution. I recognized it almost immediately because it looked just like the maps I made to track burrow pigs. My movements, their nests, and my kills.

Something was hunting these monsters. And whatever it was, I knew how to find it.

Part Three: Magic

Chapter Thirty-One

It did cross my mind that going after something or someone capable of handling black claws and other things so easily could be dangerous, and in fact not the best idea. I let that thought cross over until it was gone. Some part of me craved this kind of danger. Perhaps the part that wanted penance—or was just stupid.

But I also knew that something like this was unprecedented, and whatever was killing monsters amid the Walls, maybe we'd be on the same side or see eye-to-eye. At the very least, we'd have something to talk about. Unless it was another monster.

"Worth the gamble," I said, my pen working out some notes on another sheet. My boots were dry and I'd come quite a ways. I'd marked a total of seventeen sites where I'd found dead monsters, and going by that stretch, the decay, as well as making some assumptions about the ones I hadn't found, I knew where to go. The sites had formed a semicircle curving north, which meant that I had bypassed where I presumed the kills were stemming from. I had to double back, just a couple miles.

My destination was loose. It was an area of the map that was otherwise blank, as of course I hadn't been there yet. I'd drawn a ghostly circle through the site markings and beyond, filling out the half I couldn't yet confirm. And within it, I gently circled where I felt I needed to be.

So strange, looking at that circle, a void within a void. I wasn't prone to speculating on my map. This would be the first time I'd ever marked a spot without actually standing in it. Yet as impossible as it was to be sure about it, I was sure.

I wasted no time in turning around and heading to the center of the circle. The path there was convoluted, as all paths within the Walls were, but I made it.

And what awaited me was something the likes of which I had never seen.

The name came to me the moment I laid my eyes on the place, and I wrote it atop the circle on the map, curving the scrawl along the shape as I filled it out.

Pooled Woods.

I put the map away.

When I had started feeling roots in the dirt as I neared the circle, I had some idea of what to look for. They were thick enough to make themselves known through the soles of my boots. I expected to see a blanket canopy of branches somewhere, like what was covering Iyes.

But when I turned the final corner that brought me, roughly, into the circle I had drawn, I had to stop and stare. The Walls stretched behind and around me, but before me they were gone, and as far as the eye could see there was water and there were trees. Huge, mammoth, monster trees, with gnarled trunks comprised of thick, winding roots. Roots that had wrapped around themselves and each other dozens and dozens of times until their combined bodies were fifty feet thick and rose up in tapering length to odd points I lost in the darkness of the sky.

I pictured it as a great field of spikes, spaced far but stretching up and up to impale the heavens. Like they had pierced the clouds and spilled their contents among themselves until they flooded.

"I could write a good story, I bet," I said to no one.

So they were here. The monster, or the person, or the denizen brought up from hell—whatever was eliminating the monsters was here.

"Unless you're completely wrong." Possible, sure. But I was here.

The water was unmoving and dark. It pooled up to the entrance in the wall, which was simple and unmarked, just a gap in the great stone slabs that might otherwise lead to another hall or turn. The border of the woods dipped below me, lined by thick roots that held the water in, keeping it for themselves.

How deep do you go? I wondered. I couldn't swim through here. But if there was a working of roots under the surface, something for me to grab onto or even step right on...

I plunged my boot into the water and found solid ground a few inches in, to my relief. I was not looking forward to navigating this space wet. Still, I would tread carefully, lest the ground disappear where I couldn't see it and drop me into deeper waters.

Both my boots were in now, and with the hairs raised on the back of my neck, I drew a dagger. This was a place so unknown that I couldn't even see what the ground was made of. With absolute certainty, I knew: there was danger here.

"The edges," I said to myself, moving first to the left. The water trickled over my boots as I lifted them out of the water with each step. "Work the edges, know what you're dealing with..."

I built the map in my head rather than bring it out now. As big as this place could be, I would still eventually find the walls that surrounded it. But it had to be very big, because there was light, which meant the walls of the labyrinth were further away. I could see ahead a few hundred feet, at least. The quiet here was eerie—in a space this large, shouldn't I hear wind? And any noise in the water would surely travel to me. As quiet as I tried to be, I couldn't help but splash with my steps.

I came to one of the trees—it wasn't really a tree, more of a spire, a spear of roots twisted together into a massive weapon—and I laid my hand on its surface. I thought I might feel heat, or magic, or movement. But it was just a hard root, rough and twisted with no space between. If there was magic here, it wasn't in these things.

And it was still quiet. So quiet that it felt wrong.

I sloshed through the water until I found a wall. It was a long time. The Pooled Woods weren't nearly the size of Cartha, but they were a far cry greater than Iyes, and when I finally touched the stone I was a little out of breath from dragging my feet through the water.

Looking north, where the expanse of the woods gaped, it was clear that the trees didn't grow along the wall. I followed the stone, staying near enough to touch it, and mildly annoyed that I'd been in this place over an hour and wasn't sure what I was looking for. The path here had been so clear, but now that I was here, it was back to being lost. I was hoping to kick my boots into some half-submerged monster carcass, but that was yet to happen.

It wasn't much further north before I started to doubt what convictions I had about this place.

There was light now, more light—the water was taking on a sheen. I saw great chunks of stone on the ground, and I looked to the wall to see where they had fallen from. Ahead of me, the wall was breaking. Not broken; still standing, still dozens of feet above my head, but spreading out from a massive crack like a many-fingered hand were roots that had forced their way through the stone and crept up, down, and along its surface. It was one of many such mars in the wall. And above that, the wall had succumbed to the invasion, breaking away and falling down into the water below.

How long ago? The further I went, the more severe the damage became. I was stepping around and over huge hunks of stone, some so big I had to climb over them. The silence was still here but the light was brighter, like a very early morning in Cartha. The air was moving and smelled fresh. The elements had started to take over this place, and the northbound wall was receding, growing shorter the closer I got to its end, if it had one. Or perhaps it was just gone, some miles away from me?

The gem flared with sudden, intense light, forcing me to turn away. I stopped and pulled it from the harness. Truth be told, I had almost forgotten about the thing for a moment, not needing its light here. Had it discovered some magic hidden away?

"Show me," I told it, and it responded immediately, tugging at my fingers and drawing me away from the wall. An excited grin came across my face. I hopped down from the crumble of wall I'd been standing on, landing in the water with a splash. "Don't lead me into any monsters without giving me some kind of a warning."

The gem hadn't tugged me anywhere since leading me to Iyes, and this time it wasn't so insistent. It was more like I was holding its leash and it was guiding me. Maybe I was learning.

Or maybe the gem was.

The latter was a vast and scary thought that I didn't want to spend any more time with.

It led me across the Pooled Woods directly, towards the opposite wall. Would it take me all the way through? I had no idea how far that would be. The way these roots were growing through the place, I couldn't assume anything about its size. These things had grown into the clouds. How much stone could they have broken?

Careful, I reminded myself. The jewel wasn't a pet, and it had its own instincts. *If you feel this gem pulling in other magic—you run.*

Splash splash splash. My feet disturbed the water as I hurried, eager to find what the gem had for me, yet ready to stop at a moment's notice if something felt off. I stepped around the spear-trees, unable to resist brushing my hands across them each time I did. At this point, I wasn't afraid of making noise. I wanted whatever was here to find me. I almost wanted to yell, *Come and get me!*

The opposite wall was not as broken. The part I approached was plain stone with no trace of roots. The gem, now, was urging me to turn north once more and go up the wall, so I did, splashing through the water.

"Just give it to me," I said, hurrying forward and starting to pant a little bit. I had my dagger in one hand and the gem in the other. If I tripped over something in the water, I'd probably end up stabbing myself through the neck. "Get me there, damn it, just get me there."

I saw thin fingers of roots stretching along the wall, and the gem stopped. Dull in my hand, I made it brighten, but I couldn't get it to pull me any farther. And thankfully, it didn't seem to have unsheathed its vampiric tendencies. Perhaps it was listening to me. And yet...

"That's all you have for me?" I held it up to eye level, and when it was unresponsive, I dimmed it and put it back in the harness. I touched the roots on the wall, these ones much thinner, almost like fine hairs etched into the slab. I was at their very tips, and even in this short distance I could see they grew thicker further north.

I followed them like a trail, catching my dagger in my left hand and running my fingers along the length of these roots. These ones were different. They were smooth, even once they got to the thickness of my wrist. It was unnatural, like they had been whittled and sanded down by a master.

And there were so, so many.

They spread across the stone in a single layer, never overlapping one another. The branches they made curved away from the others like touching was a sin. They covered the wall, intricate networks of smooth, pale wood with pockets of gray stone peering out from the spaces between.

I took them to the source, my gem quiet all the while. At first I couldn't see where they led; it all looked like the same expansion of roots, though now they were too close together to see the stone underneath unless I put my face right up against it. But once I stepped away from the wall to get a better look, it made sense.

The wall was broken, but not like the walls I'd seen; like the roots, it seemed to be by design. Thousands of branches emerged from a circular hole in the wall, wrapping around the edges and sprouting out.

Between them, there was just enough space for a person to enter.

Chapter Thirty-Two

I stared at what this journey had ultimately led me to: an unwelcoming hole in a wall. It wasn't a natural occurrence, I was sure of that. From the form and gloss of the roots, to the even shape they'd pushed through the wall—this was by design.

But whose? Monster or man?

Is the latter any better? What kind of person would do something like this? And why would I be drawn here?

"Magic, of course," I said, speaking it like a curse. After all, it had brought me nothing but trouble. "I can't escape it."

I sheathed my dagger. The lip of the root-lined hole was about a foot off the ground. I put my boot on it and stepped up, keeping my head low. The inside was darker than Iyes, and the gem lit aside my shoulder with hardly a thought.

"What in the hell...?"

It was a tunnel, all right, except it led farther than should have been possible. The wall it pushed through was only so thick, about ten feet from what I'd seen elsewhere in the labyrinth. Yet this tunnel stretched on for at least two hundred feet before a turn was made.

I hate this.

I walked forward, forced to stay slightly bent down so I wouldn't scrape my hair off. The place was a death trap. If something came at me through this tunnel—say, a black claw, which would fit quite well inside the cramped space—I could barely swing my arm forward at it, let alone fend it off. This was stupid and reckless, even judging by what I'd done up to now.

Best to accept it, then.

I ran my hand along the roots, the smooth surface satisfying under my fingers. When I reached the end of the tunnel, what I thought was a branching of paths turned out to be an opening of the roots, like a field of brambles stretched out before me, but without thorns. Just a mess of tangled branches as thick as my arm, rising slightly above my head. At first glance, it looked like a dead end. I stepped out of the tunnel, gratefully stretched my neck, and stared.

The gem's light pulsed slightly as I examined the tangle of roots and chewed at the inside of my lip. To one side, I saw the carcass of a small animal caught between the roots. It had gotten stuck there and died. It was too decayed to tell what it was.

That explains the smell. Even as I mused upon the idea of sharing the same fate if I journeyed forward, my eyes caught upon the way through the mess. It was hidden, like a twist of rope inside a bale of hay. But the way this scheme of branches curved, leaving just enough space for a man to...to *wind* through, if not walk...

I dropped my pack on the ground once more, knowing it couldn't come with me but groaning all the same. It would be fine if I could find my way back, but the way this looked, it might not be so easy. I pulled the gem from the harness, keeping it in my fist. I would need the light.

I ducked under the top root while stepping over a forking pair at the bottom, taking my first steps into this maze. Each half-foot forward was a challenge, bending and twisting my body around the roots which were very unyielding despite being only a few inches thick. Even if I leaned all my weight on one and shoved against it, it was like pushing against rock. I could see how an animal might get trapped and die in here.

Easily.

Deeper in, the roots were just as thickly strung, and the gem didn't seem inclined to help me out in any way besides giving me light. Still, I was seeing what I needed to see. The path was narrow and uncomfortable, but it was there. When my shirt or pants got snagged on a root, I had to struggle to remain calm, especially when the bottom of my pant leg got stuck so firmly that I had to backtrack in order to get it loose.

By the time I'd been in here ten minutes, I was frazzled. My muscles ached from being forced to awkwardly position myself as I wove through, my head hurt from banging against the upper roots a dozen times, and my mind was strained at seeing no end in sight but finding a good number of burrowing animals who had been unfortunate enough to wander into this network of hell and never get out.

I started to hurry. The scrapes on my skin accumulated, as did the bruises to my skull, but I wanted out of here. The regret was practically pouring out of me. My curiosity endangered me almost every single time I succumbed to it, and this felt like it might be the last time I'd be allowed to be so stupid.

And then the roots started to move around me.

"No. No, no no." I thrust myself forward, practically diving through the gap I'd spotted before it closed. The roots were moving inch by inch like snakes. Spaces and lifelines were closing right in front of my eyes. And the ones around me were closing in. One pressed into my shoulder hard enough to crunch my skin against my bone, flaring bloody pain through my arm. I yanked away and moved forward, toward what I could see, which wasn't much and it was changing every ten seconds.

I tried to lunge and couldn't. My boot was stuck, stuck between two or three or god-knew how many roots and they were not just trapping it but squeezing it, inching it tighter and tighter and trying to grind my bones into powder.

I screamed. I pulled. I grabbed onto a root with both arms and yanked, and I slipped my foot out of my boot and shot forward. I got weight on the foot to check if it was broken and I could walk on it so I did, entwining myself among the roots—

How many pieces am I gonna be in when this is over?

—finding the smallest spots to force myself through, not even sure which direction I was going in anymore—

Will I be spread all throughout this patch?

—and I didn't know when I had put the gem in my pocket but it was there and it was caught on a root, damn it, caught by just an inch or two and I pulled it free and the light showed me the end, *the end,* the way out that was so close—

Roots slid in front of it, blocking it off. I cursed loudly at them, but not really so loud because I was out of air, out of breath, and there were roots pushing on my back and squeezing those last breaths out of me but still I yelled—

"Make yourself fucking useful!"

—and I slammed the gem into the roots blocking my way, expecting the gem to shatter or my knuckles to shatter or my sanity to shatter, but none of those things happened so I pressed harder and I screamed again. My vision went black for a second as a root grew onto my neck and scraped skin off in a bloody patch and I thought, *if I die here, you have nothing, gem. Nothing.*

My vision returned, a sliver. Warm blood rand down my back and shoulder. The pain was distant. Unimportant. The gem was half-buried in the tight binding of roots blocking me off, melted into it like it was hot iron even though I felt no heat on my palm. Yellow cracks radiated out from the gem and through the roots, blindingly bright. They shot like lightning in all directions through the wood and it crumbled like a rotted log.

I tore my head away from the root that was trying to close around it. I threw the gem forward into the open space and used both my hands to pull myself after it, and by all the merciful heavens I threw myself free of the brambles and landed on cold, hard stone with a click of my jaw.

I reached forward blindly for the gem. My fingertips found it and I raked it in and got shakily to my feet. The pain in my neck was fiery now, burning. My shirt had torn near the bottom at some point during all of this, so I ripped a strip free and tied it around my neck to stop the bleeding. I would have to clean the wound, but I'd need my bag for that—

I blinked, just now realizing there was an archway in front of me and someone was standing in it. The light here came from behind him; my gem was dark. He was a silhouette, featureless. Was it a man, or was it a trick?

"Is this yours?" I said, raising one arm to gesture at the place which enclosed us.

No words. He walked forward without speaking, and the light bent around him, dimly giving me his features. He was older than me, but younger than Gwin. About my height, and his skin was smudged with dark bits of soot or dirt or something else. He had a hood over his head, which he pulled down as he approached me. He wore a short beard, black and gray, with similar short, flecked hair on his head, and his face looked worn.

His garb was light but tattered, made for easy travel, dark in color and slightly bagged around his frame. Where I was somewhat wiry, this man was not. He looked like he might be able to snap one of these roots in half.

"Easy," I said.

"You don't belong here," he said to me. His voice was deep and his eyes were so starkly black and white that they looked painted.

He came at me before I could respond, immediately going for my gem. I caught his arms with my hands and pushed back, and he was as strong as he looked, but I was sick and tired of being thrown into fire after fire. With a roar, I shoved at him, breaking his grip, and the gem flashed in my hand once like a beacon of warning.

"Tell me who—" I started, and he was at me again, and he must have been holding back something before because now I couldn't stop him. He pushed me backward and I stumbled a few steps before falling, taking us both to the ground.

What? The roots—

I only got a glimpse of the space behind me, but the roots were gone, revealing a great empty stone cavern.

The man's fingers tore the gem from my hands. I reached for my dagger and pulled it free and plunged it at his side. He twisted away from a fatal blow, but I still dug into the skin of his back and he hissed in pain. His hand found my wrist and turned it, forcing the dagger out. It clattered to the stone.

He laid his hand on my forehead and held it firm, and then I was gone.

Chapter Thirty-Three

I awoke standing up. It was very disorienting. Blinking, I saw shapes in flickering light before me. Torchlight, stuck into the wall to my left. I tried to move but couldn't, and a quick look down showed me the roots wrapped around my chest and legs and arms. I was pinned to the wall, my feet slightly off the ground.

It was oddly comfortable.

My vision cleared after another moment and I could see the people before me, two men. They faced each other, muttering. I recognized one as my assailant; the other was smaller, standing perhaps six inches under his friend. He wore the same type of clothes, and both their hoods were down.

The shorter one was bald or shaved, the shine of his head dancing in the light. He looked a little younger than the other, but that might have just been because he didn't have a beard. He had a short blade strapped to his belt, hanging over his right leg.

Quite aware that I was helpless, I spoke.

"Well," I said, startling them both. "I'm awake. So you can kill me or shut up so I can go back to sleep."

"That's funny," the larger one said. "Glad you have a sense of humor."

"What do you want from me?" I asked.

"I was going to ask you the same." The shorter one approached me. The extra inches of my suspension made me a good deal taller than him. "You came all the way here. What for? If you're a wielder, why are you so far south?"

"Wielder," I said, and I smiled. "I'm no wielder. But you two...you are? The roots, all this. It's magic. Yours?"

"Yes..." The shorter man looked confused, and the taller one wasn't much clearer, but he spoke up.

"We may have a misunderstanding. Let's start with your name, stranger." The man opened his palm. "Derrick."

"Orrin," said the other, after a moment's hesitation.

"Jost." I saw that Derrick was holding my gem in his hand. He was still alive and seemingly unaffected. No surprise, I supposed, if they really were wielders.

"Jost," Orrin repeated. "Why are you here?"

"Hard to say," I said. "I saw all the dead monsters in the labyrinth, spanning out from this place. I wanted to see what was killing them all. I figured it would be here."

"You just...figured?" Orrin said. "That's impossible."

"It's his magic," Derrick cut in. "You saw this magic, Orrin. Want to see it again?" Derrick tapped the surface of the gem with one finger. "Awful lot. Probably dragged him here looking for ours."

I coughed. "I didn't use the gem to find you. I just used my brain."

Derrick laughed, but it was short. "I don't care what you say. You don't beat Hider by wandering through the maze."

"Derrick—"

"What's Hider?"

"Who," Derrick corrected, closing his fist around the gem. "Hider is the wielder who made this place. And *hid* it. And trapped it. And you just walked right through all of that and you expect us to believe you're not using magic?"

"I think he's telling the truth," came a small voice, and someone I hadn't seen before stepped out from the darkness past the torch. Orrin stepped away from me, back toward Derrick, and stopped the child from approaching any closer.

"I'm Hider," he said, and he really was a child, maybe thirteen or fourteen, with a mess of unkempt blond hair he pushed out of his eyes, which were wide and bright and amber. "I mean, my name is Will. But Hider's my um, it's my title."

Will, or Hider, or whatever name he went by, looked to both men. "If he used magic to find us, I would've known. I didn't feel anything till a little bit ago when you went to go check, Derrick. When his magic revealed itself and fought mine."

When I used the gem to break the roots.

I looked at this small boy, feeling something strange when he met my eyes, like I'd seen him before. But I knew I never had. Perhaps he resembled someone from Cartha, though I couldn't summon their face at the moment.

"Hm." Derrick broke off from Hider and came up close to me, close enough to where I could feel the breath coming out of his nose. "You tried to kill me."

I blinked.

"But I did attack you. So I don't blame you for it." He narrowed his eyes, his strange black irises peering at me. "We have not seen many humans wandering the labyrinth. None, in fact. I'll ask you plainly. Are you here to hurt us?"

"I'm not."

"Then why, really?" That was Orrin, sweeping his hand back over his bald head for reasons unknown.

So I told my story again, remembering how not long ago I was speaking the same words to Atell. These men, and even the young Hider, didn't seem surprised, though Derrick was solemn.

"How far are we from Cartha?" he asked.

I thought for a moment. "Forty, fifty miles. Maybe."

"And Iyes?"

"Twenty."

"You've come a long way." Derrick turned back to Orrin and Hider. "Let him down."

Orrin looked past Derrick's broad shoulders to catch my eye, holding that gaze for a little while, unblinking. Then he nodded.

It was Hider who approached me and laid a hand on the roots that strapped me to the wall. Without ceremony or light or any other sign of magic, the bonds began to retreat, sliding away from me. First at my feet, letting my legs free, and all the way up to my chest, until my feet touched gently down to the ground.

"Thanks," I said to Hider, and he nodded, pushing his hair away from his face again before retreating.

"Here," Derrick said, shoving something into my chest. It was my boot. Then he dropped my pack at my feet. "Found it in the pit. Looks like it's in good shape. Your pack, too."

I put the boot and pack back on and looked over the three of them. "So, I shared. What about you? What exactly are all of you doing out here in the Walls?"

Derrick and Orrin looked at each other, then back to me, but it was Hider who spoke up.

"If he got here without getting hurt, maybe he can help us," he said, his narrow shoulders going up. "We should tell him."

"Let's sit," Orrin said, casting a look of *be quiet* in Hider's direction. "Your wound needs cleaning, Jost, and we can break bread and talk."

"You have bread?"

"We have bread," Derrick said. "Come."

With what I'd seen so far of this place—a big entrance, into a massive swell of a room filled with roots, and now into this stacked-stone, torchlit hall—I expected it to just keep going and going, defying reason. So I was surprised when we turned the one corner to the left and came to a small, torchlit room with three bedrolls spaced around the walls. A dead end.

Orrin took a pack from near one of the bed spaces and brought it to the center of the floor, where there was a large blanket laid over the stone. He sat, and the other two followed, so I did the same. We rested there in a rough circle.

Derrick offered me a rag he had soaked in some kind of cleansing alcohol, which I took and used to wash my wound. It burned like hell. I tied it around my own garb to stay against the gash.

"Here." Orrin had pulled some food from the pack, including a crusty loaf of bread which he broke into four pieces for us.

I took it and smelled it, amazed at the fresh scent. Like it had just been baked this morning. I immediately tore a hunk off with my teeth. It had been a while since I'd had bread, fresh or not.

"I'll try to be concise," Orrin said. "But to address all this properly, I need to know a little more about where you come from. What ideas the people of Cartha had. If there are others like you who left the city."

I swallowed my food. "What do you mean?"

"For instance—did you, or anyone from Cartha, have contact with other towns? Cities? People, or groups? Wielders?"

"No," I said.

Derrick had produced a small but thick paper notebook, and he was flipping it open and scrawling.

"Fact-finding," he said when he noticed me looking at him. "We'll explain."

"As far as you know, then, you were the only one who ever left the city."

"The only one to survive it, at least," I said. "I was considered odd, to put it politely. Not everyone trusted me, because I was able to walk the Walls like I did."

"Okay. That helps. So tell me, what do you—you and the Cartha citizens—believe the purpose of the labyrinth is? Or why it was built in the first place?"

I exhaled. "Do you know something I don't?"

"I believe we both know things each other do not." Orrin smiled.

"Well...hundreds of years ago, monsters took over the land. Out of nowhere—or out of hell, depending who you talked to in Cartha," I said. "So the warriors of man fought them, but just enough to keep them at bay. The rest of the people built the Walls. Every day, every night, giving their lives to lay the stone. People said the builders were braver than the fighters. And it took dozens of years and all of humanity working together, but it was done. The monsters couldn't find us, and we couldn't find each other, but that's how we survived."

"What about in Iyes?" Orrin asked, not commenting or giving any indication of how he felt about what I'd said. "What did they believe?"

"They didn't care for me," I responded. "Like I said. Except for Atell, and we didn't...it didn't come up. We talked about magic, mostly."

"That's enough to go with," Derrick said, when Orrin had opened his mouth to ask something else. "We can ask more questions later. So can you, Jost," he added. "It's better for us all to be on the same page, as much as we can."

"All right." Orrin looked a little annoyed, but he moved on. "Derrick and I—and Hider—are wielders."

"I figured," I said, and I finished my bread and took the water that Derrick passed to me. "But Atell told me there were hardly any left. Or maybe none. And no one in Cartha ever even mentioned magic."

"Information is rare in these walls," Orrin said. "Often it's guesswork. That includes our society, as well. There's only so much one can surmise without actually going through the maze. So our history may be just as cloudy as yours, but we have to take it at face value.

"North of here, quite far north, is where we're from. After the labyrinth was built, the wielders who built it—"

"I agree with what this Atell woman said, by the way," Derrick cut in. "That the maze wasn't built by hands alone. Magic was involved."

"Perhaps both," Orrin said, waving a hand at Derrick. "But after the building was over, the few living wielders settled together in their own small pocket of the land among the labyrinth. Far north, which unfortunately proved to be the downfall of the town. It survived for almost two hundred years, but was taken, much like Cartha and Iyes were. As you described."

"We could have done better," Derrick said. "Truth be told, I think we got too sure of ourselves. Safe for so long, people thought we'd stay safe forever. We weren't growing our magic. We weren't binding our seals. As the generations wore on, the skill faltered. The sect was founded by our great-great-great-great-grandparents. True wielders. They'd be ashamed if they knew what harm their lines let happen."

Orrin nodded, slow and deep. "It's true. Some escaped. Some died. We are of the former. That was almost three years ago, now."

It was a lot to take in. I asked, "You said being north was the downfall. Why is that?"

"That's where they come from," Orrin said. "The beasts."

"The monsters."

"Both," Derrick said. "Whatever you want to call them."

I looked to Hider, who was looking down, picking at his bread. The question was on my lips, but Derrick answered it first.

"We found Hider in the labyrinth shortly after we fled from home. His town had been taken as well," Derrick said. "Neither Orrin nor I expected to survive. The beasts were drawn to magic, and we knew they would be on us in great numbers soon. Hider saved our lives."

"I didn't do anything," Hider said quietly, still staring down at the bread.

"He's an accidental bond," Orrin said. "But the bond is strong. He is like a force of nature. It's why he survived what killed the rest of his people."

"Like Fire," I said, without even thinking about it.

"Yes," Orrin agreed, "but his magic is deception and not destruction. Hence the name."

Of course. The 'title'. On-the-nose as it was, he was named for... "He hid you from the monsters. And he still does, right now, in this place."

Orrin nodded. "It's his specialty. Which makes it all the more curious that you were able to find your way here, Jost. The damage we have done may have led you here, but the entrance to our hideaway should have been practically invisible to you. Your magic must have made it otherwise. Another accidental bond. And powerful enough to slough away at Hider's. It's remarkable."

Orrin didn't sound awed. His gaze lingered on me, like he was waiting for me to explain myself. I didn't have anything to offer in that regard, so I said nothing.

"Here," Derrick said, handing my gem back to me. "I wanted to be a little more certain of your intentions before giving it back."

"You don't have to worry about me." I held the gem in both hands. It was warm. "Even if I wanted to use magic on you, I wouldn't know how to go about it. I just use the gem for..." I lit it, casting us all in its yellow light, soft and mellow now. "Light, I guess. That's all I can make it do."

"Well," Orrin said after I dismissed the light, "to be concise, as I had planned...we are on a journey to eradicate the beasts and free everyone from the confines of the maze. It was the ultimate goal of the society of wielders, but over time it was waylaid. We're gathering and strengthening magic so we can go north to the hold and kill the One. The being who brought forth its hellish army and swarmed over our land.

"It spawns its beasts and it moves its black empire over ours. It spreads from the north, dismantling the work of our ancestors and killing the ones it finds in the stones." Orrin breathed in deeply. "It must be stopped. Or eventually it will take us all. To think its lackeys have gone even farther south of us is disturbing. Our impeded progress is already worsening things."

"You're telling me that..." I stopped and shook my head. "I mean, I suspected something, with how these things took apart the towns—but there's really something in control. Someone. Sending an army after us, right now."

"Not just now," Derrick said. "For hundreds of years. Now is just the first time we haven't been able to fight back."

Chapter Thirty-Four

I might have been more disturbed if I had heard about this weeks ago, when I was hunting burrow pigs and trading in the outer rings. I turned to Hider, who had been mostly quiet all throughout this.

"Hider," I addressed him. "You said earlier that I might be able to help you. What were you talking about?"

Orrin made a tiny exasperated noise—*t'chah*. Derrick didn't seem comfortable, either, shifting where he sat. But neither of them tried to stop Hider, so after the child looked to both of them, he spoke.

"There's something here," Hider said. "In the trees out there. That's what we're hiding from. We've been trapped here for...two weeks, I think. Maybe longer."

"Something like what?"

"A monster," Hider whispered. "A big one."

"I didn't see anything out there," I said, and Hider nodded.

"So you can get around it. Which means you might be able to get us around it."

I glanced over at Orrin, then at Derrick, waiting for them say something. It was Derrick who sighed and then added to what Hider was telling me.

"We're not proud of it," he said, "but the thing's been besting us. Some abomination from the north that has taken to calling this place its home."

"Or it's simply waiting for us," Orrin said. "It knows we are here somewhere."

"And you're trying to move on," I said. "Why?"

Derrick said, "Because of what's in your hand right there. Magic sources like that, that were forgotten over the years. Ones we can use that aren't being used. We're going to need all we can get if we're going to challenge the One and its army."

I looked at the three of them, two men and a child who were huddled in a hidden room and hadn't been able to leave for weeks. They had the magical means to keep bread fresh in a bag, but did that equate to anything in a fight? There was a lot I didn't know about magic, and probably just as much that I didn't know about these people, but this journey sounded much more like suicide than success.

Still, it was noble, and actually rather in line with the loose plan I'd set for myself. They'd slain far more monsters than I had, so I was in no place to judge their power. We hadn't gotten off on the best foot, but they'd fed me and treated me and shared their story. Even if we went our separate ways afterward, I could do them this favor.

If I knew how.

"Okay," I said, deciding not to question their plan or its lofty goals. "I'm not sure how much I can really help, but look."

I took the map from my inside pocket and unfolded it on the blanket between us all. "This is what I know about the Pooled Woods—"

"Holy hell," Derrick exclaimed, immediately leaning over the map. "This is—Jost, this is a map of the maze. You made this?"

"I'm making it," I told him. "Every day."

Orrin leaned in, too, getting close to the paper and crawling his eyes over the lines. "I've never seen anything like it."

My pride battled with confusion. "Your society of magic people didn't have a map of the Walls?"

"No," Orrin said, eyes on the map. "The labyrinth was built by separate people, joining corners and lengths with no real communication, just markers for openings...some people might have known the whole plan, but they're dead now, and any permanent record of the routes would have been dangerous to keep then, while the battle raged..."

"So...haven't you been keeping track of your travels?" I asked this to Derrick, as Orrin seemed fully engrossed in the map, his mouth slightly open as he pored over my work. Hider was not as enthralled, glancing at the papers, but not focused on it. Perhaps he was worried about the more pressing issue of the monster.

"Not in this kind of detail," Derrick said, still excited about the map before him. "Notes and such. We search for the magic, and when we're ready, we simply have to go north. So there's no need for something so...intricate."

He grinned at me. "Still, this is amazing."

I returned his grin with a slight one of my own, feeling a little silly amid the topics we were discussing. I leaned in and pointed on the map.

"We're here," I said.

"*Pooled Woods?*" Orrin questioned.

I shrugged. "Just my name for it. And I haven't been through the whole place, so it's incomplete. But I covered this area pretty thoroughly," I continued, running my finger along the rectangular edges I'd marked, "and I didn't see anything. I wasn't attacked. So whatever it is, it must be further towards the north side. Maybe you could sneak out the south way, if you came from the other direction when you got here."

Hider shook his head, and Derrick was soon to follow.

"It strikes when we leave," Derrick said.

"Tries to," Hider added. "We get away. But I think it's just waiting out there. I don't know if it wants our magic, or if it's angry we're where it lives or something. It's not letting us leave."

"I could have just been lucky," I pointed out, breaking open an option that I thought was being unfairly ignored. "It could have been sleeping. Or just elsewhere."

"You covered a lot of space," Orrin said, waving at the map. "You must have been in the woods for hours. It's very unlikely that it just didn't notice you."

"I don't know," Hider said. "Orrin, I have a feeling like...if the monster goes to magic, why wouldn't it go after Jost? He has that big gem. So maybe your magic is like mine, Jost, but instead of hiding from stuff, you...you find it."

One of his eyes was hidden under his hair. I caught the other. "I didn't find this monster, though."

"No, but you..." Hider struggled to come up with what he wanted to say. "You found *us*. And you got past the root trap too. You can..."

"Find his way *through* things." Orrin said it slowly, and Hider was quick to nod up and down.

"Yeah! That's what I mean," Hider said. "You made it all this way. It can't all be luck, right? And you told us you thought the magic kept you safe sometimes. I think that might be how. It's not just about the light. It's about seeing things, and finding things. I mean—" He seemed to catch himself, slowing down. "I don't know. It's just a feeling."

I leaned back a bit, thinking about that. The truth was, I didn't know much more about my magic, or magic in general, than I did when I first laid hands on the gem. I could summon the light, and maybe I could stop the gem from sucking the life from things, but any other effects? I didn't have a part in those.

"You're all magic users," I said. "Wielders. Can you tell me? Is there something you can see about me or the gem?"

"I wish it were that easy," Derrick said. "We could have figured out Hider's talents much quicker and saved ourselves a lot of pain."

"We can sense magic, same as you can, because our bonded magic is attracted to it," Orrin continued for him. "But that's about as far as it goes. Trying to figure out a magic source just by looking at it, like your gem here, is impossible. We have to see how it behaves when it's bonded and make the best guesses we can."

"That's disappointing," I said.

Orrin looked a little aghast at that, but Derrick just gave a sympathetic shrug. "Hider's probably right, though," he said. "He's got a good head on his shoulders. And I follow his logic."

"Okay, sure," I said, dipping my head a little towards Hider. "But that still means that if I'm using this magic, I'm doing it by accident. Or without even realizing I'm doing it. So how can I use that to help you?"

I could just walk right out of here and that would be that, I thought, but I didn't say it aloud. It was always good to have a second plan.

It was Orrin who suggested it. "We leave. Now. We follow you and escape through the south entrance there, as marked on your map." He pressed his finger against the tiny gap in the wall that I had drawn.

"Why now?" I asked.

"For starters," Derrick said, "that was our last loaf of bread."

Chapter Thirty-Five

They had been here for three weeks, it turned out, and they were running out of food. Would be out after breakfast tomorrow, actually. Also pressing was the fact that Hider's abilities used a tremendous amount of magic, and as I learned, it was a finite source.

"Too much more of this and it'll start drinking the flesh off his bones," Derrick said. "Hiding isn't an option anymore."

I was apparently quite well-stocked with a whole lot of magic that I hadn't the faintest idea how to use, and I couldn't just hand it over to Hider, nor to Derrick and Orrin. A bond was a bond, and it couldn't be broken or parceled out. I had stolen all that magic from Cartha and Iyes and I couldn't even make use of it.

I shoved that thought down.

"What about fighting this thing?" I said. "If we can't get away?"

Hider shook his head at that, and quickly.

"It's big," he said.

"How big?"

Hider shrugged. Orrin didn't have much else to offer.

"Big enough to break the trees," Orrin told me. "Had you gone much further north, you'd see the wreckage it brought to this place. It's not a fight any of us should be looking for."

I let out my breath and leaned back on my hands. I seemed to have a knack for wandering into terrible situations, but that also meant I had a knack for getting out of them. I hoped.

The simple fact was that there was nowhere else to go. There was no forward or around; there was only out, and it led one way. It made the decision a lot easier. Sitting down and waiting had never been for me.

"Alright," I said, coming forward again and clapping my hands together. The sudden sound made Hider startle. "I know where we're headed, so you all just follow me and we'll pray to whatever we believe in that this works."

I started to fold the map back up. "And if it doesn't—nothing personal, but if this giant monster comes at us and it's every man for himself, then it's every man for himself. It's too early in my penance for me to die."

"You said that before," Derrick commented, watching me work on my papers. "You think that Cartha is your fault, and that Iyes is your fault. I told you—we told you. It was inevitable."

I didn't slow in my gatherings. "Everything was fine until I did what I did. Even if it was coming anyway, I hurried it along and cut a lot of lives short very suddenly." I pocketed the map. "I don't want to talk about it. You ready?"

I asked the question knowing full well they weren't, but I was done with the conversation. I stood up and walked over to the doorway while they got their possessions together into the three packs they carried.

It was strange to think that these three had been living in this hole while Cartha still stood. Three weeks ago, what had I been doing? I couldn't remember. And the world outside had moved onward, endlessly, into this.

I didn't feel good about the fact that my city's demise was inevitable, but it did make me feel...something. Was there a word for having the burden of thousands of deaths slightly relieved from your shoulders, but nowhere near enough?

Footsteps behind me as they approached. I pulled away from my thoughts and glanced back to them, looking at Hider. "No more traps waiting for me, right?"

Hider shook his head. "It's all gone."

"This place," I said, the thought occurring to me suddenly, "did you create it? All of it?"

"Some," Derrick answered. We walked out of the room, through the hall and into the cavern where the roots had been. "It was a hole in the wall that led underground. It's possible something burrowed it, or maybe it was even dug by man a long time ago during the building. We came in, we reinforced it a little, and we hunkered down."

"It's made of stones," I said.

"Nope," Derrick said. "Dirt. Look again."

Even as he said that, the stone walls around me changed. It happened in an instant, with no shimmer or ceremony. The thick, stacked bricks were gone, and there was just hardened dirt around me, above me, and behind me.

"Illusion," Orrin said. "My magic. For our comfort and nothing more."

I was very far from comfortable, having just learned that I couldn't even trust my own eyes around these people. "I see."

Ahead of me was the hole I had come through, and even with little light, it was clear that it led directly into the Pooled Woods, just a couple of steps deep.

"And the tunnel?" I asked, knowing the answer.

"Illusion as well," Orrin answered. "The common creatures like the shadow dogs don't come into tight places like that, particularly if it's a lengthy walk."

"Shadow dogs," I repeated. We were at the hole now, the exit into the Pooled Woods. "Are those the ones with the long front legs and the claws? And no mouth?"

"Yeah," Hider said, his voice quaking slightly.

"Hm." I liked my name for them better. I stepped out through the hole, putting my boots onto crumbly stone, then into the water of the woods, moving forward to give them room to come out.

"Forgot how dark it was," Derrick grumbled, splashing into the water with his first steps. It was still daytime, but of course he'd been used to torchlight.

"Be quiet," Orrin said, his steps almost silent. "Jost, let's go."

"Stay close," I said, turning to the left and moving fast. They would keep up or they wouldn't. I wasn't inclined to find out just how big and dangerous something that kept three wielders locked in a hole could be.

"Your illusions couldn't fool the monster?" I said back over my shoulder, quiet as I could.

"Not quite," Orrin said. "It's not how my magic works. If we all get out of this alive, I'll tell you everything you want to know."

His voice was thin with fear.

Moving quietly through the water was close to impossible, though I did my best. Orrin did better; Derrick did worse; Hider might not have been there at all, with how quiet he was. I brought us along the wall and we splashed our steps to the south. The air felt heavy and wet, and all around us it was quiet.

Orrin had been closest behind me when we exited, but now it was Derrick who was there, and whispering over my shoulder.

"There's a lot more to your magic, Jost," he said to me, so quietly that I doubt even Orrin or Hider heard him talk. "We only scratched what the surface might be. But I think you can do a lot more than wander your way around some magical roots. I think you could find true north, huh? I think you could make it through the mountain castle."

"What does that mean?" I asked him.

"True north," he repeated. "Where it's all coming from. There's a lot of maze to go through, and obstacles—not something we dare to try until we have more power. But once we're out of here...there's a lot of possibilities, Jost. If you're with us."

"Let's get out of here first," I told him. It was a lot to wrap my head around, but I knew what he was saying, and I didn't want to readily admit how much the concept excited me. To have a real goal, and a reason to press onward besides *why not*.

Mountain castle, I thought. Some fortress in the north where the master monstrosity reigned from, I imagined. What had they called it? *The One.* Quite the name, whether it was given by them or announced by the thing itself. I pictured a spiky, towering mess of spires dotting a northern mountain landscape like it was an ink drawing in a picture book. Black ink on yellowed pages, clad in shadows, each gap in the mountain making room for more of this place to thrust up through.

I had two daggers and a little yellow ball that mostly functioned as a torch. I was in no shape to storm someone's house, let alone a monster-crowded castle. One of these other three would have to do the heavy lifting if it ever came to that.

"We must be close by now," I said to myself, a low murmur. Why did it feel like it was so much longer going back? The dark water stretched ahead, looking so much deeper than it was.

I felt strange, like my head was foggy. I could hear their footsteps behind me, and at the same time they felt far away, echoing from some great distance. I turned my head to look at them and there they were, where they should be, walking along behind me in some rough semblance of a line.

"Everything all right?" Derrick asked me. Just a couple feet away, but his voice was so quiet.

"Fine," I said, and it was a lie, and my own voice brushed against my ears like a whisper, and I turned and walked forward like I knew where I was going.

Speak up, Jost. You could be leading them all to their deaths. Something's wrong and you have to tell them.

The thought pressed in my mind, but when the idea reached my lips it lost all its vigor. I let it drift away. The Pooled Woods were different now, in a way that I couldn't understand. Trying to latch onto it was like running my fingers through smoke. Was I even moving? My boots were stepping, displacing the water below me. The trees drifted toward me and then behind. But I wasn't going anywhere. We weren't going anywhere.

A tree was in my path, and it was black. It grew closer to the wall than any other I had seen, and when I moved to go around it, it moved with me.

"Huh," I said, and then the vast spire melted into the water. Its black puddle spread beneath out feet, and my foggy brain was pierced by Orrin's cry.

"It's here! Run! Run!"

Chapter Thirty-Six

My feet stuck to the ground like I was standing in tar. I pulled hard enough to feel the bones in my ankles creak, and I still didn't move.

On the other hand, my brain finally felt clear. Clear enough to see the danger I was in—that we were all in. And clear enough to act quickly.

I yanked my feet out of my boots, stepping out of the inky cloud in the water. By some stroke of luck, I had been caught right on its edge. The others weren't stuck, which made me feel less lucky; water splashed behind me as they fell back. I followed suit even as the shape rose out of the water.

From where? There's only a couple inches of water, how is it so big?

And then I thought, *It came this way to cut us off. It knew.*

Passed through us like smoke.

The monster drew up from the water like it was made of the earth below, rising up and up till it was taller than me, taller than the four of us combined. The Pooled Woods were light enough to see the thing, yet that didn't help me to understand it. It came across as thin at first, like a sheet blowing in the wind, but then as soon as my eyes latched onto part of it, it was thick, rounded, and strong. I was convinced that it was a rippling shadow and a hulking black turtle-like beast, both at the same time. It curved at the top like a big shell, but it was legless; as the four of us hurried backwards, it moved by reaching out its rippling shadow-arms and wrapping them around the spiral trees, enveloping the trunks and dragging itself forward.

Some trees creaked and cracked under the force. Its bulk made even the sparse water rush forward in a wave, splashing over the ground and wood alike. The monster brushed against the wall to the left; to the right, it stretched far enough to where running around it would take too much time. Surely it would reach its long, whiplike arms out and crush anyone who tried to pass. It was fifty feet wide, maybe more.

Orrin was still shouting at us to run, which was useless, as we already were. We just didn't know what we were running towards, or for. It was aimless panic, and it separated us amongst the trees. If we lost each other here, surely we'd be doomed. The three of them had dealt with this thing already—*the Turtle,* I thought, even though it was ridiculous—and they were strained. They knew they couldn't fight it, but with nowhere to retreat to, what choice did we have? Either handle it here, or die in a hole in the wall.

"Stop! Don't get lost!" I snapped the words out, catching up to Orrin and grabbing him by his hood. "We're faster than it, see? We should stay together. Work together."

The Turtle moved fast enough, though it definitely couldn't match our running speed. But we couldn't run forever, and the longer we spent trying to navigate around it in its own territory, the worse it would be for us.

"Derrick! Hider!" I yelled, rushing forward with Orrin to catch up to them. "Stay with us! Don't get split up!"

We reconvened, Hider's fearful panting like an urgent heartbeat in my ears.

"What's the deal with this thing?" I asked, my words quick and forced. "Tell me everything you know, fast."

Orrin looked lost, but Derrick caught onto my meaning. "It bleeds," he said. "We've seen it hurt itself on jagged stumps. So it's either stupid, or the wounds don't mean anything to it. It can turn into a shadow and glide through the water, but it can't hurt you like that. It has to re-form."

"And when it does, it can trap you," I said, my bare feet cold in the water. "Okay. If it can bleed, it can die. We have to fight it. Escape isn't an option if this monster can just appear wherever we go."

"Fight it?" Hider said.

"Your magic," I said to Derrick, looking him in the eye. "Can it help?"

I had no idea what his endowment was, but the man was a fighter—I had firsthand experience with that.

Crash! Crash! Trees fell as the Turtle approached.

Derrick nodded. "All right, listen, all three of you. We got nowhere to run, and no time to hide. Either we die, or this thing does. Don't rely on illusions, Orrin—Hider, you stay quick on your feet and yell if you see a shadow in the water. Jost, I know you're armed. Do what you can."

Derrick pulled out the sword he carried, and after a moment, Orrin did the same. Hider had no weapon to draw, and though he shivered, his face was set in grim, thin-lipped determination.

"Come to the light if we get separated," I said, and I lit the gem brightly, the yellow glow racking up in intensity where it rested against my shoulder.

The Turtle came into my light and we all saw it true, possibly for the first time—a mass of dark flesh, its arms stemming from random places in the shadows that encased it. It was pebbled and looked tough, like studded leather. The arms were different; slick and black, like they were drawn from soft inner flesh and poked through holes in the armor. They came and went seemingly at random, disappearing into the bulk and re-emerging where the beast saw fit.

It made no sound. No roar or grunts, not even breathing. All I heard was the water moving and the spiral trees suffering at its grasp.

Derrick acted first. His blade was long and slightly curved, the handle polished and shiny. It gleamed in the gem light. He had waited for the monster to grasp a tree near him and then rushed forward, and he was fast, even after living in a wall for three weeks. His blade sunk into the meat of the arm before I could see it swing, and when it didn't cut all the way through, he yanked it out and chopped again, making it a clean cut. Dark blood spurted onto the tree, onto Derrick, and into the water.

The beast made no sound, nor did it withdraw its severed limb. It rammed the remaining bulk into Derrick, who held up an arm to absorb it. It knocked him off his feet and he spun down into the water. He got back up before any of us could help him.

The Turtle seemed unbothered by its wound. It brought itself closer, making us easy to reach. For what? Did it want to eat us, or just smash us flat?

I pulled a dagger free, though it felt remarkably insignificant against this creature. This was no black claw. It was like a thousand of them.

Derrick seized the opportunity to hack at another limb, and I followed suit on the opposite side. If I could get the blade of my dagger in deep enough, I might be able to separate the thing into pieces, and it had to run out of arms eventually.

I splashed through water to reach the closest tree it was wrapped to. I lifted my dagger high, till I felt the muscles of my shoulder straining, then brought my blade down as hard as I could.

Thck.

With an unsatisfying thud, my dagger went into the arm's hide all of one inch, jarring my arm painfully. To my right and across the way, Derrick sliced through one of the tentacles with a single swing of his blade.

What the hell was this? A dagger wasn't a sword, but I should have plunged right through this thing. I pulled the tip of the dagger free and stabbed again, doing even less with the second attempt. It was like trying to chop down a tree. How was Derrick doing that?

Orrin took action while I yanked my dagger out again. I heard him draw his sword behind me, and I realized that he was making sure Hider was safe before he left him—when I glanced back, the child was nowhere to be seen.

"Derrick!" he called, and Derrick didn't look over but shouted "Aye!" and in the next instant I saw the handle of Orrin's sword flash like it had caught a beam of sunlight. He swung it down at the limb I'd been digging at and cut clean through. Dark blood splashed onto my shirt and neck. I moved away from the flailing, severed tentacle.

Even as I looked for my next target, I was trying to piece together what I had just seen. Derrick hacking through this rock-hard thing like it was nothing, and Orrin doing the same. Was that his magic? His own strength? Did he pass it on to Orrin at will? If so, why not lend it to me?

The Turtle dragged closer, and I readied myself to dodge an attack, but it didn't come for me—it swung out at Orrin, and he sidestepped the jabbing arm, slashing at it but missing. The tip of his blade cut through the water and must have stuck in the ground, because he stumbled and almost fell. He did not have the grace or balance of an experienced swordsman like Derrick. It had to be the magic.

And I had neither, so what could I do here? I tensed, waiting for an attack to come. Both Orrin and Derrick were dealing with their fair share, dodging and slashing and taking licks all the same. They couldn't get close, and my earlier thought of a finite number of arms was losing its meaning.

There had to be something else. An eye or a mouth, something I could stab into that would make a difference. Unconsciously, I asked my light to grow, and it did, bathing the hideous thing in bright yellow. It was like a living hill, a pile of glistening, sloppily-ridged armor like a roof put together by children. Its arms sprung from holes that were just the right size for them, so there was no gap to take my blade.

Where's your eyes? Your mouth? What the hell are you?

There was only one thing I noticed, and it was subtle, but my only shot. It wasn't attacking me. I had no idea why—perhaps it was drawn to their magic? I had my own magic blazing on my shoulder, yet still I stood unnoticed. We had to get closer, and I was the only one who could.

I made the decision and I ran forward, feet splashing in the water, waiting for some muscled limb to knock the wind out of my lungs. But it never came, and a few seconds later I had my hands on the monster and I was finding spots to climb. In fact, it was much easier than ascending a labyrinth wall.

But it reeked like death.

Chapter Thirty-Seven

My hands were slick and black with whatever this thing secreted, but I was still able to find grips. One of the wielders called my name, but I ignored it. Unless they wanted to throw me a climbing rope, they couldn't help me here. They needed to focus on staying alive.

"I'll find a way to kill you," I grunted, uttering a promise I didn't know that I could keep. "I will."

You could just climb over it and run the opposite way, Jost.

"Shut up," I growled.

I was unimpeded as I scaled the thing, save the tiny slips of my feet. The crags of the shell were narrow, so it was best that I didn't have my boots. But the fact that it wasn't trying to pull me off or smash me into the rough surface was disconcerting, and I didn't know why. I could hear the fight behind me, could feel the monster pull itself through the water to get closer to its enemies. It wasn't giving up and it wasn't slowing down.

An arm burst through the shell beneath me, scraping across my side and burning a rash on my skin even through my shirt. I twisted away, turning my head to see if it would wrap back around me, but it wasn't for me. It stretched out to Orrin and he cut it away.

I kept going.

My light was bright, and it reflected strongly off the slick surface of the Turtle. I saw rivulets of dark wetness spilling between crags and bluntly-pointed protrusions the size of my hand. I was tired, my muscles aching from gripping the slippery holds, and sweat and water stung at my eyes. Would what I wanted be all the way at the top? Would it be there at all? I wished I knew what I was doing.

My fingers slipped on an edge, and my heart gave one wild thump as I thought I was going to fall—then I saw that I still had my grip, and I was just clinging to the inside of one of the armholes. Empty, either not yet used or retracted or something else.

I pulled my dagger free and dug it inside, and there it was, the sensation of the blade sliding into yielding flesh. Dark blood spurted from the hole, onto my hand and up my arm. I forced the blade in as deep as it could go, twisting it, my hand and sleeve getting soaked in the foul ichor.

The hilt stopped me, and despite my forceful stabs and turns, there was no reaction from the monster. What seemed like a lot of blood to me was probably a mere drop to something this big. It wasn't enough. I had a feeling that even a three-foot blade plunged into the same spot wouldn't be enough.

Disgusted, I yanked out my dagger and wiped my hand on my clothes so I could get another grip higher up. Below me, words were shouted, lost amid the splashing water, the thuds of tentacles on trees, and my own harsh breathing. I wasn't going to last much longer up here.

I sped up, working my way toward the top, my fingers aching and my shoulders trembling. The hard shell scratched at my palms and feet even underneath the slick blackness that coated it. I pulled myself up and up until I at last reached the top, where I lowered myself against the curve and caught my breath.

Now what?

While I searched in vain for some lucky opening in the shell, Derrick whipped around a waving tentacle and dashed forward, so loud and fast that I could hear the water clearly even this high up. The man was incredibly quick, moving around the arms before they had a chance to grab him or knock his off his feet. And when a tentacle swung around to go at his back, there was Orrin, slicing it away.

When Derrick reached the shell, he delivered a massive, two-handed swing to the Turtle. The blasting crack of the shell rippled the water around us, and then the monster did roar, a rumble that shook the shell. Derrick pulled his sword back with one hand and reached the other into the beast where he'd cracked it, able to wedge his fingers beneath the fracture. He pulled. I heard the sound of tearing flesh, and the Turtle roared again.

I couldn't fathom Derrick's strength. The fracture in the shell raced upward as he peeled it away from the creature, Orrin defending every onslaught that came toward Derrick's back. Severed tentacles fell into the water, hunks of dead meat polluting it with black blood.

The Turtle wrapped one tentacle around a rooted tree. I watched it try to pull itself in vain and remembered the roots I'd been wrapped in just hours ago. My gem was bright, and when I touched my fingers to it, I felt the heat there.

So do it, even if you have no idea how. There's no time!

I abandoned my mountaintop goal and slipped back down the side of the monster, to where Derrick was ripping the shell apart with his bare hands. The air filled with cracks and the grotesque tearing sounds spewing from the wound. The Turtle paid me no mind; its attentions were focused on Derrick and stymied by Orrin. I saw the sweat gleaming on both their faces, cast in the light.

I dropped into the water before the crack in the shell, which was now more of a gaping maw, like a hanging sheet blown upward by the wind. Dark, stinking meat laid hidden inside. I saw Derrick's face, strained and confused as I ducked underneath his arm and went into the wound.

"Jost?" he managed, before I disappeared inside the shell.

I held my breath. It was unbearably hot in here. The water burned my feet. I expected to run into a wall of flesh, but there was a surprising amount of room. My light showed me the shell: glistening, stretching above me like a labyrinth wall, ropes of wet flesh connecting it to the bulbous, pulsing core of the Turtle. Though there was a few feet of gap between the shell and the body, it was still massive. Putrid black flesh piled unto itself, with extensions of arms flitting outward. Did it know I was in here? Could it? What would happen to me if it turned into a shadow while I was inside?

It didn't matter; I wouldn't survive in here much longer. I could hardly breathe and my feet were being parboiled. I ripped the gem free and shoved it against the bulk of the monster. The hot meat singed my fingertips. I grimaced and pressed the gem against it as hard as I could.

"Come on!" I pleaded. "Come on! Do something!"

Burning, burning pain. I yanked my hand back, hissing, and pocketed the gem in disgust. Gritting my teeth, I retrieved a dagger and eyed the fleshy ropes in the muted light. I reached up to grab one and it squished under my fingers but held strong. Fine, then. I would start from the top and work down. Above me was a network of crossing vines flowing with monster blood. I chomped the flat of my dagger blade between my teeth and climbed.

The flesh here wasn't as hot, and it was a relief to get my feet out of the water. I got up as high as I could—it was a much easier climb than the outside had been. Then I started to cut.

Fwap! Fwap! My blade sunk into the living ropes with ease, the tension snapping them back to the bulk as I sliced through. I cut the ones above my head, then the ones I was hanging onto, then dropped down and did it again. Sweat poured from my face. I panted and got spattered with blood. I cut everything I could reach and fell back into the water.

Rumbles above me, then creaks, then whiplike cracks and snaps. The shell was breaking. I wiped sweat and sticky blood from my eyes to find the gap and stumbled out of the monster. My feet caught something heavy and I sprawled forward, landing facedown in the water. It was dirty but cool, easing my tender skin. I wanted to stay in it for hours.

Behind me, the creaks and snaps grew louder, mixing with the rumbling roars of the Turtle. I pushed myself out of the water, running forward blind until I caught a tree and righted myself. My whole body radiated with pain, and I turned back and cleared my eyes again to see the Turtle collapsing in on itself like a poorly-dug grave.

The shell buckled where Derrick had cracked it, pulling inward where I'd climbed and cut the tendons. But it didn't stop there—all the support was crumbling, snapping, and it started slow then happened very quickly as its body gave in. Whatever hole it loosed its cries from became gurgled, filled with blood. The shell broke into massive, jagged chunks, some falling loose, but most being yanked into the center and piercing deep into its heart.

So much blood, blackened spray and shell filling the water and air. I watched it collapse into a pile of bleeding flesh and pointed shell fragments, and then the sounds stopped.

It was over. We made it.

Orrin was there, to my left, some yards away. He looked exhausted, his sword hanging from weak fingers and his face grim. I didn't see Hider. With his power, I imagined that I couldn't unless he wanted me to. The only sound was the panting of our breath.

Orrin started to walk forward, and he muttered something I couldn't hear, repeating it. I blinked, following his gaze, and that was when I saw the body on the ground, close to the corpse of the Turtle. Close enough that it had long spears of fallen shell sticking up out of it like it was a pincushion.

Derrick.

"No," Orrin was saying, louder now. "No, no no..."

My throat tightened and I felt sickness rise in me suddenly, but I held it in and made myself move to see. Maybe he was still alive. Maybe...

He was facedown in the water, not breathing. The ragged pieces of shell that stuck in him were shallow, weak wounds. What had killed him was the pair of tentacle arms driven through his chest and stomach. They stuck out the back of him, draped lifelessly over his body.

"No, no." Orrin pulled out the shell fragments. He'd been stuck with four of them, and Orrin yanked them out with two hands, not being careful, probably because he knew his friend was dead. "No, no, no..."

I tripped over his body, I thought. *I ran blind out from the shell and tripped right over him and thought he was a rock.*

Orrin fell to his knees after tearing out the last piece, a two-handed job that made a wet sound. The shell splashed into the water and Orrin had his hands on Derrick's back, his lips moving but no sound coming out.

Footsteps behind me; Hider, emerging from wherever he'd been. He looked smaller and more frail than ever, his eyes so wide that even the hair over them couldn't hide them all the way.

"Orrin, is he okay?" Hider called, and his voice cracked, and I gritted my teeth and held out a hand to stop him going forward, not sure what to say. Maybe nothing. It wasn't my place.

Before Hider could get closer, Orrin stood up fast, pushing up off Derrick's body. It rocked slightly in the water. Then he rounded on me, squeezing the handle of his sword so fiercely his knuckles were white.

"*You,*" he said, vitriol spraying out of him like a mist. "You did this."

"What?" The accusation caught me so off-guard that it took me a moment longer than usual to get angry. "What did you just say?"

"Orrin—" Hider started, but Orrin swung his hand out and shoved him, hard, and the young boy stumbled back and fell.

"Hey," I said, and I still had my dagger in my hand. "Don't you take another step."

"It didn't touch you." Orrin raised his sword, pointed it at me. It trembled. "You walked on it. *In* it. And look at you. Look at Derrick and look at you."

There was no arguing that. Hider stood up again, but kept his mouth shut.

"You're the monster," Orrin said, standing beside the dead body of his friend.

"I'm sorry about Derrick," I said, and that was where I should have stopped, but I didn't. The rage was there, quick inside of me like it had been waiting. "But you're very fucking welcome for saving your life, too. And Hider's. I boiled alive inside that thing, and you're here accusing me of being its friend?"

I pointed my own blade at him, smaller but steadier. My other hand hovered above my pocket where the gem rested, lighting our feud. "Don't forget that you all tried to kill me first. I forgave you for that. You drop that sword and you step back, because I won't do it again."

My words were strong, and it felt good. Inside, I swirled with anger, pain, and sorrow. Death had found me once more and laid its tidings at my feet. Orrin was right, maybe—not all the way, not that I came here to sabotage and kill them—but what I brought with me was not escape or salvation. It was death, and it littered the path behind me too.

"Orrin," Hider said, daring to speak again. "Don't. Don't do this. We have to..."

His eyes rested on Derrick's body, and he shut them, lowering his head. "We have to go, Orrin. There's other monsters here, they'll smell the blood, the magic, they'll come and they'll kill us. Don't start another fight."

Orrin's eyes locked on me like he didn't hear Hider at all. The man was strong of mind but hurt of body, and without him borrowing Derrick's magic, I was sure I could beat him. Kill him, if I had to.

But I didn't want that. Did he?

No. He lowered his sword, tip piercing into the water. The bald man looked from me to Derrick, then to Hider, who was wiping at his eyes.

"Don't come near us," Orrin said. He sheathed his sword. "If I see you again, I will strike you down like a beast."

The analogy rang in my ears, but I lowered my own dagger as well. "Go on then, before the real monsters come."

Chapter Thirty-Eight

I was alone again, as I'd been for most of this journey. Most of my life. Derrick's corpse could hardly count as company. Hider had seemed saddened to leave it, but what could they do, carry it with them? They left southward, to tread the same path I'd already bloodied. Safe from me, surely. I had no intention of going back that way.

Anyone I found ended up dying, so it was better for me to keep a wide berth. On the surface I could make light of it, but if I lingered on the thought, it burrowed painfully into my consciousness—was this what I was meant for, now? To never find a place where I belonged, to have death at my heels wherever I went? Could I possibly dare to enter another town, to involve myself in someone's life?

Right now, I was tired. I found my boots somewhere past the Turtle's body and climbed atop the dead monster like it was some great statue. When my feet were dry, I got the boots back on. It didn't take long. The monster was still hot enough to make the swaths of shell stuck to him roasting warm, like a fire roared underneath. I found comfort on one not too hot.

I lied there for a while, trying not to think about how content I was to relax atop this thing's dead body where it was warm and dry. I drifted to sleep at some point, or at least into a hazy version of consciousness, and when I snapped out of it I was a little more rested.

And hungry, terribly so. I'd had no opportunity to hunt, and the stores I'd taken from Cartha were running low. I had some, yes, but...

My stomach growled. I closed my eyes and listened to the hot shell around me sizzle like a cookfire. And before I could think about it, I knew what I wanted, and I was climbing back down to the ground and stepping my boots into the water. I stared into the body of the Turtle, a mess of broken shell fragments, drooping tendons...and meat.

There was no foul odor like there had been when it was alive. This might as well be a gigantic dead burrow pig. It didn't smell spoiled, and if it tasted foul I'd just spit it out. But something about it was intriguing, the dark meat reminding me of the water fowl the farmers raised, which would hang in the stalls on the inner rings. I'd traded for it a rare few times. It was delicious and rich.

I stepped in and I cut off a hunk from the mass. It was tough and still a little warm, but the monster's heat was contained in its core, and these outer parts had cooled. I squeezed it, the striated muscle squishing under my fingers like a slab of steak. I sniffed it and it smelled fine, bloody and raw like anything I'd cooked up before. Monster or not, this thing was made of meat. And I was hungry.

I climbed back up and threw the meat down on a hot section of shell. It sizzled immediately, and the sound made my mouth water. Somewhere inside I thought, *Am I really about to eat a piece of this monster?* But that was distant enough for me to be able to ignore. The smell of the meat drowned it out even further.

I stood while it cooked, surveying the Pooled Woods. Despite Hider's fears, I wasn't receiving any company. My light was muted; I cast it wider to be sure, then pulled it back in when all I saw was the trees. I was alone here.

"I'm the monster in the woods now," I said, and with a grin, I stabbed the meat with my dagger and pulled it up. It looked like a rough cut of steak, but darker, and it dripped with a very dark red.

I bit into it and the hot juice dribbled down my chin. It was tough on the outside, but tender where it wasn't seared. It tasted *hot* somehow, not from the heat, but inside my stomach, warming me as I swallowed. I was reluctant to admit it to myself, but I did: the meat was delicious.

I ate the whole thing in a couple minutes, and then I cut away another piece, climbed back up, and did it all over again.

I'm the monster in the woods now.

When I was full to the point of discomfort, I rested on the cool shell a few minutes before finally getting back down to the water, washing my hands and face. Orrin and Hider were long gone by now, disemboweled by a black claw for all I knew.

I dried my hands on my shirt and pulled my map from its pocket. Something was stirring in me, the same thing that drew me to circle this area on the map before. North. What had felt vague and drifting was starting to weave itself into a rope, the threads coming together to pull me in one direction. North was where the monsters spawned; north was where *the One* was, whatever that meant. The person in charge. Or monster in charge.

The emptiness of the northern reaches stretched out on my map. I knew in my heart, my bones, my soul—whatever it was, I knew that my penance would be served there, delivered in blood. My blood or that of the creatures roaming the Walls, so be it. I would stab till my blades were broken, and then I would use my hands.

The swirling feeling in my chest stopped as I stared at the blank paper, and I was not driven to mark anything. The woven threads directing my attention pointed me to the north, toward the unexplored remains of the Pooled Woods, but I could see no farther.

"Fine."

Beside me was Derrick's body. His sword had been hidden by cloudy blood, but now the water had cleared some, and my light shone off the blade. I lowered myself and picked up his weapon.

It was heavy. I would be able to wield it, though not to Derrick's effect. The scabbard and belt were still on his body. I knelt down and worried it off him, looking at his pair of deep wounds.

"Sorry," I said, the only apology I could muster, but I meant it. I wasn't so paranoid as Orrin that I assumed my survival led to Derrick's death, but I had changed the course of events. Perhaps they would have all died without me, yes. But they might have made it out alive, too.

The scabbard belt was far too wide for me, even if I adjusted it to the narrowest clasp. I used my dagger to work a hole through the leather, a task that made my forearm burn, and used that spot to secure it around my own waist, tucking the hanging end in. I'd never worn something like this before. It was odd.

"If I don't like it, I'll dump it off," I said, carefully sliding the sword into the sheath. "You don't mind, do you, Derrick? No?"

That joke didn't feel great, and neither did the idea of searching the rest of his corpse. I walked away before I could give the idea any more merit. Not comfortable with the sword, I kept my dagger out and had my light back in the shoulder harness. Yet as harrowing as that battle had been, I felt safe now, like all the danger here had been erased and I was sure of it.

"Finder magic," I said to myself. It wasn't a very snappy name, but I wasn't expecting anyone to write a book about me, anyway. Were the wielders right? It felt right, and certainly this magic had led me to things, whether I was aware of it or not. It acted in subtle ways, like tracing me to the wielders. Or more boldly, like dragging me to the gates of Iyes because it was hungry for the magic that protected them.

That memory stung. I gritted my teeth and sloshed through the water until it went away.

It's good they left. Anyone who spends time with me ends up dead.

"That includes the monsters," I said.

How many more do I have to kill to make up for Derrick?

"Not my fault."

North. I would go north, and leave this place behind with the others.

Chapter Thirty-Nine

The Pooled Woods did not stretch on much farther, and they were as quiet as they'd been when I first arrived. I left through the massive northern gap, gratefully putting my feet onto dirt. Not completely dry dirt, but at least no longer submerged.

I walked with my map in my hand and drew, drew, drew. I squared off the Pooled Woods and branched the walls that led away from them, but I wouldn't expand on those. My goal was north, and as vague as that was, it gave me a sense of purpose, trappings of urgency. I imagined Orrin and Hider progressing south, probably having reached Iyes by now—what was left of it. Would I find signs of their journey during my own?

"I should have taken Derrick's notebook," I said, remembering him jotting things down as we talked in the hole.

I walked for hours, filling each day with tens of thousands of my footprints. When a lone black claw first threatened me, I used Derrick's sword. Inexperienced, I landed a shallow wound on its back, and to my surprise, the creature tried to turn tail and flee.

I chased it down. I cleaved the heavy sword into its back, a mortal blow that sounded like the butcher's block. And when it was dead, I used my dagger to cut it open and I cooked its meat over a small fire. The dirt was dry here, drier even than it was near Cartha, and I could find dead roots to make easy tinder.

The meat was good. Not as good as the Turtle, but as good as a burrow pig. Better, maybe. It had been some time since I'd eaten pig, and there were none here.

Monster eater, I thought, and I ripped off more with my teeth. I hoped the other black claws would see their eviscerated fellow and be scared, and then I thought, no. Come to me and let me eat you.

Orrin's finger, pointing at me. His wide eyes. His anger. His fear.

These memories latched their claws onto my ankles as I went north, farther and farther. I slept in the dirt and I ate what I killed. There was no shortage of monster meat, and whatever attempts they made on my life felt feeble; half-hearted. They never came when my gem was alight, and it stayed on through the night. It felt more like I was running into them.

I wondered again, time after time, *How smart are you, little gem? Are you keeping me alive for your own benefit? Can you construct such an idea, a plan that might stretch years and years?*

There were times it glowed without my insistence, times it yanked on my harness and urged me one way or another. I pointedly steered around those areas, even if they were directly on my path. The gem no longer pulled hard enough to move me. Was it understanding, or was I simply better at controlling it?

Better to go around them than to wander in. Better to take longer than to steal magic someone else might need.

The gem didn't make any movements toward Derrick's sword, even when I brought it close. Either the sword didn't hold Derrick's magic, or it was released when he died.

Or you already took it, I thought, holding the cold jewel in my fingertips as I walked. *Took it without me knowing and got Derrick killed.*

The scenario was so likely that it made me uncomfortable, the same as the memory of Atell being pulled into the water while she looked into my eyes. There was no company here to keep me away from my thoughts, from the images that floated behind my eyelids, so I had to do my best on my own. I suppressed some, and I let some torture me.

I covered miles, with no real measurement of how far I traveled any given day, but how far can one go when he walks for twelve or fifteen hours? My map grew in narrow fashion, a small berth that kept stretching upward on the paper. Ugly. As it was, I wouldn't come close to using all that paper I'd taken from Cartha. But that didn't feel as important anymore.

It was eight days after leaving the Pooled Woods when I started to notice the changes around me. Not the monsters or the magic; those were manageable and invisible, respectively. But to the dirt and the sky. To the Walls themselves. I didn't know when, but at some point I had walked through a transition to a different stage of this maze, and I only noticed when I kept having to step over big chunks of stone in the dirt.

Here, the labyrinth was crumbling.

I cast my gaze up on the ninth morning after leaving the Pooled Woods and realized that I was actually squinting. The sky was brighter than it ever had been before. Still muted, and nowhere near as bright as Cartha had been when the sun passed over, but the light was there. I didn't even need my gem. And the lit sky showed me that the stone walls all around me were full of holes.

It was like some disease had spread across them, causing great chunks to fall out that broke apart when they hit the earth. Some spots along the top were simply gone, like a giant had come and scooped his hand through the stone. There were no healthy spots; it was all pockmarked and gouged. One great crack led all the way through a huge swath of wall, arcing up to the top, and if that piece were to fall I was sure it would shake the whole world.

I knelt down and grabbed a fistful of dirt. It was mostly dry, which was unheard of in the Walls. The ground here had always been wet, always sinking under my feet. Now I could look back and struggle to identify my footsteps. Even the air was drier. I'd been mindlessly walking for so long that I missed the small signs that led to these bigger changes. I pulled in a deep breath to taste it, and took a moment to assess myself.

My pack on my back, still heavy, with strips of meat hanging off the back, drying. Derrick's sword on my waist, looming large over my daggers. I was getting better with it, but it still made my shoulders burn if I swung it more than a few times. My boots, thankfully whole. My clothes a little worse for the wear, but still keeping me warm enough, and I'd patched together the few tears that threatened to rip them apart.

On top of that, I was well-fed. The monsters came and then they went—but only if I let them go. I'd had two meetings where I ended up with a gash big enough to stitch up, but nothing worse than that. My magic was unconscious and obedient, but I wondered if it had been secretly growing without me noticing, and if it was keeping the black claws at bay.

Stopping to look over things helped to set my mind back in some semblance of order. These last few days of mindless walking had put it into the clouds. I stretched my shoulders, the right one popping in my ear, and rolled my neck from right to left and back again, working out the stiffness and creaks. Tonight I'd rest longer than usual. It would be good for me.

But there was plenty of daylight left, and with the parts of the Walls that were missing, that light went a long way.

I let my own light die and kept moving, taking more time to avoid stumbling over rocks and hoping a random sharp edge wouldn't pierce the tough leather of my boots. Or my skin.

I marked on the map in tiny notes where there was severe damage, not sure why I was doing so. Perhaps I'd come back later to see if it had deteriorated more. I took the occasional turn where I was forced to, but ultimately continued north.

"Why aren't all you monsters dismantling this labyrinth?" I asked myself, as well as any monsters that could hear me. "Plenty of time. No one to stop you. And you can cut through stone like water. What's the problem?"

These gouges, these crumbles and cracks, did not look like the efficient work I'd seen done on Cartha. It was natural, but—only here? Cartha's walls were solid, as were those of Iyes. Any damage done had been done by the people who built them.

If the construction started up here, it would have been many years before the southern Walls were built. So these are older.

"How much older?" I stopped and laid my hand on a fallen piece that was five times my height, a hunk of stone so big that there might have been another thirty feet buried in the dirt below. It had come from above, leaving a massive wound in the top of the wall.

The air was warmer than normal, but the stone was cold, stuck in the shadows. I scratched my nails across its surface, and it wasn't until I went around the huge thing that I realized it had somehow splintered something below it.

"A gate," I said, observationally, and then repeated, "a gate!"

It was once a gate. The stone covered most of it; the fallen angle of the piece had crashed through the wood and iron and reduced it to sawdust. From where I stood past the chunk, there was enough room to slide between the rock and the wall and force my way through the wreckage. My heart inched toward my throat.

A town. Should I even go in? Should I...

But what was I thinking? What could this town be, if the gate was broken and all was quiet?

I knew, but I took my pack off and dropped Derrick's sword and moved between the stones anyway.

Chapter Forty

It was a tight squeeze. I had to hold my breath to fit through the narrowest stretch, a few agonizing feet where the heavy stone pressed against me on both sides and I thought I'd crack my ribs if I drew in a breath.

What a way to go, I thought, because I couldn't talk to myself aloud. *All this, and I get stuck like a rat in a trap.*

But I pushed through, losing a fair amount of skin off my forearms and taking a red scrape across my cheekbone.

"Better find a different way out," I said, and I sucked in a few breaths now that I was able. My foot kicked through dirt and sawdust that had been churned together and stuck here for...how long? Windless, lightless, trapped. I turned the mixture over with the side of my boot once more before ducking under the splintered portion of gate that remained and emerging into open air.

As I expected it to be, the town was gone. By the looks of things, it had been gone for a long time. I stood atop a gradual slope that led downward into an area probably half the size of Cartha, which is to say it was massive. There was evidence that buildings once stood here, but whether it was ten years ago, or fifty, or a hundred, was anyone's guess.

And there was something else here, rising from the ground like the spiral root trees of the Pooled Woods, but not quite the same.

"Crystal spears?" I murmured, straining my eyes to catch the detail of the closest one, which was too far away to see in detail. There were many of them scattered over the land, and they were all pointed in one direction—at me. It was alarming. They caught the light (and here there was open sunlight like we had in Cartha) and spilled it back onto the ground in shattered pools of rainbow big enough to hide a house in.

I walked forward through thick, unruly grass. In some places, it was taller than me, wiggling with the slight movements of the air caught by its feathery tips. The whole place might have been beautiful if it wasn't marred by my conviction that something horrible had happened here.

Neat squares of buildings were set into the ground like old, forgotten runes. I could practically see the black wave from the north descending on this place, taking it apart with calculated precision. When I neared the remains of a structure near the edge, a simple square etched into the grass, I saw stone dust littered there. Just as trapped and ageless as the sawdust I'd come through.

"This isn't the first town," I said, kneeling down and running my fingers along the top edge of stone still buried in the ground. "I must have passed so many more...missed them. Ones that are gone."

The place was easy to denote on the map; I'd been able to see its expanse from the entrance, the irregular shape of the walls, rounded at the far end with elongated corners stretching out beneath it. To the right, not too far away down the slope of the hill, was a hole in the wall, a massive one. Just like the one in Cartha, where—presumably— the monsters had come through. Though this breach had been made a long time ago.

In ink, I named the ghost town *Axhead* and thought about what it used to be called when people lived here. The world was so big and full of deadly mystery, yet my map could shrink it down and let me examine it.

I put the map away after I finished the tiny outline of the place, not bothering to mark the damage to the walls because it was so plentiful. Anywhere the wall met the ground, there was a pile of crumbled, fallen stone. When it was all worn down and collapsed, there'd be enough stone to cover the town forever.

I approached the closest of the crystal spears, observing its shape as it became more clear. It was odd—just as strange as the fact that it was here at all, was the way it was formed. It was pointed at the tip and appeared to have sprouted up from the ground, tilting forward like it was a pike ready to spear an oncoming army. Around its length were many rings of the same crystal with blunt points swept forward, like crowns. The whole thing rose five feet above my head.

When I reached up to touch it, my gem murmured from my pocket. Not speaking, of course, but *murmuring* was what I had come to call it when it had a muted resonation, something that could only mean magic.

"In the spear?" I hesitated, thinking of killer branches and life-stealing gems. But my own gem wasn't rearing for it, so whatever magic was here, it mustn't be too powerful.

Hell with it, I thought, and I laid my hand flat on the lower part of the crystal sprout. A chill passed through me, but it might have just been me working myself up. The clear growth was smooth but naturally ridged, appearing to have formed on its own rather than have been sculpted by a stoneworker.

"Hm." Touching the thing brought me no insight. I walked forward, letting my hand run across the smooth surface, lifting my palm over the bluntly-pointed crowns that encircled it. Scanning across the town—

Not really a town anymore, is it?

—I figured there were about twenty or twenty-five of these sprouts, all the same size, spaced more or less evenly around. None of them stood where a building had been. Maybe they'd been some sort of magical defensive system, triggered when the town had been overrun.

"Thanks for not killing me, then," I said, giving the spear a pat and walking away. I moved through the open space, appreciating the sun and the moments not spent mindlessly drilling northward. None of the other spears did anything when I neared them, though they solicited that same hum from my gem.

Axhead was big, and I wandered around it until the sun disappeared behind the wall and left the place in darkness. I walked through alleys that no longer existed, through homes and walls and doors that were long gone, and I thought that this was what Cartha must look like now.

The thought struck me like cold, heavy iron. I rested my hand against a nearby crystal and stopped, catching my breath, which was stuck in my chest like a half-chewed lump of food. The image of the great beast crushing my home under its palm came to me, and I could at once see myself as though I were flying above my own body. Bent over, staring at the ground but not seeing it, my dirty black hair matted to the sides of my head. A field stretching around me, a sea of grass with the forgotten stone of dead families. The walls around me; the Walls around them. On and on, and it was just me, standing amidst all of this as night curled itself into the cracks where the light had fled. No reason to turn back; nowhere to turn back to. I was on an ocean, floating on a little raft that could only go in one direction, with no one to pull me back up if I fell off into the water.

What did they do to the cows? The pigs, the chickens? Did the monsters have a hearty feast, or did they hunger only for the flesh of man? Did they hunger at all? What happened—*what happened to everyone I knew?*

The lost, anguished thought brought me to my knees. I would never know what horrors had befallen them. Did I want to? I'd seen what happened to Gwin; maybe that was enough.

The world pressed on me. I went flat to the ground and I closed my eyes and pushed out the wetness there. I let go, drifting away to escape my thoughts, the reality, and praying I wouldn't have any dreams. I was a vessel of guilt and regret, running from things I couldn't possibly escape; seeking things that couldn't possibly fix me.

I fell asleep alone.

I awoke in company.

Chapter Forty-One

It was nighttime when I opened my eyes, deep night—*the same night? Is it tomorrow?*—black enough to be well before the morning. There was moonlight, interrupted only briefly by ragged clouds. I could see it gleam dully off my fingernails when I opened my eyes.

I blinked, regaining my senses, and pushed myself up off the ground. I was fully awake, the best I'd slept since dozing atop the carcass of the Turtle, and I—

Boots. I saw boots that weren't mine.

I hurried to my feet and instinctively pulled a dagger free as I righted myself, thinking, *Who is it, could it be Orrin, could it be someone from Iyes, who—*

My dagger hung from limp fingers and I croaked, "Franz?"

It was him, no mistaking it. His hair was dusted with stone powder, like he'd just been working in Cartha. Sleeves rolled up, like always.

"You're a long ways away, Jost," his raspy voice grated, teasing me. "You shouldn't have left."

"You're not real," I whispered.

You're not real.

"Don't tell me what's real," Franz said to me, and he stomped his foot on the ground and I saw the grass tremble in the moonlight.

I lowered my dagger. What was I going to do, stab him? A ghost? Because he had to be a ghost. A vision. Something.

"Come with me," he said, holding out his hand. It was dusty with stone. His eyes were black, hidden in shadow with the rest of his face. "Come with me and bring your magic."

"You don't know anything about magic, Franz," I said, hating that my voice was trembling even more than my fingers. "You're not Franz."

Franz smiled, and he had no teeth or gums or anything behind his lips. Just blackness.

He said, "Then who are we?"

I turned around as Franz's grin spread wider, and there were bodies there, some lying down, some standing up and staring at me. The ones on the ground got up with a fluidity that made my stomach crawl.

It took me only a moment to see the meaning of Franz's words, because the faces beginning to surround me were ones I recognized. Some only fleetingly; some with gut-clenching certainty. People in my ring, the poor ones like me that haggled for hours at the inner markets to get enough food for the week. But also the farmers, looking out of place without their manses and fields over their shoulders. Harvey the jeweler and Santelle, who traded in live and dead animals alike but usually smelled of the latter. Nem, who bought my pig meat but had me swear to never tell anyone about it.

All these people stared at me, and when they opened their mouths I saw the emptiness there, not just the pit that stretched to the back of their necks but a *void* within them, a frigid world stretching further than their insides could show, clamoring to be filled.

I didn't have the breath to scream. My heart beat for two, and if I stayed there, the circle of these *not real not real* people would grow smaller and smaller until I was one of them and empty inside.

Ahead of me was only Franz. I ran at him and he didn't try to stop me, my shoulder bumping him out of the way

—no it didn't, you didn't feel a thing Jost, you just—

and leaving me to stumble forward through the grass and almost lose my footing before I caught a crystal spear with my hand and stayed upright.

"Out, out," I panted, and I yanked my hand away from the spear like it was ablaze. I looked wildly around, running forward again just because I had to, just because I didn't know where to go. I regained my bearings after a moment and turned east, where the big hole in the wall was.

I saw them side-eye, a throng of people so large that it could only have grown since I last whirled my head around. Would it swell to the size of Cartha, until my entire city swept my trail, opening thousands and thousands of endless mouths to swallow me?

They were coming, hundreds now, thousands soon, and they all moved together, all without a sound, like they were a floating shadow. To call it eerie would be tame. It was a hammer blow to my sanity.

Moonlight cast my frantic shadow beside me, made jagged by the grass. My boots scraped across the edges of stone as I tore through the fallen town, the giant crystals seeming closer together than they were before, one on my side each time I turned my head.

Before me was the wound in the wall, the ground littered with chunks of rock. I stomped the smaller ones into the dirt as I ran to my escape.

The voices came to me when I got close to the hole, Franz's and Harvey's and so many others, whispers of my name that sank hooks into my ears and dragged me down. Invitations to turn back and go with them. To Cartha? To nothing?

I was crying. I noticed when the world got blurry and I tripped, slamming my elbow hard against a hunk of stone and wetting it with my blood. The pain was immediate and sharp, clearing my vision. I scrubbed at my eyes with the back of my wrist, still gripping my dagger, avoiding blinding myself only by luck.

I grabbed the edge of the hole, heaving myself over the stone below me. I expected a fight, for icy hands to land on my shoulders and ankles, yanking me back into oblivion. But they didn't come, and the voices were weaker.

The panic drove me out, scrambling up and over the rubble that blocked my way. Stone gave way, shifting under me and eventually mixing with dirt. I sprung forward and rolled, sliding down the rocks and into the dirt of the Walls, landing on my back and gasping for breath.

My gaze went to the exit and found eyes staring at me. They were standing there, enough of them to fill the massive gap shoulder-to-shoulder, watching me like I was some caged animal.

I'd only come some few hundred yards, but my body felt rubbery and weak. Still, I got to my feet, an ungainly ascent.

And they came, making their silent steps down the same rocks that had cut at my stomach and arms and legs in my desperate escape. I moved to the right, staying up against the wall until I was fast enough to break away. At some point I had sheathed my dagger, and now my empty hands caught the next corner and hauled me past it, deeper into the maze.

Don't get lost.

But it was either lose them or be lost to them. When I dared to look behind me, they were there, ghostly. In the Walls, the moonlight was gone, but my gem cast itself onto them, a wall of yellow pallor.

My fear drove me forward. Looking back, they were farther away, and farther, till I couldn't see them anymore. They were left behind.

I was elsewhere. The dirt beneath my boots was churning instead of packing down, carrying moisture and making it harder to run, then harder to walk as my legs started to give. In the darkness, in the constant turning of my neck to be sure I was alone, I didn't see the water until I was practically stepping in it, and when I stopped myself I fell forward into the shallow pool, catching myself with my hands so I avoided submerging my face.

My breath, heavy, rippled at the surface of the water after its motion subsided. I was on my hands and knees in a body of water that circled out from a deep corner of the maze. The slope beneath me was apparent; even inching my fingers forward, I could tell that the drop-off was sudden and steep. It could be that this water stretched beneath the wall.

I wasn't eager to look behind my back because I knew I couldn't run anymore. Perhaps better to be taken blind than to watch it happen. But instinct forced my neck up and around, and behind me was wet dirt and stone walls and nothing else.

Were they gone? Or just late?

I blinked and Derrick was there. Somehow, I wasn't even surprised. It was too dark to see if his wounds had come with him as well, but his sword was strapped on to his body, a tiny piece of reality that I knew was wrong, and it calmed me.

"Sorry," I said. My voice was very small, even though I'd caught my breath. "It wasn't my fault."

Another blink and he was gone.

I stared into the water and now I saw a face there that wasn't my own reflection. A face I'd forgotten on my surface, but one that haunted me below that. Atell. She was far away, deep in the water, but the gem's light revealed her. The jewel throbbed against me, hot on my leg. I felt it pulsing.

"Who's doing this to me?" I asked quietly, keeping my eyes on the vision in the water. "You, gem? Why?"

It didn't answer.

I didn't want to blink and make Atell disappear, so I kept my eyes open until they burned. Her face got closer to mine, rising upward. Her eyes opened, seeing me.

And when her arm burst through the water and grabbed me, I knew she was real.

Chapter Forty-Two

There was no time to think. I grabbed her arm with my free hand, tilting back and getting leverage with my feet, pulling her free of the water and falling backwards so that my head hit the dirt and she was on top of me.

"No, no, no," I said to myself, quiet at first and then louder as I reached for my dagger. Maybe the ghosts were behind me still—they'd corralled me into this dark corner of the Walls to be killed by something that looked like Atell.

The hilt was warm in my hand. I drew it back, my other hand wrapped around her arm. It was so thin that I could feel the bones there, and she had no strength to keep me away. It had no strength. It wore the face of Atell, the body of Atell, but she was dead and there was a monster pleading with me.

"—me, me, Jost, please, *Jost*—"

Atell's voice. Atell's eyes, dripping wet, Atell's mouth gasping for breath while squeezing out the words. It wasn't fighting me. She wasn't fighting me.

"Atell," I said, not a question but a breath of disbelief, and she rolled off me into the dirt and I let my dagger fall on the other side.

Our panting breath filled the air, and we lied there long enough for me to feel sure the ghosts from Axhead weren't coming to smother me. Us. I thought maybe that they were spawned from the crystals, tied in to where they were sprouted, and then I let it leave my mind.

I finally looked over at her. She was still there, staring straight up at the sky like I had been.

"This is impossible," I said.

"Where are we?" she asked.

"I can show you on the map," I said, and I looked back up at the sky. It was dark, the moon hidden away from us, but the strip of sky we could see was cloudless and dotted with stars. "If this is really you and I'm not just crazy."

"You want me to tell you what happened." Slight rustling as she shifted. "I don't know."

"I know what I saw," I told her. "I saw that thing grab you and pull you into the water. I saw bubbles come up and then nothing. And now you're here. And it's been...hell, nine, ten days? I'm crazy. I'm definitely crazy."

Although it would be nice if insanity led me to things like Atell instead of Franz.

"Thanks for thinking I'm not real," Atell said, "but I am. Stop being ridiculous."

I breathed in through my nose. "So tell me."

I heard her shrug. Her bare feet moved idly in the water, heels dragging at the wet dirt. "I don't remember a lot. It was like being asleep, until I woke up underwater and I was about to drown. I didn't realize so much time had gone by."

"You can't live for ten days underwater," I said, a thin dread washing over me. I was certain that this blink, or the next, I'd turn my head and she would be gone.

"I'm thinking," she said, and went silent for a while.

Blink.

Blink. Blink.

She was still there.

"I remember getting pulled down. I took a breath right before, but I still got some water in me." She spoke like she was walking through the labyrinth, pausing at turns and trying to figure out the right way to go. "And I tried not to cough, but my chest was burning. And when I couldn't hold it in any more, I hacked up the water. But it..."

She paused, breathing.

"I remember...it ran down my chin. And it was warm. And it was impossible because the lake was cold. Colder the deeper you went, and I was deep. Underwater. I shouldn't have been able to choke and cough and *breathe* but I did."

"You..." I could hear her breath quickening, stirred by the memory.

"It was dark, but I was *in* something. I remember thinking that, one of the last things I thought before it all went to sleep. Like something had eaten me and I was in its belly." She stopped, splashing the water with her foot. "But...that's it. Really."

I relaxed a little, soothed by the passage of time. "Everything that has happened to me has been crazy. There hasn't been a single normal thing since I left Cartha. It's only natural that something crazy would happen to you after being in my company."

"Not your fault," she said.

Tell her about the broken gem you found. She deserves to know.

The thought was intrusive and dark, coming from some other part of me. It stopped me dead in the middle of speaking.

"Jost?"

It is your *fault, of course. She'll realize it eventually. She's smarter than you.*

I cleared my throat. "So this monster pulled you into the water and swallowed you and then spit you out and here you are, huh?"

"I don't know," she replied. "I really...it feels like all this happened yesterday. Or hours ago. Are you really sure it's been this long?"

"I'm sure," I said, picturing Atell in some monster's belly, suspended in some kind of unconscious bubble. I'd yet to see a monster eat someone. Attack them, yes, kill them, yes, but eating people didn't seem to be on their list of priorities. So if this one in the Iyes pond decided to grab someone and not kill them, what other purpose could it have but to keep them? Had it decided Atell wouldn't make a good pet and just spat her into the water?

The idea of a huge underground network of water-filled tunnels beneath our feet, crawling with waterborne monsters, scared the hell out of me.

"You're right," Atell said. "It's crazy. But it's all I know."

I let it go, knowing there was nothing else to be gained by speculating or questioning something I couldn't possibly understand, probably not even if Atell had consciously witnessed her entire journey.

But she was *alive*. She was *here*. And though it was bizarre, it was good. I was in no position to pick at its seams and try to make it unravel. I'd accepted the truth of far stranger things, and faced them head-on.

"Are you okay?" I asked her, surprised that it took me this long to say.

"I'm not hurt." She paused. "But I'm hungry. Very hungry."

"I have—" I was going to say that I had some food, but I didn't have my pack. We weren't too far from where I'd left it. "My pack is back a ways. Can you walk?"

"I said I'm not hurt," she repeated, but got to her feet slowly, and when she did, she fell against me after one shaky step.

I caught her gently, like her bones were hollow. She weighed so little, but she was warm.

"Take it slow," I said.

"Yeah." She lingered against me for a moment, then pulled away, bending down to stretch her legs and dig her fingers into her thighs and calves. "I feel like I haven't moved in days. Well...I guess I haven't."

She got to walking just fine after a little while, and I brought us back the way I had come, only somewhat wary of my former pursuers. They weren't there waiting for me, and we bypassed the large hole in the wall, heading back south to where I'd left my bag. I stayed close to Atell in case her legs would give in, but she stayed upright.

We rounded the exterior of Axhead without incident, and I was relieved to come across my pack laying at the destroyed southern gate. I knew I'd find it, but after being chased away over a mile...

"Here," I said, unnecessarily, because Atell could see my pack just fine.

"Is that a sword?" She walked over to Derrick's blade, sheathed and clasped to its strap. "You didn't bring this into Iyes."

"I...picked it up after I left," I told her, not ready to go into the whole story. "Go on and sit, I'll see what I have."

Atell stepped away from the sword and brought herself down on a flat part of the big stone that was crashed through the gate. "Thank you, Jost. Whatever you have, I'll take."

I was hungry too, now that the adrenaline was finally all the way gone. I took a look at the meat I had hanging from my pack.

It's monster meat, I thought. It hadn't occurred to me that this might be strange for Atell, as I'd been eating it since I left the Pooled Woods. But it was all I had, and it wasn't hurting me.

Just another thing I won't tell her. I untied some and got the rest of the materials I needed for a small fire from my bag. I collected tinder wherever I could as I walked, so I had plenty. And I'd learned something new with the gem ever since cooking the monster meat.

Atell watched me assemble a small bunch of dried roots and grasses atop the rock nearby her. I took the gem from my pocket and pressed it against the bunch, then closed my eyes. Where calling the light had become second-nature, this one took a little more cajoling, like I was unspooling the idea from my mind each time I used it. But in the same way that I could call out the gem's light, I could make it produce heat.

The first time, it had burnt my hand, so I'd had to lay the gem alone in the fire and then poke it out afterwards with my dagger for the next few attempts.

Now, I kept the heat away from me and solely to the sticks, until they smoked and then cherry embers came into being at their tips. I blew those into life and the cookfire was on.

Atell smiled. "That's incredible."

The fire was warm on my face, and I pulled away from it with a small grin of my own. I hesitated before spearing a piece of meat on my dagger.

"If you've never..." I paused. "Fish is the only meat you've ever had?"

She nodded, her eyes dipping down to the wet slab on the tip of my dagger.

"Probably start slow then. I hunted some creatures I've, ah, never hunted before." I set the meat on the rock near the fire and carved off a chunk. "I've been eating it just fine, but if you're not used to it..."

I wished I had something else for her. Where were all the goddamn burrow pigs? I hadn't seen a single one north of the Pooled Woods.

"You look guilty," Atell said with a little laugh. Her fingers trembled, even lying flat on the rock. She must have felt very weak. "So these aren't the pigs you told me about."

"Not exactly."

Her eyes stayed on the meat for another moment, then came back up to mine. "Black claw?"

Of course she figured it out.

I let a little air out of my nose. "Yeah. It's all I've got."

"So you're eating monsters," she mused, seeming more entertained by the idea than disgusted by it. "Are they good?"

That made me laugh, and my smile came back. "Honestly? The best thing I've ever had in my life."

I don't know if Atell agreed with that, but she and I both ate until I had to cook some more.

Chapter Forty-Three

After making the fire, cooking and eating, the sun was starting to make itself known to the Walls. Atell had moved to the ground, sitting in the dirt with her back up against the stone, and I was doing the same next to her.

"Did we eat it all?" Atell asked me, worried. "I didn't mean to—"

I raised my hand, waving away her concerns. "The meat is plentiful out here. Don't worry about it."

She started to say more but let the words go, tilting her head back against the rock. "Iyes is gone by now."

"Yes." It wasn't a question, but I answered it anyway. She'd been there to see it empty, and she knew what happened to Cartha. There was no sense giving her hope that it might have gone another way.

It would be a long journey back to find nothing.

Atell let her arm fall off her lap and into the dirt, close to me. "I imagined leaving Iyes. It was never like this."

"I sure hope not," I said, trying a joke. It fell flat, and I abandoned it. "I'm sorry."

She didn't say anything, but she brought her head back down to her chest and closed her eyes. I saw her body hitch once, briefly, and then her tears came, just barely visible in the slowly-growing light. She cried quietly, hardly moving.

There was nothing I could think of to say, and that was for the best, because I wasn't really equipped to handle something like this. I bit into my bottom lip. I was a little uncomfortable, but in a much greater way I was feeling Atell's pain; pain that I had been through personally only weeks before; pain I never let myself stop to reflect on.

Her hand still rested atop the dirt. I took it in my own, enveloping her cold fingers in mine, which were only a little warmer and streaked with dirt and the blood of other things.

I held her hand for a while. She was lost in her grieving for long minutes as the day's light came, still mostly hidden by the Walls, but less so this far north.

When she pulled her hand away, it was to wipe the tears from her face, and only once. After that, she was done, and she took in a deep breath and said two words.

"What now?"

Two words, and all the frightening possibilities of the world to follow. I looked at her, knowing that behind her was nothing, and before her was the open world she'd always wanted, forced upon her in the worst possible way. Her situation was like mine, but also drastically different.

"I'm going north," I said simply. "I met some people— wielders, actually—after I left Iyes. We parted ways, but they told me the truth behind what happened to the world."

Atell's bright curiosity came back at that. Her eyes still shone, but they were wide as she implored that I share with her.

Ready to go into it now, I held nothing back of the wielders' story, save some details I might not fully remember.

"I took his sword," I told her when I was finishing, nodding my head toward it where it laid on the ground. "Derrick's. They just left it there, and I figured I could put it to use."

"Can I?" Atell hovered her hand over it, and I nodded.

"There doesn't seem to be any magic in it. You should be safe."

She lifted the sword, struggling to get it off the ground with just one hand and eventually using two. The weapon probably weighed a significant portion of what she did.

"It's beautiful," she said, running her fingers along the scabbard. "I've never held a sword. Closest I've come was your dagger."

The tough steel-and-leather scabbard was indeed finely crafted, though I wouldn't call it beautiful. The sword itself—silver, wire-wrapped handle, with shiny twists at either end of the hilt where the blade rested, and a long blade that was wide but thin enough to make one question how it could be so heavy—I thought that was beautiful. And when she pulled it from the sheath, I could see Atell felt the same way, her mouth falling slightly open as she cast her eyes down its length.

"So you're going north," Atell said, her eyes still down on the blade. She ran a finger down the steel.

"Yes. I...have a lot to make up for, and I have no other place to be. I'd like to die trying to make things right, if this maze is going to kill me one way or the other."

That was the honest truth. I didn't believe what I could do would make any difference, but it was all I had.

"You should have gone with the wielders," Atell said, looking up from the sword. "How else do you stand a chance? Your plan is to face something a whole village of magic users couldn't?"

I smirked. "I guess so."

Atell slid the sword back into the sheath and set it down, letting out a small relieved noise when it hit the dirt. "What about waiting for them to come back?"

"Trust me," I said, "Orrin doesn't want to see me again. The look in his eyes when he saw Derrick...he would have tried to kill me if Hider wasn't there to urge him away. It's better for both of us if we never see each other."

"We couldn't find them, anyway, with Hider." She paused. "Well, you could, actually."

"No thanks," I said. "I'm going to go in one direction. No more looping back."

"You'll finish your map on the return path, then."

"Maybe." I smiled. "And maybe if I die, you can take it up."

"That's stupid," she said, flexing her fingers. "We'll die at the same time. I'm going with you."

The question had been on my mind ever since I'd been sure Atell was real and not a figment of my imagination—what would she do? Coming with me was the only real answer, with no home to return to and no real experience surviving out here.

Truth be told, even though I had no right to, I was planning on asking her to join me. There was still plenty of the book to be read, and she had a deeper understanding of magic than I might ever have, never mind the fact that she didn't wield it.

And it would be nice to have her along. Her face was one I'd missed dearly.

I coughed, clearing those thoughts from my head even as they brought a tingle to my cheeks. Atell was looking at me, waiting for me to respond.

I gave her a nod, then cracked a smile. It was very easy to do, because as much as I might not want to put her in danger, I was glad she would be with me. The Walls outside of Cartha were my territory, something I'd grown to love exploring alone. This was a different world now, and I was a different Jost than the one who used to hunt burrow pigs. Atell was part of that.

"Okay, then," I agreed, wearing my easy smile. "We'll both die somewhere between here and where the labyrinth ends up north."

It was she who took my hand then, wrapping her fingers over the back of it and into my palm. Her nails cut half-moon marks into the dirt on my skin.

"I can feel it," she said, whispering. "Like this is what I'm meant to do. What we're both meant to do."

I wanted to agree, but I couldn't. On a good day, I could tell myself this was destiny or fate. But the reality rang far louder. This was something we'd been pinned against, where life's maze had shunned us at turn after turn until we came across this long, straight pathway with no way out but forward. No way of seeing what awaited us at the end. No way of knowing if we'd even make it further than a few steps.

But...

I turned my hand, catching hers and squeezing it once.

It'll be better not to face it alone.

Part Four: The World

Chapter Forty-Four

It was three weeks later that the world changed.

Our progress through the labyrinth was mostly unhindered, to our surprise. I'd expected Atell's company to encourage the presence of monsters, but no such horrors occurred. With blades in hand, we were the predators.

Atell ate more monster meat than I did, and she at first asked, then soon insisted, that she be the one to carry Derrick's sword.

"You have your daggers," she said, adding bluntly: "I need to be stronger."

So she carried the sword. I took it back when she was struggling, but soon she held the weapon all day and all night, though she didn't yet have the strength to use it.

Her awe at the curves and corners of the maze had come and gone right around the time her town had been destroyed. Her eyes had lit with wonder at her first steps outside of Iyes back then; now she was gritty and focused, and her determination was inspiring. I wanted to ask her, how can you do this? How can you move forward so well, so smoothly, without looking behind you? I'd gotten lost in my thoughts among these walls more times than I could count, but I never saw that happen to her.

The nights were different. We weren't opposed to night travel, but a day filled with walking, navigating, marking, hunting, cooking, dressing, and eating took its toll.

And when we took to the dirt or among fallen stone to rest, the silence came with it, and I would hear Atell fidget. Shifting in the dirt, or lightly scratching her nails against a hunk of stone. Running her fingers over the leather of the scabbard. Breathing just a little quicker than usual.

I would listen for a sound of despair, a sob, but she never made it obvious, and I never knew what to say. Nor to do. The thought of going over to hold her made me twist up in a lot of different ways. I'd been with women in Cartha, but this wasn't about sex. I'd held Atell's hand for all of ten seconds and that was the extent of our contact, excluding when she tried to kill me at first sight.

It just didn't feel like my place, like I would impose compassion over something she was hiding. It was clear she didn't want me to know her struggles, the same as I didn't want her to deal with them alone.

The nights grew shorter as we went north. Our pace was quick; I'd at first thought we would make time to read Gwin's book, but the time wasn't there. We ate the day with travel, and the night brought needed rest. I steered us pointedly away from any path that might lead to a town, any direction that made my gem tremble. I hated those small moments, when tingling fear pulled at my heart, my gem vibrating. I pictured it like a salivating maw, chomping at flesh that was just out of its reach. Atell didn't question my navigation. We both knew which way north was; that was all that mattered.

Atell had been carrying the sword the last three days when we came upon the rise.

We'd been surging northward for weeks, and we'd only recently stumbled across a body of water to wash ourselves in. Atell had been hesitant at first, looking at the pool tucked away in the corner of the walls, surely recalling how she'd been taken. But to her credit, the hesitation was brief, and she then laid down the sword and stripped to clean herself off.

I had looked away politely, but not without noticing the narrow bands of muscle on her arms and the curve of her neck down to her shoulders. She was thin, and beautiful, and clearly getting stronger than she had ever been. The meat and the sword-carrying were having their effect. Had all the Iyes people been so frail just due to their limited diet?

So now, three weeks after I fled from Axhead and Atell burst from the water, we stood staring at something neither of us had ever seen in all our miles of walking in the labyrinth: a sudden and steep change in elevation.

The ground rose up and up, past our own heights, and the Walls were built on this slope, the bottoms arcing upward and following it to the horizon. It stretched far, so far that the tall stone walls appeared to pinch in on themselves and grow shorter. And at the end—far, far on the horizon—was the faintest glow of light, still bright enough to make itself stand out amid the weak daylight of the labyrinth.

Both of us stopped in our tracks, partly because we were exhausted, and ahead of us rose a miles-long challenge to our beaten legs.

"Can't imagine there's any way around this," I said, letting out an inadvertent sigh while I marked the area on my map. I mused on how to indicate the slope, and eventually settled on drawing an arrow through the path. There were spots where the Walls diverged into the various twists and turns of the labyrinth, but the straightaway led north and extended to the horizon, so that's what we'd be taking.

"We should probably rest first," Atell said. The heel of her hand sat on the sword's pommel, fingers hanging loosely in the air. "There's some monster left, right?"

"Yes—and you can just call it meat," I said, not for the first time, as we settled onto the ground with relieved groans. My legs tingled with warmth as the muscles cooled down. It was late into the afternoon now. "Sits better."

"It's monster. I call fish, fish." Atell reached into my pack, which I'd dropped down between us. She'd gotten adept at building fires, forming the proper root arrangement quickly.

I set my gem to it and let the embers burn and flare. "You cook, I'm gonna stretch a little bit."

Atell tsked. "I keep telling you."

"Yeah." I bent over my extended legs, letting them stretch till they burned, feeling that odd sensation of shared pain and relief that came with working on a tired part of one's body. I moved the stretch from my legs to my chest and shoulders, all movements Atell had shown me once I complained about being sore some days ago. She was much more flexible than I was, something she'd gained from years of doing these stretches to keep her strong when swimming.

"I don't think we can make it all the way up there before nightfall." I got close to the fire again, finished stretching, with Atell sitting on the other side. "It's such a long path that I can't even tell how long it is. Not from here."

"It's odd, is it not?" Atell held a speared piece of meat over the fire, her eyes on that northern horizon. "Like there's a mountain underneath the dirt."

I nodded. "I've never seen this sort of thing before. I guess the world isn't just perfectly flat."

Atell cast her eyes to me and then flicked them to the side, a gesture of mild annoyance. I tended to get a little lighthearted when we set our things down. She handled it well enough, even if she didn't laugh much. It was fine. I wasn't very funny.

Neither of us were terribly hungry, so we finished that cooked piece, threw some dirt over the fire, and sat back on our hands. It was a middling hour, late enough in the afternoon that we felt the day was coming to a close, but still with light coming in, light that was especially bright at the end of the long hall. It stared at us, beckoning.

Despite my joke, this truly was something I hadn't seen before. There was a tingling sense inside of me, an invisible string that wound around my brain, ran down the back of my neck, and attached itself at the other side to my gem. When it was plucked, the skin of my neck glossed with a chill, and my eyes never wanted to close. Now, they were drawn to the pathway.

We didn't travel in the dark, not when there was so much day to be had here. But I couldn't resist.

"We should go," I said, still staring down the northern way. "I'm feeling it."

Atell raised an eyebrow at me, but she knew what I meant. I'd been mostly open with her about the magic, excluding some details I wanted to keep for myself. Like the way the gem sought out other magic and consumed it. Against my will.

"Like there's something at the end?" she asked.

"I'm not sure," I answered. "Maybe. It's like…"

I paused; closed my eyes; took a breath. I pictured cresting that tall hill, my legs burning from the exertion, my breath heavy in my chest but my hearth thrumming with the thrill of what awaited us…

"There's *more*," I said, opening my eyes. "More path, maybe, but it could be something else. I think…no, I can't tell anymore. It's gone."

The tingly feeling—the *find*, as I was coming to call it, since I hadn't been able get Hider's words from my head—was capricious. At times it felt like it wasn't part of me at all, but more like a bird flitting past the corner of my vision or a dream I'd left in the night. If I tried, I could catch some details, but only for a moment.

"Okay then. Let's go." Atell was quick to get to her feet, limber and swift despite the strain of all these miles traveled by foot. I got up a little slower, but still full of energy. The find was gone to wherever it went, but it left me with an urgency that revitalized me down to the tips of my toes.

We strapped up and walked, leaving behind the charred remains of dried roots and a few burned drips of meat juice.

Our small camp was right at the bottom of the incline, and the slope was noticeable as we went up, reaching higher with our steps. There were no words to say, our breath saved for the exertion. Atell started panting not long after I did, but neither of us slowed, nor did she ask me to take the sword.

Were I to estimate the distance, in my half-delirious state of exhaustion upon reaching the top, I would have put it at about three arduous miles over the course of an hour, with tiny rests on the way up. But I couldn't be sure, and the spot I later marked on my map was most assuredly inaccurate because for the first time ever, I neglected to draw my lines. I was transfixed—we both were. We sat down hard at the top, for the weakness of our legs and the awe of what expanded before us.

For what we saw atop the rise was a completely different world.

Chapter Forty-Five

The late afternoon sun spilled glorious colors onto the land, orange and yellow and pink, things I'd never seen. The sky was like a painter's pallet. We had come up so high, and it was so clear, that I wanted to reach out and touch it. Behind us was the dark path, still hidden by the walls. And below us stretched out the world, so incredibly and wonderfully...open.

We had not reached the end of the labyrinth. Rather, the labyrinth had reached its own end. As we ascended the rise, the walls on either side of us had gotten shorter and shorter, until they stood above us by only a dozen feet, and over the rise and back down the ensuing slope, they narrowed down into almost nothing.

Atell and I sat upon an apex, and as far as we could see stretched the open world mixed with the incredibly complex and vast array of the labyrinth, but the stone was mostly destroyed and gone. The huge field before us transitioned from dirt into a sea of wild grass growing amongst the remains.

In some places closer to us, sections of walls and even entire maze segments still stood, but they were short and worn. Further out, there was nothing like that, and we could see large swaths of the maze simply etched into the ground, an echo of where it once stood.

There was rubble almost everywhere, but the further out my eyes went, the cleaner it was. The walls near us rose and fell almost randomly, in various stages of decay, like a gargantuan carcass picked clean, leaving only its fading bones behind.

And beyond all that to the north, perhaps one day's walk away, were...

"Mountains?" I whispered, not believing it even as I said it. Would mountains be so perfectly black, as though the light shined on everything but them? I'd never seen mountains before, so I couldn't say, but it still felt wrong.

"It looks like it," Atell said. "Mountains..."

She fell silent, which was strange, because Atell wasn't one to trail off. She spoke her mind and she did it in short order.

"Something's wrong about it," she finally stated, not taking her eyes off what laid far away.

"You're right," I said. It really did look like a mountain range, so much that it felt foolish to suspect otherwise, but at the same time...

We watched it until the sun went all the way down. I waited for the world to become as black as it was inside of the walls, but that hour didn't come. The sky was peppered with stars, and the half-moon was bright as a torch.

Atell and I looked over this soft-lit evening until we couldn't keep our eyes open any more, and we fell to sleep shortly before the monsters came.

Scritch. Scritch.

The sound woke me, flashing my mind back to Cartha, to Iyes. I hurried to my feet, bleary, with one hand on my dagger while I looked around for the black claw scraping at the wall.

Nothing. I lit the gem, and the light roused Atell, who started to ask me what was happening before she heard the noises herself. Her hand quickly found the sword where it laid next to her.

I cast the light back behind us first, down the hall, sweeping it side to side. I saw nothing, nowhere close. Before us, where the north drop-off began, I could see very clearly in the light of the evening sky that we were alone.

I snapped my head up to look at the walls. Were they on the stone, climbing up? Sitting on the edge and waiting to strike?

But no—nothing around us. Nothing near us.

Scritch. Scriiiiiiiiitch.

"Where are they?" Atell said, a small amount of panic in her voice.

I took a breath and listened, but it was somehow impossible to tell where the sound was coming from. It felt like it was all around us, like it was in the air. And it wasn't until I stopped looking that I could see.

I grabbed Atell's arm with one hand and pointed with the other, drawing her attention to the landscape. There, amid the rises and falls of the wasted labyrinth walls, were the monsters. So, so many monsters, just black shapes in the moonlight, too far away to tell if they were black claws or not, but without a doubt they were the same colorless beings who tread through the labyrinth all around us. We were hearing their sounds, carried through the open air, even this far away. They were working on the stone.

Atell didn't speak, her breath caught in her throat and the sword hanging from her limp hand. The tip rested in the dirt, keeping it upright.

"So they really do come from the north," I said quietly. The black mountains were invisible now, not catching any light. "At night. To do their work."

They'd been working on it for years and years and years, their progress methodical, if sloppy. Eventually, they would tear it all down.

"It's horrible," Atell whispered, and I knew she was thinking about Iyes. Imagining these creatures roaming through the roads and alleys she'd lived her whole life in, tearing down walls that had been there since she was a child. Tearing down her home. I knew, because I was thinking the same thing. Hadn't been able to stop myself from thinking about it every time I heard a scrape against stone.

But I was more used to it than she was.

"They're far away," I told her, and indeed, the closest ones we could see must have been miles from us. The sound just carried so well out here that it made them seem much closer. "We can rest until the daylight comes."

Atell exhaled and sat back down. "I can't believe I want to sleep right now. But I'm exhausted."

"It's fine." I saw the heaviness in her eyes. "Sleep an hour or two. I'll wake you and we'll switch. If anything gets close, we'll know."

The monsters before hadn't been very aggressive toward us, a blessing that made me uneasy. It could be that these ones from the mountains were different. It was better not to take any chances.

Atell fell asleep clutching the sword, and I stood over her, watching the monsters tear the world apart.

Chapter Forty-Six

The daylight came without incident, both of us getting enough rest to be a little fidgety when we were finally ready to go down the hill. The monsters had dispersed as the morning came, and Atell had been awake to see it.

"I don't think they like the sun," she said. "It didn't seem to hurt them. But when it came, they retreated further and further."

"Hmm." That could be helpful later on, if it was truly the case. "Then let's keep traveling during the day. And we'll try to keep to areas where the Walls have been totally destroyed—where the monsters have no reason to come."

I made quick markings on my map, not bothering to draw in labyrinthine paths that were no longer fully impeded by walls, instead lightly circling areas where we could see that grass had overtaken what was left of the stone. There were many of them.

We descended, and I savored the relief in my legs with going downhill. The path down was even longer than the path up, and we kept as straight as we could, turning when a wall was too high to climb over, and going up ten or twelve feet to cross over the ones we could. With the advanced state of decay and destruction, there was plenty to grab onto.

"It's the magic wearing," Atell said when I pointed this out, panting after coming fifteen feet over a wall and working her way down the other side. "The monsters haven't come this far. But their effect is spreading this way. Whatever magic holds the Walls together, they're making it crumble."

She admitted it was only a theory, but it held water to me. Like Derrick had told me, all of this was only a matter of time.

When the ground finally leveled out, a couple of hours had passed and my legs hurt in a different kind of way. I rubbed at the tops of my thighs when we stopped at the bottom of the slope and realized something.

"It's a lot closer than I thought," I remarked, looking at the horizon, which was almost wholly dominated by the mountains. "Some trick from being all the way up high, I guess."

"Do you see that?" Atell asked me.

"What?" I followed her gaze, but she was just looking off into the distance. "What do you see?"

"It's..." She made a sound in her throat, like the next word was an odd shape and she was forcing it out. "Moving."

"The mountains?"

"The whole—just look."

So I did, and it only took a few moments to see what she meant. It was incredibly subtle, something you'd only see if you were looking for it (or if you were as observant as Atell, apparently). But it was true. Ever so slightly, the mountain range that spanned most of the horizon and stretched up to the sky was...*shifting*. The lines of the many rises looked less like mountains and more like vast, pointed humps with blurred edges. It was like staring at a cloud on a windless day— you almost couldn't tell it was moving at all, but it was.

Seeing this gave me a heavy pit in my stomach for a lot of reasons I didn't care to sort out. But it explained why we had felt so uneasy staring at these mountains from atop the hill. Something had been off, and we just couldn't tell. Now we could.

"What the hell are they?" I asked, not looking for an answer. I shook my head. "Doesn't matter. It's where we have to go, and we'll find out when we get there."

I looked over to her. "You okay?"

She flashed me a smile, one far too big for the circumstances. "Just fine. Let's get over there."

She was scared. That was okay. I was, too. It just happened to be easy to go forward because going backward wasn't any better.

It was very different, walking through a landscape that wasn't dominated by the towering heights of the Walls, seeing sunlight shine off of grass for miles in some directions. It was almost like walking through the city of Cartha, but even Cartha had more obstructions, more houses and businesses arranged in the many rings, than what remained out here. Some of the Walls were still dozens of feet tall, but those stretches were short and appeared on the brink of collapsing, enough for us to avoid them. But there were many more sections of wall here that we could climb over—or simply walk over, being careful not to catch the edge of a rock and twist an ankle.

Atell had grown up with a canopy over her head her entire life. Seeing the sun, the sky, the clouds, and the stretch of the land around us—I think if she were anyone else from Iyes, someone who hadn't read and sought stories about the outside world, then that person would have broken or run away. There simply had to be a part of Atell that felt overwhelmed. Even I, who'd done this sort of thing all my life, who'd grown up in a city hundreds of times the size of Iyes, was taken aback at seeing this.

But the part of Atell that made her the person she is was much stronger, much grander. And she usually moved on ahead of me when I was going too slow. It made me smile—something nothing else out here could do. Not even the sun in all its glory.

The daylight got us to where the Walls were gone, and just traces of stone marked the grass that led up to the moving mountains. After all these days of travel, and the final stint across the skeletal remains of the northern labyrinth, we stood in the open world. Hundreds of years ago, everywhere would have looked like this. It was beautiful in the fading light, save for the mountains.

Of course now, we could see that what was before us was no mountain range. No anomaly of nature, and no trick of the light.

It was alive.

I thought of the Turtle, and how its bulk had reached around and over me, looming so large in the Pooled Woods. That was nothing compared to this. You don't mistake something for being a mountain without it being incomprehensibly massive, and by the time we were within a half-mile of it, the great creation swallowed our entire field of vision except for the sky it didn't quite touch.

The daylight had gone from yellow to pink and orange, but it didn't change how the expanse looked. It was pure black, so black that I might have thought it was a shadow except for the tiny spots that glistened when it moved. Its great, inexorable motions were like slow breathing, fractions of fractions of an inch at a time.

And it was hot. The heat radiated off it, and the grass near its edge was dead in a radius of a few feet. Like how the grass by the Walls in Cartha died from not getting enough sunlight, except this crop was sweltered to death. Another similarity with the Turtle, though there was no shell over this thing, just simmering flesh like the black claws wore. The kind I'd cut into and pulled the meat out of a good dozen times in the last few weeks.

"I hate to say it," Atell murmured, rolling her neck as we approached the thing, "but it feels good. The heat."

I chuckled. She wasn't wrong; when the sun went away, it got chilly fast, and the night was upon us. "Still, I don't exactly want to make camp here."

"But..."

"But night's coming, and that means the monsters are going to come out."

We stopped in the grass, well before the ground started to die at the foot of the range.

"This is it, then," I said, remembering what Orrin had told me, which I had shared with Atell in turn. "The mountain castle of the One."

"You're kidding," she said, letting out a little laugh.

"What else could it be?" I said, not answering her humor. "I admit, I had pictured it more like a castle and less like a mountain."

"Gods above and below," she said quietly, casting her eyes up as far as they would go. "I've never...they...it must have been building this for hundreds of years."

"Yeah."

Atell exhaled a long breath. "Remember when I told you that you should have waited for the wielders? I still think that."

I nodded, then glanced at the western horizon, where the sun was slowly disappearing.

"Come on," I said. "We have to find somewhere safe to be when the monsters come out. We'll figure out what we want to do after that."

I already knew what I wanted, and it wouldn't leave Atell with much choice. But there was only one place to go.

Chapter Forty-Seven

We found shelter after backtracking to where some walls still stood, sliding ourselves into an alcove formed by great sheets of fallen stone. With our combined strength, we managed to shove over a big slate to give us cover once we were inside. Maybe these monsters wouldn't care to go after us, but it was better to be safe than to be eviscerated some hundreds of yards from your goal.

There was no light inside the stone except for mine. We couldn't see the outside world except for a crack that looked toward the ground, but we knew that night would fall in just minutes, and the swarms of creatures would head deeper into the labyrinth to do their work. Where we were, with the walls mostly destroyed, they seemed to consider their work completed. They should pass us by.

We keep ourselves alive on an awful lot of assumptions, I thought, and grimaced.

"What?" Atell said, seeing my face and reminding me that my gem was still lit.

I quashed it, washing us in almost perfect darkness. "I'm going in there. It's the only time to do it—when the monsters pass, leaving the fortress empty."

"And?" She shifted, the soft noise very loud inside this space. "Then what?"

"I don't know," I said, and I felt the overwhelming urge to laugh—to simply cackle with the madness of it all. "Go find the big bad monster and stab it in the eye? Sneak up on it and cut its throat? I'm not much of a planner. I'm only good at drawing things I've already done."

I couldn't see it, but I was sure Atell rolled her eyes at that. "You're ridiculous. But you can't make a plan without knowing what you're up against. So I don't blame you."

"Thanks," I said, still on the verge of laughing but managing to hold it back. "What about you, then? I hated dragging you this far, honest. I know you made the decision pretty easy, but this is something else."

"It is."

In the moments before she gave her answer, I realized that I was hoping that she would say she couldn't go with me. It was better for her to hide here and wait for me to return—or if I were to die, for her to wander amidst death, rather than march straight towards it alongside me.

It was a selfish hope, and I kept it to myself. She didn't have to deal with my opinion on top of everything. And her answer was about what I expected.

"I didn't come all this way just to abandon you at the final stretch," she told me. Her tone was accusatory, like she'd been reading my mind and wanted to smack me for it. She added with sarcasm, "I hope that's all right."

I gave a little laugh—just a small one, not the crazed belly-laugh I'd been fighting—and said, "Then all that's left is to wait."

The sounds came soon after, the myriad thuds and wet tearing noises of claws gashing the ground around us. The creatures were eager and hurried, and whatever fear we felt when their footsteps first surrounded us began to dissipate as they went on.

And on. And on.

Neither of us were willing to speak, but I thought, *How many are there? I've heard hundreds...thousands. How many can there be? How can we hope to do anything against this horde?*

My heart was quickening, and I took a deep breath as silently as I could. I reminded myself that absolutely everything, from the very first moment I'd laid my hands on the gem, to this instant here where I was surrounded by an army of monsters and sitting next to a girl who'd never seen the sun until hours ago—all of it was *insane*. It was insane for me to be here, plotting an invasion of my own with an army of two. It was insane for me to have survived this long, insane for Atell to have reunited with me, insane for the two of us to have made it this far. There was no making sense of it or wishing for the best. We just had to do it, and if we died trying, then at least we'd borrowed a whole heap of time in the process.

I found Atell's hand, and we sat there and let hell funnel around us.

Between the sounds thudding off the walls and with how quietly Atell was able to move, I didn't notice that she got closer to me until I felt her breath on my shoulder. I felt her heat even amidst the warmth of our alcove, and for once I knew what I wanted.

I found her in the darkness and I kissed her.

I couldn't see a thing, could just feel the warmth of her skin and the touch of her kiss as she gave it back. I brought a hand up her side and shoulder before I got my fingers on her nape and pulled her in closer till we both pressed against the wall. Her tongue was strong and tasted faintly of iron. Her hands moved from my arms to my chest and she put her weight on me, holding still for a long moment.

We broke the kiss and caught our mutual breath as quietly as we could. The world raged on outside. Even with her forehead pressed to mine, I couldn't see her.

She didn't say a word; just kissed me again. And this time, when it broke, we were alone.

I lit my gem softly so that I could see her eyes, wide and green. Gorgeous, and tense. Our breath filled the air.

I said, "It's time."

Chapter Forty-Eight

I left our hiding spot first, shoving the makeshift door inch by inch. Each grating scrape of stone on stone was torturously loud. I made the smallest possible space, shoved my pack through, then followed suit, leaving a good amount of my skin behind on the rough edges. Atell slipped through with no problem.

It was almost pitch-black outside, with the stars and moon covered by clouds. I quieted the gem once we were out, not wanting to draw any attention in case there were lingering monsters. Our eyes were fairly well-adjusted from being tucked away in the alcove, so we could see enough to run north and not worry about tripping over some errant rock.

The stone and grass fell into the distance behind us amid the sounds of the monsters doing their work, and it wasn't long before we were approaching the castle. Our steps crunched on the dead grass. I pushed my lower lip out and blew cool air up onto my face. It was hot near this thing, hot enough to make sweat spring out on my forehead.

With no other way to see, I lit the gem, casting the light forward to shine it on the black wall before us. It was like a sheet of rock, a cliff shooting almost straight up, so high that I could raise my light up and up and up and not see the top.

I swung the light to the left, then the right. "I don't see a door."

"The monsters had to come from somewhere," Atell said.

We moved down the wall. At first we walked, and then we ran as more and more of the wall passed by us with no means of entry. We went the other way, covering a half-mile. Nothing.

"This is ridiculous," I said, growing angry as our time slipped away. "Where did they come from? How do they get back in?"

"Something only they can see?" Atell suggested. "Underground?"

But the ground wasn't disturbed, and we both knew it. I strapped the gem to my pack and walked to the wall. It was so hot that we'd kept our distance, but there had to be something we were missing, some detail that would make itself known to us.

I braced myself and laid my hand on it, tentative, expecting a burn. But just as I touched it, the wall peeled open before my eyes. *Peeled,* like someone had stuck a knife through a hunk of flesh and yanked it down. There was a disgusting sound of wrenching flesh and a blast of hot air, and I was suddenly staring at a dark doorway that led into the castle.

"God," I croaked, my fingers hanging limp. If I had been holding the gem, I would have dropped it onto the grass. "The whole thing...the whole thing really is alive. It's all flesh. All of it."

Hungry, Jost? Cut a chunk out of this doorframe and cook it up.

Gorge rose up inside me and I swallowed it down. Every single thing I came across out here was worse than what I had left behind. I wished someone in Cartha had cared about me enough to stop me from going out into the labyrinth over and over and over. Now I was out, and this was where it had led me?

If hell manifested itself in front of me, it would look like this.

"Jost." Atell's voice in my ear; her hand on my shoulder. Shaky, like me. "It's okay. We knew it...that it was alive."

I took a breath and got my composure back. "Sorry. It's just a lot. I'm picturing what this must look like, the whole thing, if we were to climb it, you know? I mean...how big would it be? How much of the world is taken over by this?"

Atell shook her head. "I don't know. I never read anything about this. Never heard a story about it."

"Even the wielders didn't know," I said, still staring into the dark, wet depths of the castle. "They would have told me that something like this was out here."

"Maybe," Atell said. "Or maybe that's why they were going in the other direction."

Orrin and Derrick, fleeing? Maybe. It might be the smart thing to do. What did they really hope to find in the labyrinth that would let them go up against this?

Will you knock it off?

"It's just a big pile of meat," I said, perhaps the largest understatement of my life. "If it was...if this whole thing was the One, the king of the monsters, we'd be dead already, right? It can't be. We build our walls out of stone and the monster builds its walls out of flesh. That's all. And we're going to go inside and we're going to find its bedroom and we're going to kill it."

I turned to Atell and smiled and hoped I didn't look crazy. "Let's do this."

Her hand slid off my shoulder and I walked forward, her steps falling in close behind mine. The doorway's opening stretched right to the ground, as inviting as could be except for everything about it. How big was this thing—this place? For all I knew, we'd be cooked alive inside before we managed to explore half of it.

I finally walked in, setting my foot onto the floor inside and finding it stiff as stone, which eased my spirit some. My boots even made a solid *thud* stepping inside.

"It's okay so far," I said, turning back to Atell. "And it's—"

I only caught a glimpse of the shock on her face before the door disappeared, closing back up and leaving me alone inside the castle.

"Hey!" I spun and pounded my fists and the wall, which was just as unforgiving and solid as the floor. I hammered it, the sound muted. When my fists did nothing, I pulled my dagger out and stabbed it. The tip went in a half-inch and gave no more.

I swore and let the dagger clatter to the ground, calling Atell's name. I pressed my ear to the wall but couldn't hear anything except the beating of my own heart.

"Shit." It was no use, just like trying to hack away at those tentacles in the Pooled Woods. She'd been locked out. At least she hadn't been cut in half by the door.

It had all happened very fast, but it really seemed like the door had opened for *me*, and once I was in...well, that was it. Why? Maybe it could sense the magic in my gem, and it wanted it. It was setting a trap, a lure, to get me close enough to take my magic and then crush my puny body.

Fine, then. It wouldn't have let me in without the magic anyway, so that was the coin I was laying on the table. That and my life. At least Atell didn't have to risk hers in the same bargain.

Except...

I picked my dagger up from the ground. She was trapped outside at night, with the threat of daylight on the horizon in a matter of hours. When it came, the monsters would be driven back to the castle. And they would surely kill us both—her first, trapped alone on the outside. She couldn't go back to our hiding spot. The rock was way too heavy to move on her own, and that was if she could even find it in the dark.

"Easy. I just have to find the One, kill it, and get out of here before daylight." When I knew things really were completely hopeless, it made it easier to be sarcastic. I turned around and got my first really good look at the place, trying not to picture Atell scrambling around the wall outside, looking for a way in.

I was in a larger space that branched out into various rounded tunnels, like I was inside of a giant black heart. At first I thought it was all pitch-black darkness, an environment that I found strangely comforting after being confronted with the opposite after so long. But as I watched, narrow tracings of blue light came into existence, wound through the floors, the walls, and the curved ceiling that was fifty feet above my head. They were like narrow veins, and when one's light faded, another's came to life. In the vast space, they didn't offer much light beyond seeing the general shape of the walls, so I lit my gem to see better.

The pattern of blue light was reminiscent of very slow breathing, fading in and out, disappearing almost completely before coming back. The thought made the hairs on my neck tingle.

It wasn't as hot inside as I expected it to be. It was still warm, enough to make me pull at my collar, but it was nothing like the inside of the Turtle had been.

"Lucky me," I muttered.

It was quiet here. I heard my voice very well, and I sounded scared.

I chose to just go straight. The tunnels were all different sizes, some so small I'd be forced to crawl through, and some too small even for that option. Others were cavernous, tall enough to build a house in, and then another couple of houses on top of the first one. Keeping track was laughable, I realized, as I considered pulling out my pen and paper and marking my trail. There were hundreds of ways to go. It would take me years to even start a map.

I clutched my gem in one hand. Looking ahead, I knew there was only one way I'd get through this. I needed the magic. All of it. There was no need to be afraid of it anymore—either it would kill me, or I'd die here without it. If it found some other magic and got hungry, so be it. More for me. Us.

I'd kept a close eye on the magic ever since Iyes, constantly aware, constantly checking at it and pulling it back. Now I held the gem in front of my eyes and spoke to it like it could hear me.

"You are unleashed," I said.

I closed my eyes and felt its power stir.

Chapter Forty-Nine

I'd done this warily before—just brushed myself across the gem's consciousness. A silly word, because it wasn't alive any more than a plant growing towards the sun was alive. But I could *feel* it there when I tried, and it was terrifying. Like I was holding an entire ocean in my hand, an endless pit in my palm that could swallow me whole and leave me drowning in darkness forever. The feeling of standing backward on the edge of a cliff while the fall stretched out under my heels.

The gem reached out to me like an animal sniffing meat and deciding if it was fit for consumption. It touched whatever part of my soul it was able to touch, and I felt that connection, bright and hot, like when I'd first laid my fingertips on the gem.

My eyes were closed, but the gem shone so brightly I could practically see through my eyelids. Its heat crept into me, starting in my fingers and palms and traveling up my arm like it was hot pitch in my veins.

The pain was slow-moving and intense. I gritted my teeth so hard I expected them to chip, squeezing strained tears out of my eyes.

Is this what the people of Iyes felt when the gem tried to consume them? What an awful way to die.

I tried not to picture their pain-wracked faces, and failed.

This wasn't me trying to find some wielders in a hole, or confirm true north through the labyrinth. I was standing in a nightmare tunnel spooled from hell. To make it through this place, for my *finding* to be strong enough, I needed more from the gem. And for that, the gem needed more from me.

Just hopefully not all of me.

I let the fiery pain spread and tried to stay silent, thinking and hoping the gem could hear me, could understand: *Don't kill me.*

Silence, pain, and yellow light, tinged red by the flesh of my eyelids. My brain felt waterlogged; overwhelmed. But I understood something, even if that something wasn't words or ideas or thoughts. The magic was creeping over me like hot tar, falling and folding into every crevice, learning me. Knowing me. I felt regret and it knew my feelings. It didn't care for my pain, but it probed at my intent with purpose. It was judging me, as thoroughly as anything possibly could.

I was enveloped, in far too deep to go back. I let it go on because I didn't have any choice, and when it finally withdrew, I felt weight lift off my chest and I breathed like I hadn't had the chance to take a breath in the last five minutes. In an instant, I went from being completely smothered to feeling wholly alone.

I opened my eyes and the gem was dark.

"What..." I muttered, turning it around in my hand. Had it rejected me? No, it couldn't. We were bonded, whether I liked it or not, whether the magic liked it or not. That was something I knew from Atell, from the book, and from the wielders too. The magic and I would live and die together, unless it was taken by someone else.

It was then, as I stared into the silent gem, that the floor beneath my feet tilted forward. I stumbled, leaning backward, and then fell down, sliding toward the tunnel in front of me.

What the—

Grasping the gem with one hand, I scrabbled for something to grab onto, but my fingers only found the ground, bent under me and pushing me forward like a great beast's tongue swallowing me up.

I slid forward and then a hole opened up in the ground before me. I managed to tuck the gem in my pocket as I fell in and got my fingers around the lip, holding myself in the air. It was warm, all the blackness around me heating up. Beneath my fingers, the lip flattened and my grip slid off and I fell, yelling until I hit the ground and the air was knocked out of me. Then I was sliding again, a helpless doll in the grasp of a much larger player.

So this is it, I thought as I descended into darkness and the walls around me grew more and more narrow. *It found me, and it's going to kill me.*

There was no stopping it; anytime I reached out for something, it wasn't there. Anytime I caught onto something, it disappeared. I stopped trying and let it take me, catching images of the world around me through the breath of the light veins. It slid me down, then forward, then dropped me on my feet and pushed me onward with a wall at my back, over and over and over again for interminable minutes until at last I was pushed forward on my stomach, shielding my face with my hands, into the first room in some time that wasn't moving beneath me.

With the world around me finally stopped, I stood. My breath came heavy and fast, and I immediately reached for the gem, pulling it from my pocket and trying to light it. Nothing. My pack was still whole, though anything inside had taken a serious beating, and my daggers were still strapped to my legs. But they wouldn't do me any good if I couldn't see a damned thing. What the hell was wrong with the gem?

I squeezed it again and was about to swear at it to see if that would help when it was suddenly plucked from my hand.

Before I could react, the room of rockflesh where I stood was lit by a network of blue veins like a million streaks of lightning across the sky. I saw my hand, empty. I saw the vast stretch of the room, like a long, flattened dome, black and cut with blue light, curving up above my head.

And there, just a few feet away from me, stood what could only be the One.

Chapter Fifty

The monster reminded me of the mountains. The castle had looked like a mountain range, but we knew that it wasn't. In that same way, the One looked human.

But I knew that it wasn't.

At a glance, passing in the streets of Cartha, maybe I'd be fooled. It was tall, but not towering. It wore a long shock of white hair that went down past its shoulders and for all I knew, well down its back.

But its face was *just* too narrow, *just* too pointed, to be human. A nose like a blade, eyes that were slitted one moment, wide open the next, and too-white around their black irises. Like a child's drawing of eyes. Perfectly hairless, so smooth it was inconceivable that anything might grow from this creature's skin besides the white hair from its head. It didn't have eyelashes. The skin inside its nostrils was the same creamy color as its nose and face. It looked like it was wearing a dark, formal suit, but I soon realized that was also its skin, demarcated in an approximation of clothing. Its arms hung too far below the waist. Its legs didn't meet the ground, but were part of it, like it had sprouted up out of the castle. It didn't have feet. When it closed its mouth, the lips disappeared completely.

It was haunted, something I could never unsee. Something out of a nightmare. Something out of hell.

It smiled at me, showing the teeth of a human but having far, far too many. And it spoke.

"Welcome home...Jost."

Chapter Fifty-One

I didn't react to its words, the way its voice billowed out of its mouth and didn't match how its lips moved. My dagger in my hand, I struck. It was the fastest I'd ever moved.

In a simple gesture, it brought up my gem in its long-fingered hand. The point of my dagger struck it and the blade broke in half.

Pain jolted up my arm. I dropped the hilt to the ground and reached for my other dagger and then it laid its hand on me, long fingers draping across my forearm. It didn't have fingernails, and the tips were pointed. Though it didn't grip me particularly hard, I couldn't wriggle my arm free.

"Stop this," it said, and its voice was deep and misplaced. It sounded like someone else was inside its chest, speaking for it.

"What are you?" I said, my words weak.

"So you try to kill things without even...learning their name." The smile returned, and the creature shoved me backward.

That tiny motion from its hands pushed me through the air. I landed on my heels and fell hard on my back, my pack taking the worst of the fall.

I scrambled to my feet, but it didn't approach me. It just watched as I slipped my other dagger free and pointed it outward.

"The One?" I asked.

"So you found Hider," the monster responded, and its smile grew wider, showing more teeth yet. "I waited a long...time for my creations to grow. He was fast. You are slower, but so...much more accomplished."

I exhaled through my nose, and pointing the dagger now, I saw that it was steady. I didn't shake, now that I had a moment to think. This thing held my gem with no problem, and the gem was still unlit. I didn't believe that my magic had taken me here.

"You brought me here," I said to it. "Why?"

The monster stood eerily still. Its mouth moved only after it had begun to speak. "Hider told you nothing. It must have been for good...reason. He had others with him?"

"How do you know about Hider?"

"I had...hoped he would tell you. This would be less confrontational." The One lifted its arm and pointed an inhuman finger at me. "I will be...clear. The old humans called me Titheu when they were alive, and I kept it. I am Titheu. You are one of my children.

"The...first. Jost. Born of my limb and the life of seventy-one humans. Sent first into the human maze to find a stronghold and report back...to me. Your journey was too long. I thought you lost, until you found the seal gem. Now you come to report...or so I had thought."

My mouth was open, and I snapped it shut. I'd pictured many different things happening if I got to this place, but this wasn't one of them. That the One...Titheu? That it would know my name. That it would speak to me, and that it would tell me things. Things that were crazy.

But it knew. It knew about Hider. And Hider and I both were accidental magical bonds, something that would kill—

Kill what? A human?

"Learn it," Titheu said, "if it has been unlearned."

I never knew my parents. I couldn't remember anything about my life before I was eight years old. Where I came from. No one knew, not even Gwin.

"I..." My grip faltered; the dagger wiggled. I clenched it again. "I'm not like you. I'm a human. I grew up in Cartha..."

"Cartha," Titheu breathed, mouth unmoving. "I presumed you found a...city. To live so long, to grow. It would be the broken seal. The one I hold here."

The gem, still in its hand.

"So it's true," I said. "That magic was keeping Cartha safe. And Iyes. And I took it away."

"Unexpected," Titheu said. "But welcome. I did not believe...you could touch the seal. But now that you have carried this, I can...too. The magic was transformed to accommodate your form. Your being. And mine."

What is happening?

"You are in doubt. I did not predict...the memories would be so far gone." Titheu paused, lowering its hand. "Defects with the first are to be expected. I used too many humans with...you. The others responded better. But you are one of few to...bond with magic. Your return is good for me."

Titheu turned its head slightly, looking past me to the wall. It let the gem fall from its hand and it rolled across the floor all the way to my boots, nudging my toe.

I bent down and picked it up, and to my surprise, it lit, bathing me in yellow light and casting a soft circle on the floor. Had Titheu been suppressing it?

"Your fear is precious, but unnecessary," Titheu said, turning its head back to me. "You know I do not wish to kill you. You must learn again of the grander purpose you...serve. This is one of many concentrated magics we must gather before we can take the...maze and the rest."

There was a new kind of sick inside me, something I didn't think was possible. It sat curling in my stomach. I looked away from the monster's eyes and down into my gem, where a small reflection of my face curved around the yellow surface.

"I'm one of you," I said, watching my lips move in the reflection. "That's why I could walk through the Walls without getting killed. The monsters didn't care."

"Yes," Titheu said, breathing the word out. "They fear you. You are greater than the empty guard could ever be."

Some black claws had attacked me, but not very many. If Titheu's goal was to gather magic and its progeny had the same intent, then some may have been drawn to me because of the gem. I didn't have to kill more than a few to scare them off.

I remembered the black claw in Cartha slithering by me while my heart stopped in fear. It hadn't even noticed me—the gem, perhaps? Of course. The seal magic, once hiding the city, hid me for that time. Before I took over the magic and learned how to use it. Maybe its residual touch even hid Gwin so that he could escape. But once he left Cartha, that magic was gone.

That first black claw I had killed—it must have come for the gem while the gem was still figuring me out. A short crossroads that almost got me killed, and gave me scars for the rest of my life. The gem didn't hide me in the maze. Maybe it couldn't.

And the Turtle...Orrin had been right. He'd noticed right away, while I was blind to it. Hider would have known, too, and of course he wouldn't have wanted to incite Orrin against me...

It was too much to think about.

Deep breath.

What was I going to do, question this creature? As if it would have any reason to lie to me so plainly. As though if it wanted me dead, it couldn't have killed me the moment I knocked on its door.

So I wasn't a human, but some kind of part-monster put together like a mud sculpture? The One waited for me here with open arms, ready to take me back into the fold and rejoin it in its conquest of man?

It made me sick to consider, no matter how slim the odds were, no matter how much I didn't want to believe it. That, in essence, I was part of this plague spreading over the world. That there were parts of me I shared with the black claws. With the giant monster that crushed Cartha.

With Titheu.

My life had not been easy. I hadn't been happy in Cartha, outside of some fleeting moments. I trusted almost no one, I was quick to anger and lash out, and I craved the call of the labyrinth despite its dangers. Were these parts of me truly *me*—truly *Jost*—or parts of Titheu? Parts of the monster I was learning about—the monster that I was?

Do you believe it?

I didn't. I did. I wasn't sure.

These things destroyed Cartha. They killed your friends.

I never had friends.

They forced humanity to hide in the Walls to survive. They took everything from them.

And what had I done for my fellow man? Sold them meat and put them all at risk with my jaunts through the Walls, until I inevitably invited disaster.

Now Titheu wants to take your humanity away from you.

My shock bled into anger, the feeling I was familiar with, the one I'd turned to all my life. I looked at the cool, emotionless face of Titheu and knew I couldn't be like this thing. Not in the way it described. Not its child, nor its lackey, nor its monster slave, thralled to do its bidding.

The one advantage I had was that Titheu didn't know that. I needed to keep my own cool, accept its words without thinking about it too much—for now.

I was terrified to learn more, but I needed to. So, fine.

We could talk.

Chapter Fifty-Two

I set my jaw and lowered my dagger, meeting Titheu's eyes once again. I let the gem shine on. Its light was comforting; familiar. The only thing here that was a part of my world.

This is your world, Jost.

No. I had to keep it together.

I walked toward the monster, which watched me impassively.

"How many are there?" I asked it. "How many like me?"

The smile was gone, its mouth once more that thin line that disappeared into the smooth flesh of its face, and then re-emerged to say, "You were the first I made. After you...a good deal more. I had to improve the craft. Making humans is difficult and takes time and captured...lives. Hider was the first I truly perfected."

"But Hider is so much younger than me."

"One of your defects," Titheu said, and its smile curved upward. "Too human. You are not meant to age or grow as you have been doing. Perhaps something I...can fix."

Immortality? Maybe being a monster wouldn't be so bad after all.

As though I'd want to live forever in this world.

"Cartha," I said, my mouth drying up as I approached the question I really wanted the answer to. "The city. What happened to the people? I was there. There were hardly any bodies in the maze. The city was empty. What happened to them?"

Titheu blinked, very, very slowly. "They are with the horde, like the rest. With no magical protection, we are able...to take them into assimilation, and kill the resistant."

I almost lost my composure then. I bit the inside of my lip bloody.

Assimilation?

"They turn into things like me?"

"Simply horde," Titheu said with another slow blink. "Empty guard. The large ones are made new entities. The smaller ones are merged...into other entities, or many into one new entity. I have little use for small horde. My children are...specially crafted for me. Your mission is grander than the horde."

Not dead. Worse. Assimilated. All of them, so suddenly? Iyes, too? No dead bodies there, no one strong enough to resist...hell on earth, they are all monsters now, I might have killed them myself, I might have eaten them—

I couldn't dwell on that. I couldn't. It would kill me.

"So you and your monsters can't handle raw magic, is that it?" My voice shook despite my efforts. I was close now, close enough to reach out and touch the thing. I felt heaviness in the air, like a storm was above my head. "You made these half-human, half-monster hybrids—"

—like me—

"—to go and fetch it for you. Yet you've already destroyed so much of the maze."

"It is all a matter of strategy, Jost," Titheu breathed. "Too much of me was lost tearing down the stone risers with the magic protecting them. Too much...time was taken. And when we do come to where the cities are, there will...be far more magic."

"Then I can keep mine," I said. "To use in the maze."

"For now."

"I understand."

I was close enough now. I had to assume it was telling the truth. And as complex and horrifying as that was, it didn't make my goal here any different.

Kill this monster and get the hell out of this place.

I swung at its head, bringing the dagger in a high arc with my left hand. I strayed from its black armor, from its hidden mouth, and aimed for its right eye. My charade must have been convincing enough, because the tiniest flicker of disbelief actually flashed across the One's face before the tip of my dagger found its eye and slid into it with a satisfying squelch of flesh until it was buried.

I had the chance to form a narrow grin before Titheu spoke.

"It is a shame."

It shoved me again, but this time it was no tease. Its palm smashed my chest and my ribs creaked. Still clenching the dagger, I ripped it free of its eye as I flew backward, tumbling and rolling across the ground. I managed not to stab myself, but the rest of me ached like I'd fallen down a cliff.

Titheu was not bothered by the dagger to the eye. There wasn't even any blood; no wince of pain; no evidence that I'd done anything.

I got to my feet.

This is bad.

"I had thought the first was lost," Titheu said again, "so your death will...not hinder us. Hider and the others will be more than sufficient. Still, a...shame."

I looked around, spreading my light and taking in my surroundings. But where could I run, where could I go, when the thing I was fighting was part of the room around me? Even as Titheu moved toward me, its legs did not walk. It simply glided, its root to the floor traveling with it.

Nowhere to run, Jost—so you fight.

Its arms were outstretched and its fingers were longer now, darker and more pointed. Weapons to impale me. I couldn't just wait; I would have to strike first.

But when I tried to move, my feet didn't give. I looked down to see that the floor had grown around them, covering the tops of my boots. I grunted, trying to pull free and not moving one single inch.

There was no humor in Titheu's eyes while it approached me. I threw my dagger at its head, but throwing knives was something I'd never practiced. The monster didn't even bother evading the poor throw; the weapon bounced harmlessly off its face.

I wished that somehow, some way, I could scream at Atell to run, to run and keep running until she reached the end of the world. But I would never get the chance to tell her that now.

The One was here before me, the gem's bright light casting itself into every crevice and seam of the creature. Its hair, long and white, glistened like a corona around its head. Its boneless movements reached for me.

I wondered, *How could I ever think this thing was human?*

When it pressed the needles of its fingers into my chest, cutting through my shirt, cutting through the strap of my pack, cutting through my skin, I lifted the gem and shoved it forward into the monster's neck, finding the hollow beneath its pointed chin. I thought of Hider's roots, pinning me. How I'd been inches from death, and how I must have felt, then, the exact same way that I did now. Desperate. Trapped.

The gem glowed brightly beneath the monster's head, and Titheu paused, its fingers still resting beneath the surface of my skin. The magic flared, a miniature sun inches from my eyes, forcing me to shut them and turn away. But still, I willed that little yellow ball, pouring myself into it, leaning into the flow of energy that was starting to make my blood boil in my veins and kill me from the inside out.

If you need me, gem—

"Then take me!" I grunted through gritted teeth, tasting blood and feeling it drip down my stomach and soak into my shirt. I couldn't even feel my hand anymore. Maybe it had been burned away. By inches, my body seemed to disappear from my sense of being, like I was just a pair of tightly-shut eyes floating above the ground and shying away from the blinding light before me.

The world was dark and bright at the same time, for a long time.

When I was able to open my eyes, the flash of yellow light stayed burned in for a moment. I blinked a few times and the world returned. My sight returned. The pain in my chest returned, burning and dripping like a melting candle.

Titheu stood before me, halted however-briefly by the surge of magic from my gem, but not broken. Not burned, nor shattered like the roots had been. Its expressionless face did not change. It raised its other hand up, the long fingers getting longer and sharper and pointing directly at my face.

I knew that two would slide into my eyes, one into my forehead, two into the ridges of my cheekbones, and—seeing now that this monster actually had seven fingers and not five—the last two would pierce my throat.

I let the gem drop from my fingers and accepted my death.

Pain flared in my chest and the walls around me rumbled. But—no, that wasn't it. It was the sound of footsteps, the sound of someone running.

Someone else was here.

Chapter Fifty-Three

The first thing I saw was the blade of the sword, coming down from above and cleaving straight through Titheu's arm. Its pointed claws slipped from my flesh and its dismembered limb fell to the floor, which swallowed it like a pit of tar.

I recoiled, bringing a hand to my chest and pressing into the hot blood leaking there. Titheu glided backward, the flat stump of its arm starting to bubble.

Atell stood between us. The tip of Derrick's sword plunged into the floor. Around it, the dark meat of the castle shied away, writhing and wriggling. She pulled it free.

"Jost," she panted. Her brow was coated in sweat and her hands were trembling, even the one wrapped tightly around the hilt of the sword. Black, tacky blood was sprayed across her body. She'd been through hell to get here. But she was here.

I put my bloody hands on her and held her up. She was ready to collapse.

"Have to...go," she said.

"Atell." I spoke her name with concern, gratitude, worry and a million other things mixed in, forgetting everything else. I took the hilt of the sword and she let me pull it from her hand. The blade was filthy. For her to be carrying this heavy thing, to have swung it however many times she did...it was no wonder she was trembling.

I left my other hand on her shoulder and looked past her to Titheu, whose severed arm was hissing and glowing like there was a blazing fire there we couldn't see. That was when I realized the heavy sword weighed hardly anything in my hand, and that same whitish glow that consumed the stump of Titheu's arm was spread beneath my fingers on the grip. It traced across the hilt and traveled up the blade in a neat curve that followed the sharp edge of the sword.

"There's magic in this," I whispered, and as I said that, my gem radiated too, rolling towards the tip of the sword in an attempt to make contact. I stopped it with my boot and picked it up, securing it in the harness.

"Yes," Atell said, and then, "I think it's eating me."

Shit. That was why she was so weak.

"Just hold on a little longer," I said, drawing the sword up from the floor and leveling it at Titheu. "I'll finish this and we are out of here."

I ran at the One. It was clear as day that it was in pain, that this sword had an effect that my daggers and my magic couldn't hope to match, and now was the time to thrust the blade through its heart and end this.

The blade was feather-light, and my strike was true, driving forward while a scream ripped from my lips. The sword pushed through the monster's skin like butter, right where the heart would be in a man.

But Titheu was not human.

The wound burst white around the blade, and the sound that came from Titheu's motionless mouth was horrific, a keening howl that shook my eyeballs in their sockets. The monster melted around the blade, simply fell into the floor like it was dumped from a bucket. Its form disappeared into the flesh of its castle.

Very suddenly, it was quiet. Yet I didn't feel like celebrating.

I rushed back to Atell. "Are you okay?"

She nodded and asked, "Was that it? The One?"

"Yeah."

"Dead?"

"I..." I glanced back at where Titheu had stood. "I don't think so."

"We have to find it," Atell said, reaching for the sword. "We have to—"

She fell, almost onto the blade. I drew it away at the last moment and caught her with my free hand. She was heavier now, with muscle on her bones, but still so thin and light.

"No," I said, pulling her to her feet. "We stay here, we die. Titheu—the One isn't just a monster. It's this whole place, and I don't know how to kill it. It's hurt, but if we stay here, it will come back and crush us."

The idea of sacrificing my life in a vain attempt to kill Titheu had its merits minutes ago, when it was just me. Now it seemed stupid and wasteful. If I was going to fight Titheu, I needed to know more. I needed to *be* more. And I had an idea how.

But first we had to get out of here alive.

Chapter Fifty-Four

C ome on," I said, pulling at her hand until I was sure she
was able to move well enough on her own. Even being
away from the sword for just a little while seemed to be helping. "We
have to get out."

"How?" Atell asked, looking around the place like she was
seeing it for the first time.

"How did you get in?" Without waiting for an answer, I ran
into the closest tunnel to us with Atell behind me.

"I just cut through the wall," Atell said, catching her breath a
little more. "After we got separated. I—I panicked a little. I cut at the
wall, but it wasn't working. Until the magic woke up in the sword."

"You bonded with it?"

Down the hall, running in the sphere of light that my gem gave
to us. I had no idea where I was going, but I had a feeling towards
where south was. I followed any slope that led upward, remembering
my fall on the way down here.

"No," she breathed, "it's just in the sword. Imbued. If we
bonded it wouldn't be trying to eat me."

I didn't feel any sensation like that, even with the sword
gripped between my bloody fingers, so I presumed that my own magic
was holding it at bay.

Around us, it appeared that the castle of the One was asleep, in that it was acting like a normal structure and not moving, and its intermittent veins of light were dead and dull in the walls. The gem was our only light now, but it was plenty.

I trusted my sense of direction, but we were still buried under tons and tons of mountain-flesh. I assumed Titheu had drawn me to its lair inside the castle, and that since I had come from the south, it would have no reason to wrap me around the back or side of its cavernous hangout before bringing me in. It would have just brought me to the side I was closest to. Right?

It was a very small hook to hang our lives on, and it was strained by many other things. I prayed it would not break.

Up, through, following curves that we had no choice but to follow. At one point, we reached a bend in a tunnel that I was certain was taking us away from where needed to go. I felt it in my gut and even in the invisible bond that threaded me with the gem.

"Stop," I said to Atell, halting before the turn and raising the sword. It worked for Atell, and it worked just fine slicing through Titheu's chest, so—

Schk!

I sank the sword into the wall, cutting across it in a broad diagonal. It opened up like an animal hide, though the sword didn't feel magically strong to me.

Still, it worked as a tool. I sliced away thick strips until it was a big enough hole for us to step through, into a new tunnel that led straight south.

Once we were through the hole, the world around us came to life in a slow, rumbling way. The veined lights breathed into existence, and the whole place seemed to shift, like the entire castle was rousing but we could barely feel it.

"Whoops," I said under my breath.

I woke it up.

"Run!"

I think we both said it at the same time. We tore down the long hall, our feet smacking against the ground, our breath coming in gasps. There was no time to stop; no time to slow down. If it found us in here, we would die. There would be no chance to fight back. Probably not even time to scream.

Panting, running forward with the sword held out in front of me, I tried to imagine how far we'd come. Were we close to the end?

The end? Jost, this isn't some big building. It's not even a labyrinth. There is no end, and there is no way out. You have to make it yourself.

The path was ending—really ending. No left and no right, just a block of black, blue-veined flesh. A dead end, the first one we'd seen in this entire place.

I brought the sword up again and slashed through, knowing it was both the wrong thing and only thing to do. If taking down one wall was enough to stir Titheu from its wounded retreat, then another would tell it where we were. The alternative was to run in circles until it found us anyway.

We squeezed through the gap and the wall bled on us, steaming hot. The air around us warmed as Titheu continued to stir. Glancing back, I saw the wound in the wall close up before my eyes, strings of flesh stretching to knit it together.

"We have to be close," Atell said, between heavy breaths. "We have to. I know it."

And I believed her. I'm some kind of optimist, even while the world collapses around me.

"Here!" she cried, thrusting a finger at the wall we ran towards. "It's—no light!"

The wall ahead of us, where the path split flatly left and right, wasn't veined. I cast my gem-light forward onto it and just saw black, ridged flesh like the dried meat hung in the circles of Cartha.

"I'll cut it," I panted.

If this isn't it, we're found.

My chest hurt and the waist of my pants was soaked with my blood.

No more running.

The blue light swept behind us, not alive in its breathing pattern anymore, but rather an arch sliding down the hall, looking for us. Trying to focus and shine on our sweaty, bloody flesh so that Titheu could see us. It knew we were here, and once it pinpointed us, it would flatten us in the walls of its body.

I knew this, because I could see it happening behind us. The tunnel collapsed inward, faster than we could run.

At least we'll die fast, I thought, and I raised the sword.

Chapter Fifty-Five

The blue light, so much brighter now, swept over us as I cut through the wall, screaming in fury, in need, in agony as the wounds on my chest ripped open wider. I let the fire burn and pour out through my blood and drew the blade all the way down to the ground, and when the slice in the wall opened up, the air behind us rushed forward in a big swell, escaping the castle.

It was the end of the line. We'd made it.

I squinted my eyes, the light above us shining bright and hot.

To my horror, the gap in the wall reached tendrils of black flesh across itself and pulled, healing. Closing us in. Behind us, the tunnel flattened, smashing the walls together less like flesh and more like sheets of rock. It was so loud that I couldn't hear what Atell was saying; could just see her lips moving frantically.

She was grabbing at the tendrils, and they must have been hot because steam rose from her clenched fists. She pulled at them, trying to stop the healing. Outside, past her, I could see the night sky and the moonlit grass. The ether was dotted with stars.

I didn't have the strength for it, but I swung the sword again, narrowly missing her. I cut through the tendrils and they snapped back into the walls. I dropped the sword and shoved Atell forward through the hole, using my weight to push her because my shoulders didn't have the strength. I was the weakest I'd ever felt, my life slipping through the gashes Titheu had left in my chest.

But I pushed her out, and she fell forward onto the grass. The tendrils came back like dungeon bars. I kicked the sword out through the gap. Better for her to have it than it be lost in here with me.

She was shaking her head, yelling something, but I still couldn't hear. The world was loud and it filled my head. More tendrils came, cutting away my sight of her neck, her torso, her cheeks. Her eyes. Her hand moved and something came hurtling at me, and it stuck into my boot.

My dagger, the one that wasn't broken. I remembered throwing it at Titheu. So she had picked it up.

I pulled it from my boot, blinking. My mind was fuzzy and my ears rang with the crashing sounds of hell, like the Walls themselves were falling apart around me. It was so hard to think. But the grip felt familiar and warm in my hand. The sword was nice, but these daggers had raised me.

It was Gwin who had given them to me, a trade I thought was fair at the time. Later I learned I'd gotten fleeced. But I got him back since then. Plenty of times—

Focus! Cut it, Jost. It's new flesh. It's not strong like rest.

I held the dagger point-down and drew it up, getting in close to the wall. The heat was intense, so hot that I couldn't breathe. I found the center of the tendrils and I cut down, and when one hand wasn't enough I brought up two and there it was, the give, the first snapping of the tendril that led to more, to momentum bringing me down through the rest, and either through perfect timing or pure exhaustion I fell forward and out, catching a tendril on the hip. It left a burn mark across my pants.

I landed on Derrick's sword, thankfully the flat of the blade. The cool outside air enveloped me. My ears were able to hear again as the breeze curled inside them.

Atell grabbed my collar and I grabbed the grass and we pulled, moving farther away from the wall. With whatever vestiges of energy remained between us, we stumbled and crawled away from the castle, leaving a messy trail in the grass. The wound in the wall closed, and nothing came out.

Maybe Titheu thought we'd been killed. Maybe the monster was looking for us still. But we were out.

Somewhat revitalized by fresh air and the thrill of escape, we made it to some decrepit part of the labyrinth and leaned our backs against cold stone, able to breathe for the first time in too long a while. I let her take the sword back and sheathe it, its hunger apparently sated.

In the distance, the destructive sounds of the monsters filled the horizon.

"In my pack," I said, my voice weak. "There's gut. Silver needle. Can you..."

"Yes," Atell said, and she helped me slip my pack off and dug through it until she found what she needed. She tore open my shirt so she could see my wounds, five narrow but deep cuts.

"I can't see the bone," Atell said. "That's good. It probably feels worse than it is."

"Feels pretty bad," I managed. "Thought I might die."

"I've seen worse," Atell told me, handing me my water skin. "Here, drink. As much as you can. You didn't lose that much blood. Really. The heat and the running made it worse. Someone in Iyes fell off the wall and broke both his legs and cut open his head. That was a lot of blood."

"That makes me feel better," I said.

"Shut up and drink." The sting of the needle followed her words, and I tried to move as little as I could while she sewed me up like a piece of fabric. My bloody, ruined shirt stained the grass next to me. I swallowed water, then swallowed more when I realized how good it felt going down my raw throat.

"There," Atell said, finishing up with dressing her work. "Not bad at all."

"Thanks," I said. "For this. And finding my dagger. And...well, everything, really."

"I can't believe you," Atell admonished, cleaning the needle and stowing it back in my bag. I took it from her and dug through for a clean shirt. "You were just going to shove me out and die? What's the matter with you?"

"That's a big question," I said. I wasn't bleeding very much, so I slipped on my shirt. "Not sure how to answer it."

"Stop giving up," she told me. "You're stronger than you think."

I gave her a little nod and she shook her head, then sat back down next to me. We both looked straight ahead, towards the east, where the night sky and dark horizon stretched endlessly.

"You trust me, right?" I said.

"Maybe not with your own life," she teased, then stopped when she saw the look on my face. "What is it?"

"I talked to him. It. The One," I said. "I learned some things, stuff I can't forget. I want you to know, but I also want you to know that I'm still...hell, I don't know. I'm still Jost. It's...it's..."

"Go on," she said.

Complicated. I finished the sentence inside my head—lamely, at that, because I didn't know how to describe all of this. How much was truth, and how much was lies? There were things I would probably never know. But the least I could do was share it with Atell.

"I never knew my parents," I finally said. "And now, well...I know why."

I told her the truth. Not just what Titheu told me, but how I felt. About Hider and Orrin, and the monsters. How I survived Cartha, how I survived the gem—all of it. And how the more I thought about it, the more I talked about it, the more the horrible truth made sense.

Atell's response was simple. She asked, "Do you feel any different?"

It caught me by surprise, because I hadn't thought about that. So it was easy to be honest.

"No," I said. "I feel the same. Just maybe a little pissed off."

She smiled. "Sounds the same to me."

"Do you really not care, or do you just not believe me?"

"I believe you," she said, choosing not to tease me, which I appreciated. "And why should I care? I thought you were a monster when we first met, you know. I tried to kill you."

"I vaguely recall that."

"You're not a monster just because your—"

"Please don't call it my father."

"—because of where you came from," she finished, going a little red in the face. "Monsters hurt people. They destroy our lives. They take us and don't give us back. That's not you. And even if you never learned this, you stopped being a normal person the moment you touched that gem. So this...it's nothing."

I understood, in that moment, that Atell was the only person in the entire world that I cared about, and that her opinion meant the entire world to me. Hearing her words cleared a fog in my mind that I didn't even know was there. That dreadful feeling of everything being different, being *wrong*, was gone. And I just saw her.

Ignoring how it hurt my chest, I pulled her to me, close. I smelled the sweat in her hair and felt her breath against my neck.

"Thank you," I said.

"I'm just telling you the truth," she answered, but she held me the same.

The world stopped for a little while, but nothing could stop it forever.

Chapter Fifty-Six

"This isn't over," I said to her after those long, pleasant minutes. "We didn't kill Titheu. Until the One is dead, there won't be any peace. Not for us. Not for anybody."

"No," Atell said, sitting back up. "And there's no hiding, either. What are we going to do?"

"I told you there were others like me," I said, coming up with the name for them—us—in that moment. "*Inhumans.*"

"Inhumans," she repeated. "Hider, too."

I licked my lips. "Yeah. It seemed very attached to Hider. But Titheu, the monster, it's not perfect. It's not a god. It made a mistake with me, and that means it probably made mistakes with the other ones."

"How many are there?" Atell asked.

"I have no idea," I said. "Dozens, maybe? If I was the first, it's been almost twelve, thirteen years. Assuming I...well, if my earliest memories really are my earliest memories."

And the first years of my life never really happened. I just...came into being.

I said, "Plenty of time for Titheu to make more. And they were sent out into the maze to find cities. Maybe to live there. Some might know their purpose. Some might be like me. If I can find them...get them on our side. Between the Inhumans and the wielders that are still out there, we would be able to do something. We'd be able to fight."

"Hm." Atell shrugged. "It's a lot better than the first plan. Which was no plan at all."

"Yeah," I said with a laugh. "I'm understanding more of my magic now. I can communicate with it, a lot better than I could before. It'll help. I hope. I felt something when I saw Hider, and he surely did too."

"Orrin's in serious danger, then," Atell said, understanding the implications of that before I did. "The two of them are looking for exactly what Hider wants. What Titheu wants."

"You're right," I breathed.

"So we find them first," she said, stating it plainly. Like it was going to be easy.

"You'll come with me then?" I asked. "On this insane hunt?"

"Obviously," she answered, and rapped my arm with her knuckles. "Stop thinking I'm trying to run away."

"Heh. Sorry."

It was a nice feeling, to be out of the woods and about to set off on a new journey, even if that landscape was vast and colored only with danger and uncertainty.

Except we weren't out of the woods. Far from it, in fact, and it was the reddish haze of the rising sun that called us back to attention. Because we were sitting in open grass, nudged against short stacks of stone, with an army of monsters to the south on their way back north.

The morning was about to drive them right through us.

"Atell—"

"The sun."

"There's nowhere to hide," I said. "This isn't good."

We both rose, looking over the stone wall that didn't even reach our shoulders. In the distance, in the spreading light of the new day, were hundreds of shadows spread across the horizon, growing larger as they tore their way towards the castle in the distance behind us.

Atell pulled the sword from its scabbard, the thin line of power lit across the blade. The last bout had almost killed her; would she survive this one?

I had my dagger in one hand and my gem in the other.

"If we can make it through this," I said to her, "it's a good start."

There is something oddly comforting about life-and-death situations. You lived to fight the next day, or you died and you never had to worry about it again. The monsters were close enough now that I didn't even have time to think about how this particular swell of clawed, mindless killers was likely the simplest challenge that laid ahead of us, and how from here it would be uphill until the very end.

All of that would have to come later. Now, I could hear the claws tear up dirt and scrape against the half-buried stone.

The sword had been interesting, but I'd raised myself on the dagger. I held it tightly now, just a small knife, but one I could put the whole force of my body into. A short blade, but one that could be shoved where it hurt. Where it killed. And then pulled free to do it again and again, as I would have to.

When this was over, we'd run far enough to be out of reach of the One and its castle until we were ready. For now, we'd have to live.

The monsters came to us, and we began to draw their blood.

TO BE CONTINUED...

IN *BOOK 2: INHUMANS*

Jost's adventure continues in **Inhumans**, Book 2 of the *World of the Stone Maze* series, now available!

Visit **www.ShaneLeeBooks.com** to get your copy!

Thank you for reading.

- Shane Lee

For more from Shane Lee, visit

www.ShaneLeeBooks.com and say hi on Facebook

and Twitter, @ShaneLeeBooks.

Also from Shane Lee...

Black Forest: A Horror Novel

Monty can't believe it. His little sister, Terra, went into the cursed Dromm Forest. And after rescuing her from the black trees, he knows one thing.

No one can ever find out.

But now people in their village are dying, their living bodies shriveling and turning black. It's no plague, and it's no coincidence...

When Monty saved Terra from the forest, something else came out with her.

Now it's up to the two of them to destroy an enemy no one believes is real—one that gets stronger with every life it takes.

ABOUT THE AUTHOR

Shane Lee is a lover of both horror and fantasy, so it's only natural he would merge the two into fantastical worlds with terrors around every corner and magic waiting to be uncovered. It's just his favorite thing to do. Outside of that, he knows his way around the kitchen and a computer, and his wife is a bit better at both of those things.

But he'll catch up one day. Maybe.

CPSIA information can be obtained
at www.ICGtesting.com
Printed in the USA
BVHW042146080322
630980BV00013B/670